"Pull the reins down and back! Keep it low!"

Blake carefully got off the horse and wanted to kiss the ground. It took a while for Amanda to catch up, but as soon as she did, she was off her horse.

"Are you okay? Were you trying to give me a heart attack?" She wrapped her arms around him and his whole body relaxed. "I'm so glad you're all right."

"Good thing we don't have to call Nadia and tell her we accidentally killed her fiancé," Amanda's sister said. "You still have a way of keeping things interesting."

A near-death experience wasn't exactly how he wanted to cap off the day, but it had made one thing crystal clear: when Blake had been on that horse, afraid he might die, there was only one person he was thinking about. There was only one person he wished he could say *I love you* to, and it wasn't his fiancée.

It was the woman in his arms.

Dear Reader,

As soon as one of my writing buddies suggested going back to the Blackwell Ranch, I was on board! I could not be more excited to revisit the guest ranch in Falcon Creek, Montana, this time with a new set of eyes.

Amanda Harrison is feeling a bit lost. Her sister ran away from her own wedding and didn't come back. Instead, she's marrying a cowboy in Montana who works on a ranch owned by a family that—surprise!—is also Amanda's family. The Harrison women aren't Harrisons at all. They are long-lost Blackwells, and anyone who knows Big E from the first set of books knows that he's going to do everything he can to reunite those ladies on his home turf.

Amanda brings along her newly engaged best friend, Blake Collins. She's been friends with Blake since middle school and has been in love with him for about as long. Unfortunately, his engagement isn't the only obstacle in their way. Amanda has to learn the true meaning of family to tear down the walls she has between her and Blake so they can find that happily-ever-after we're all looking for!

Welcome back to Montana. Wishing you a good ol' time!

Amy Vastine

HEARTWARMING

Montana Wishes

———

Amy Vastine

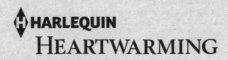

(H) HARLEQUIN®
HEARTWARMING™

ISBN-13: 978-1-335-88985-0

PLEASE RECYCLE
THIS PRODUCT IS RECYCLABLE

Recycling programs
for this product may
not exist in your area.

Montana Wishes

Harlequin Enterprises ULC
22 Adelaide St. West, 40th Floor
Toronto, Ontario M5H 4E3, Canada
www.Harlequin.com

Printed in U.S.A.

PROLOGUE

BLAKE COLLINS STOOD in the Harrisons' driveway with arms waving above his head like
he was trying to flag down a rescue vehicle.
Thirteen-year-old Amanda was stuck in the
back of the minivan with her younger sister
Fiona, who couldn't stop touching the new stud
earrings in her ears. Amanda didn't have earrings, but she wouldn't dwell on it or she'd cry.

Blake was there to offer her the perfect distraction. Of course, there was no fast escape
to get to her friend. Climbing over any of the
triplets sitting in the middle row would only
lead to a huge shouting match and Mom sending them all inside to think about how they
should speak to one another. She couldn't risk
missing out on why Blake was here. Whenever
he came over unexpectedly, he had a surprise.

"Don't forget you all have chores to finish before dinner. Your father will be home

soon," Mom reminded them all, but Amanda knew it was directed at her.

Lily groaned. Sixteen-year-old Peyton turned around in the front passenger seat. "Hey, Lil, no worries. I'll help you get yours done. Please don't give Mom a hard time."

"You're going to help her? She doesn't even have the hardest chore, and I have a ton of homework," Georgie complained.

Lily, Georgie and Amanda were the triplets. The middle children in this lively family of seven. If there was one thing the triplets constantly fought over, it was fairness. It always seemed nothing was fair, however.

"I have a broken wrist." Lily held up her bright yellow cast as if none of them could see it from a mile away. "I need the help more than you."

"Well, maybe you should stop trying to copy everything Danny does and you wouldn't get hurt so often," Georgie said, folding her arms across her chest.

"Maybe if you didn't study so much, you could get your chores done and have some fun like Danny and I do."

"Girls, we just spent an hour at the mall

Amy Vastine has been plotting stories in her head for as long as she can remember. An eternal optimist, she studied social work, hoping to teach others how to find their silver lining. Now she enjoys creating happily-ever-afters for all to read. Amy lives outside Chicago with her high-school-sweetheart husband, three teenagers who keep her on her toes and their two sweet but mischievous pups. Visit her at amyvastine.com.

Visit the Author Profile page
at Harlequin.com for more titles.

Big thank you to my Blackwell sisters—Anna, Cari, Carol and Melinda. Without your support, creativity and senses of humor, I don't know where I would be in this world. There's no other group of ladies I would rather have on my team.

having some fun. Can we not argue for like five minutes?" Mom was getting irritated.

Amanda tried to keep the peace like Peyton. "I'll help you, Georgie. Let me see what Blake needs first."

Her mom pulled into the driveway and Blake rested his hands on his hips.

"I still can't believe you're friends with Blake Collins," Lily said. "That boy is hotter than hot. And Tanya said he's the best kisser in the entire middle school."

"And why would your friend Tanya know how all the boys in the middle school kiss?" Mom asked, staring hard at Lily in the rearview mirror.

"It's not like she's actually kissed every boy in school. She has standards."

"That means he's the best kisser out of the *popular* guys at school," Georgie explained.

"He better not be trying to kiss you, Amanda. You know our rule about dating."

No dating until sixteen and only after Mom and Dad met the boy. Peyton had yet to subject some poor kid to that torture.

"Oh, my gosh. We're just friends, Mom. There's no kissing going on. Please never talk about it again." Amanda didn't want to think about Blake kissing her, Tanya or anyone else. Their friendship wasn't about kissing. It was about having the same interests and volunteering at the animal shelter. Kissing at this age would definitely just ruin their friendship. No one married their middle-school boyfriend.

Lily and Georgie both opened their doors and got out. Amanda jumped up, nudging Fiona out of the way ever so slightly.

"Please tell me you did not find another stray dog to wash in my bathtub, Mr. Collins," Mom said. "I'm positive they do that at the shelter."

"I did not come here with a stray dog, Mrs. Harrison." His gaze flicked to Amanda. He wasn't lying, but he was sure leaving something out.

"Do you like my new earrings?" Fiona asked, pushing her earlobes out with her fingers.

"Um, they're nice."

"Just so you know, getting these is a big deal."

Blake nodded but looked confused. "Cool."

Amanda touched her own naked earlobe. It didn't matter, she told herself. Blake didn't care about earrings. She grabbed his hand and pulled him away.

"What's going on?" she asked when she got farther from her family.

"I wish you had a cell phone, Harrison. I would have called you and told you to hurry."

Blake was one of the only kids in school with a cool new flip phone. Benefits of being an only child.

"Well, I'm right here. You don't have to call me. You can tell me."

"I found something. I had to hide them." Them? Behind Amanda's house there was a shed. Her dad kept his lawn mower in there and other tools. Blake grabbed the door handle. "Are you ready?"

Amanda could feel her heart pounding in her chest. The excitement was almost too much. "Open the door!"

Inside the shed was a box with a cat and three little kittens. The mama was busy cleaning her babies.

"Triplets!" Amanda felt connected to the kittens instantly. "They're so cute!"

"Kyle found them under his deck and called me," Blake said. "I would have taken them to the shelter, but it's closed for the night. You know my dad is allergic or I would take them home. It's supposed to rain tonight. I'd hate to leave them in here. What if they get scared? You think your mom would—?"

He was so adorable. Sweeter than all three kittens combined. "We're going to have to sneak them in. We'll hide them in my room."

"What about your sisters? Will they tell?"

Amanda shook her head. She and her sisters could argue, but when it mattered, they were there for one another. "They'll help us. We might have to bribe Peyton, but she should have our backs."

"I'll grab the box. You go ask your sisters to cause a distraction."

Not a problem for the Harrison girls. Amanda rallied the troops. She found Lily first because she was the only one not doing chores. She got Fiona up to speed while Amanda brought Georgie on board.

"I'll have Mom come inspect my work in the kitchen. That should give you enough time to get them inside," Georgie said.

"Perfect."

Blake came in through the back door. "We have a problem."

"What?"

"I brought the box out of the shed and they all hopped out," he whispered. "And scattered in four different directions."

Fiona and Lily came in the room. Amanda looked at Georgie.

"I got Mom. You guys get the you-know-whats," Georgie said.

"You two, come help," Amanda told her other sisters.

"What are you guys up to?" Peyton appeared and there was no way they could lie. They needed her to help.

"Peyton, I need you to think about how much you love us and not how much we annoy you right now."

Her older sister narrowed her eyes. "What did you do?" She focused her glare on Blake. She knew there could be only one reason he was here and that it had to do with a helpless animal. She softened immediately.

"It's a rescue mission. Are you in or are you out?" Lily asked.

Peyton took a deep breath and tightened her ponytail. "I can only imagine what I'm getting involved in. I'm in."

Georgie went to distract Mom, and the rest of them went out to find the kittens and their mama.

The four girls and Blake went on a kitten hunt. Peyton found the first one under their mom's rosebushes in the far corner of the backyard. "Oh, my gosh, it's so cute!"

"Found one!" Fiona had snatched up the mama cat.

"Here's one," Lily said as she chased a kitten out from behind the air conditioner. Blake and Amanda both tried to corner it by the side of the house.

Amanda thought they had it, but it managed to run right through Blake's legs.

"Blake!"

"I got her!" Lily and her broken wrist dived for the kitten and somehow caught it.

Amanda thought her heart stopped. If Lily hurt herself again, Dad would be so mad. Her ever-resilient sister jumped up like it was nothing.

"The last one is all yours, Amanda," Lily called out.

"Come on, Harrison. We've got this," Blake said. His belief in her meant everything.

Where could the last one be? Blake spotted it hiding under the table they had on the patio. Amanda didn't want the kitten to be afraid. She tried coaxing him to come to her.

"Hey, little buddy. It's okay. We're here to help. We want you to be with your family.

Don't you want to be with your family? Your mom is missing you. Come on. I promise I'll take care of you."

Without hesitation, the kitten came scampering into her arms.

"You're the kitten whisperer," Blake said. "So cool."

No one called Amanda cool. No one but Blake.

"Let's get these guys inside before Dad gets home," Peyton said.

The five of them sneaked back in the house with the four cats and the box. They would have to hide them in Amanda and Lily's closet. Once they got them all settled, Georgie came in with a bowl and a cup of water.

"For the mom. She's going to need to stay hydrated so she can keep up feeding the babies."

"Hello!" their dad called out when he came in the house.

Amanda closed the closet doors and thanked her sisters for getting them this far. She tried to ignore the fear that was coursing through her veins. If her dad knew about the kittens, he would make them sleep outside.

Her dad appeared in the doorway. He was quite the imposing figure, dressed in his naval uniform. He crossed his arms against his broad chest. "What are you all doing in here?"

Georgie sat on the bed like there was nothing unusual to see here. "We're hanging out." She giggled awkwardly. She hated lying.

Dad didn't care what the girls were doing in there. He was much more interested in Blake. "Mr. Collins, I thought we had an understanding. Amanda, you know boys aren't allowed in the bedrooms."

"We were practicing this thing we need to do for drama class. Peyton and Fiona were giving us some feedback," Lily lied.

One of the kittens meowed and the girls froze.

"What was that?" their dad asked.

"Me," Amanda said. "Meow. Meow."

"We have to play cats in the skit we're doing for class," Lily added.

The cat meowed again, so Blake started meowing over it. Lily joined in, too. Georgie acted like she was a cat swatting at something invisible dangling in front of her.

"I think you need to meow a little deeper," Peyton said, critiquing Blake. She showed him how to do it.

Dad looked suspicious but started to back

out of the room. "Is this really what they're teaching you in school?"

Everyone nodded.

"Okay, well, you can practice your little cat routine in the family room. No boys in the bedrooms. Ever."

"Yes, sir," they all said at the same time and followed him out.

Amanda and Blake slyly high-fived. They had done it. Thanks to the help of her sisters. She and Blake were an awesome team. Always would be, she hoped.

"I wish I was a Harrison," Blake said. "You guys are awesome."

Amanda's heart swelled in her chest. As chaotic as it was sometimes, she was proud to be a Harrison. There wasn't anything she'd rather be.

CHAPTER ONE

"SHE SAID YES."

"She said yes to what?" Amanda tightened her grip on Clancy's leash. The Irish wolfhound had a good forty pounds on her. If he wanted to take her on this walk instead of the other way around, he could. Had it been anyone other than her best friend and business partner on the phone, she wouldn't have answered it during this particular walk.

"I asked Nadia to marry me and she said yes!"

For some reason this news was a punch in the gut. Amanda had the wind knocked right out of her. Blake had been dating Nadia for no more than two months. Two months! She stilled to catch her breath. Clancy, however, had no intention of taking a break and nearly yanked her arm from her body, causing her to lose her balance and tumble forward. Her phone went flying as she put her hands out to break her fall.

Her knees and palms burned as they scraped on the pavement. She felt like that clumsy adolescent Blake had befriended back in middle school. She'd been the girl who had grown over three inches taller in less than a year, completely throwing off her center of gravity. He had been the popular three-sport athlete all the girls loved. Even though Amanda had been the least cool of the Harrison sisters, she and Blake had bonded over their mutual love of animals while volunteering at the local animal shelter and remained friends for over fifteen years.

Amanda brushed some gravel from her palm and took hold of the dog's leash. Thankfully, Clancy was more worried about his human companion's well-being than he was excited to be free. He sniffed her from head to toe to make sure she was okay.

"Good boy. I'll be all right. Don't worry about me," she said, giving the giant pup a pat and getting to her feet again. Her hands and knees would heal. Her heart was another matter. She needed to find her phone, which had ended upside down a few feet away. She picked it up and groaned when she flipped it over and saw it was cracked.

"Amanda? Amanda!" Blake called out from the other end of the line.

She put it to her ear. "I'm here. Clancy gave me a lesson on how not to walk a hundred-and-sixty-pound dog."

"What happened?"

"I fell and did so with all the awkwardness you have come to expect from me."

"You fell? Are you okay?"

It was sweet that he had been worried. Blake always worried about her and he always had her back. When she let him, at least.

"I'm fine. Georgie would tell me it's nothing a little hydrogen peroxide and some antibiotic gel can't fix."

"Don't give me a heart attack like that, Harrison. You know better." She could picture him shaking his head.

The only one handing out heart attacks today was him. Had he really told her that he'd proposed to Nadia? Had he thought this through? Was he sure he wanted to spend the rest of his life with Nadia? Not that there was anything wrong with her. She seemed nice enough, but… There was something holding Amanda back from rejoicing.

"Are you going to say something about the fact that I told you I'm getting married?" Blake asked.

"I would, but…I'm speechless." She cringed, knowing she had to come up with something better than that. Blake desperately wanted Amanda and Nadia to be friends. His favorite pastime had become sharing all the ways in which the two women were alike. He couldn't believe they both liked vinaigrette salad dressing and thought the movie *Sixteen Candles* was the best. Apparently, that made them practically twins!

As a triplet, Amanda had an identical twin and a fraternal twin. She didn't need to play twinsies with anyone else.

Deep breath, she told herself and silently scolded herself for being rude. Nadia was… nice. Amanda should be happy for them. Blake was her best friend. There was no one in this world who deserved good things more than he did.

"That's all you have to say? Amanda Harrison is never speechless. What does that mean?" She could hear the worry in his voice. She was the worst best friend.

"Well, you have to give me a minute. I'm still reeling from the fact that you didn't tell me you were even thinking about this before you actually did it." In other words, she was mad that he hadn't said something earlier so she could have talked him out of doing something so rash.

"I know. It was sort of spur of the moment. It's all your sister's fault. Lily inspired me."

Until right now Amanda didn't think she could be angrier with Lily for leaving her and her sisters to clean up the mess after she ran away from her own wedding. Adding to that, the runaway bride had since accepted a marriage proposal from someone else she'd known for all of a hot minute. Blake had decided to spontaneously propose to someone he barely knew because Lily was foolish enough to get engaged to a stranger? Lily also jumped out of airplanes and skied down double black diamond slopes. Of all of her sisters, did he really want to follow Lily's lead?

"My sister agreed to marry someone after knowing him ten days, Blake. I'm not sure she really knows what she's doing. Are you sure Nadia is the one? Is she your happy-ever-after?"

Blake didn't answer right away. Amanda had made it back to her tiny bungalow and grabbed her mail from the mailbox before opening the door for Clancy. Was it selfish that she wanted him to admit he'd made a mistake?

"We're twenty-nine, Amanda. I want kids. Lots of kids. And I want to be young enough to be a fun dad. Nadia wants a big family, too. She'll be a great mom. I think that could make for a darn good happy-ever-after."

The lump in Amanda's throat made it impossible to respond. Blake was an only child, and for as long as she could remember, the only thing he'd wanted was a home filled to the brim with family. He used to love coming over to her house because there was never a dull moment in the Harrison household. With four sisters, Amanda had grown up in the midst of constant chaos. The good kind, most of the time.

"Amanda, are you there?" he asked.

A big family of her own wasn't something Amanda would ever have. She pushed that pain aside and tried to focus on what was best

for Blake. If Nadia could give Blake everything he ever wanted, who was she to not
want that for him?

Holding her broken phone to her ear with
her shoulder, she tossed her mail on the
kitchen table and tightened her long blond
ponytail. She needed to man up. "I'm here.
I'm really happy for you. Both of you. I can't
wait to see the ring."

"Oh, well, no ring yet. Like I said, it was
pretty spontaneous. I asked her before I even
thought to get a ring. You'll help me pick
something out, right?"

"Sure," she forced out. What could be more
fun than shopping with the perfect man for
the wedding ring he planned to put on someone else's finger? Jumping out of an airplane
while deathly afraid of heights sounded like
a pretty good alternative.

"You are the best. You know that, right?"

"Only the best for my best friend," she said.

"Thanks. I have to go. Looks like Nadia is
finishing up her call to her parents and I still
have to call mine."

Amanda's heart clenched. She had been his
first call. "Tell your mom I said hi."

"I would, but then she'll know I called you

first. I'm sure she'll call you sooner than later to get all the gossip. She's going to need to hear it from you that Nadia is good enough for her one and only baby boy."

"I'll talk her up."

"Thanks, Harrison. Like I said, you're the best."

The best. Not the one. She tried not to acknowledge the way that stung.

Amanda hung up and stared down at the crack running across her screen. Like a river with its streams, there were smaller cracks branching off it. She and her phone had one thing in common. Both of them were broken. Someone could repair the phone, though. No one could fix Amanda.

After washing her hands and taking care of her scraped palms, she sat down to flip through her mail. Junk, junk, bill from Dr. Waters's office. Dr. Waters, the best ob-gyn in town, according to everyone on the internet. Endometriosis specialist, they had said. A miracle worker who had helped those who had been told they were infertile to have precious little babies of their own. There were no miracles for Amanda, however. Dr. Waters simply confirmed what the other three doctors before her had said. The probability of Amanda ever having a baby was basically 0 percent. Given her pain and condition, she might want to consider a hysterectomy. A hysterectomy at age twenty-nine. There was something so wrong about that scenario.

She fiddled with one of her stud earrings. She was the last of the Harrison girls to get her ears pierced. It was a tradition for the girls to get their ears pierced when they "became a woman." Their mom then bought them earrings for every major milestone—turning sixteen, graduating from high school, getting their first real job. Now, not only did she not have her mom, but there were no other milestones for Amanda. There would be no wedding. No baby someday. No daughter to whom she would pass on the tradition.

Amanda let out a somber sigh. She'd pay the doctor's bill and be done with it. Done with doctors. Done with searching the internet for success stories. Done with hoping for some miracle to make her fertile.

Her email popped up when she opened her laptop. There were several work-related emails. When she and Blake had started Sit, Stay, Play, they never imagined how quickly their little customizable pet swag subscription box company would take off. No more living paycheck to paycheck. Amanda could afford to do things for herself and give more than she'd imagined to causes she cared about.

She noticed the message from the DNA kit company. Running away from her wedding day wasn't the only mess Lily had made. She had run away, leaving with no explanation other than a note that said she was sorry scrawled on the back of her birth certificate. According to that, the man they called their dad was *not*. The Harrison girls were actually Blackwells. Even after her strong, tough-minded dad had broken down and admitted it was true when she had confronted him with the birth certificate, Amanda clung to her denial. She immediately sent in a swab, needing scientific proof that her entire life was a lie.

She clicked on the email and her ancestry was revealed. Nothing too unexpected. They were mostly European. Her blond hair, blue eyes and pale complexion could have told her that. Where her ancestors came from wasn't as important to Amanda as the list of people in the relative finder portion of the report. It didn't take long to scan the list and find the name she feared would be on there.

Elias Blackwell.

She slumped in her scat. It was true. She shared 25 percent of Elias Blackwell's DNA. He had been the man who helped Lily run away from the wedding. He owned the ranch where she was currently living. He claimed to be their grandfather.

How could this be? Their father was their rock, their biggest supporter. He had always been there for all five of them. Amanda couldn't remember a time he wasn't her dad. But there was another man out there. Someone named Thomas Blackwell, and he was their biological father.

She typed out an email to Fiona and Georgie. No need to tell Peyton, who apparently had known this their entire life and never bothered to tell any of her sisters. She had sent a letter explaining herself, so Amanda was less mad than she had been. These results, however, reignited some of her anger. It was true. Elias Blackwell was their grandfather. The DNA test confirmed it. What that meant, she wasn't sure. Did it matter that these people were related to them by blood?

If she asked Blake, she knew he would say yes. When he heard there was a huge family they didn't know about in Montana, he thought it was the coolest thing in the entire world. He had actually been jealous.

Clancy sauntered over and sat down in front of her, laying his big head on her lap and looking up at her with those soulful eyes. He understood when she needed comfort better than most. She scratched him behind the ear.

"You're a sweet boy. You're my sweet, sweet boy." Amanda had fostered Clancy when he was a pup and had fallen in love. When he wasn't adopted right away, she decided to keep him.

The doorbell rang and Clancy went from completely chill to totally out of his mind. His bark was as big as his body. Amanda tried to quiet him down as she shuffled to the door.

"Sit, Clancy," she commanded. He stopped barking and sat. "Stay." She prayed he'd listen when she opened the door.

Standing on her front porch was her dad, and behind him stood an elderly gentleman in black jeans, a blue-and-black plaid shirt and a big ol' cowboy hat. She didn't need to be introduced to know who that was.

"Daddy!" She wrapped her arms around his neck and made it clear that the only dad she cared about was the one right in front of her.

"Hi, sweetheart." He gave her the tightest squeeze back. She knew how painful all this had been for him. She had spent the last month assuring him that he would always be her father, but there had been a sadness in his eyes that broke her heart every time they had been together since Lily's canceled wedding.

"Miss Amanda," the man standing behind her father said, taking off his hat and holding it against his chest. "You'd think after basically raising a set of identical twins, I wouldn't be so shocked that you look exactly like your sister."

Elias Blackwell.

He didn't need to introduce himself. Amanda had no doubt she was standing face-to-face with her grandfather.

"What are you doing bringing Mr. Blackwell here?" she asked her father, forgetting all about her manners.

"Please, if you aren't going to call me

Grandpa, at least call me Big E." He placed his hat back on his head.

Her father's jaw was tight. He seemed to be about as pleased as she was that the man was there. "This is why I asked you to wait in the RV. Do you have no compassion for what my girls are going through?"

"Oh, well, excuse me," Elias replied, all sassy and frustrated. "I thought we were here to get acquainted. Not sure how that was going to happen if I'm hiding in the RV."

Her father gave it right back. "I wanted to explain a few things to her before I introduced you. But you're more stubborn than that mule you were yapping on about. I don't know how I'm going to survive this trip."

Amanda was confused and it surely showed on her face. She could feel her brows pinch together. "Trip? Where are you going? How come Lily didn't come home with you? Maybe I could talk some sense into her face-to-face."

"She's too busy plannin' her wedding," Elias answered, causing her father to loudly sigh. "Not to mention she loves it on the ranch. You should see her learning to train our horses. She's a natural. Of course, she would be. It's in her blood."

Amanda closed her eyes and wished the old man away. How in the world could her father stand traveling with him? When she opened her eyes, she was sadly disappointed to find he had moved closer and was making his way up her porch steps.

"Listen, Mr. Blackwell—"

"Big E, please," he interrupted.

What kind of grown man called himself Big E? Was there a Little E? Or was he saying "Biggie," like the deceased rapper? Either way, it was strange. "Listen, Mr. Big E. I don't need a stranger to tell me what my sister is good at or what she's up to. I am aware that she is engaged…again. My sister and I have a close relationship."

"Of course you do." He shifted his weight from foot to foot. "She spoke about you quite a bit. Said you were the sister she's closest to. That's why I'm surprised she didn't tell you she wants you to come help her."

Panic replaced her indignation. "Help her with what? Is something wrong?"

Clancy stood up and pressed against her leg. He didn't bark, but he made his presence known. Her father threw his hands up. He shot his military glare at the old man before turning back toward Amanda.

"Don't listen to him, Mandy. Lily's fine. She didn't come home because she's decided that she wants to move to Montana. She and Conner have decided on a Christmas wedding on the Blackwell Ranch."

Amanda smacked her forehead with her hand. The last wedding took a solid year to plan, and Amanda had been there every step of the way, keeping Lily on task. "How is she going to plan a wedding by herself in less than four months?"

"The ranch is the perfect place to plan a wedding, darlin'!" Big E bragged. "It's one of the most premier wedding destinations in the entire northwest mountain states. We have an entire staff to help her with that."

This man clearly had no idea how all the words coming out of his mouth were like daggers in Amanda's heart. Usually, Lily asked Amanda to help her when she was in over her head.

She couldn't continue this conversation about her family with this man who was nothing more than an interloper. He might share their blood, but that was it. She turned her gaze on her father. "What is going on with this RV? Did you drive that thing all the way from Montana?"

"We did," her father said, as if it had been the most exasperating journey of his life. She could only imagine, given the few minutes she'd been around Mr. Blackwell. "Elias and I have decided to go looking for Thomas."

Thomas? Thomas Blackwell? The name on the birth certificate? "Why would you do that?" she asked.

"Maybe I can take you to dinner? We can talk about it over some crab legs?"

"I heard Ocean's Dream has some of the best seafood in the area," Big E said, joining them on the porch. "My treat."

Apparently, he had missed the part where her father asked if he could take her to dinner. She had assumed they would leave Big E behind. Unfortunately, it was obvious that they must have talked about how Ocean's Dream was Amanda's favorite restaurant. It was the place she and her dad had dinner whenever they met to catch up. It was a sacred place and not somewhere she would go with this stranger. All Amanda had wanted to do when she saw her dad at the front door was fall into his arms and cry. She wished she could tell him all about what the doctor had said, about Blake's engagement. She just wanted her dad to tell her everything would be all right. That wasn't going to happen with this wannabe grandpa following them around.

"I appreciate that you have an interest in getting to know me," she said to Big E. "I'm sure finding out you have five granddaughters is very exciting, but all of this is nothing but totally overwhelming to me. To be honest, I am not ready to deal with my expanding family tree yet. I will be sure to let you know when I am."

Big E gave her a sharp nod.

Her father looked chagrined, not something the retired navy admiral looked very often. "I know all this is unsettling. I'm sorry about that. I know this past month has been nothing but one shock after another. I'm so sorry about that. Your mother and I never wanted you girls to find out like this."

Had they really wanted Amanda and her sisters to find out at all? It didn't seem like it. The lies were another thing that Amanda was trying to wrap her head around. Their father was a man of honor. *Honest* and *hard-*

working were the first two adjectives to pop in anyone's head when they thought of him. This lie about who her biological father was had her questioning everything, even though she still loved him with her whole heart.

"I know you didn't, Dad, but here we are. With him." She waved her hand in Big E's direction. "When are you two leaving on this adventure of yours?"

"Tomorrow morning. We only stopped by to check in with you."

Well, that was sooner than expected. "Dad, have you really thought about this?"

He stared at his feet. "I have. It's the right thing to do. I probably should have done it years ago."

This whole thing was unbelievable and heartbreaking. "Maybe he doesn't want to be found. Have you thought about that?"

His eyes lifted. "It's possible, but I still have to try."

"There's nothing more important in this world than your family," Big E chimed in.

Amanda had had enough of his opinions on the world. She was very clear about how important family was. Her father might not survive this trip. The two of them seemed to have very different personalities.

She threw her arms around her dad. "Keep me posted on where you are and what is going on."

"I will. I promise." He squeezed her tight, and she had to swallow the emotion threatening to burst forward. "Call your sister. I'm sure she needs you as much as she always has. Maybe you and Blake can take a road trip. Check in on her."

That wasn't helping her keep her tears at bay. She was losing Lily and Blake. Lily had always welcomed Amanda coming to her rescue, but in one of her darkest moments, she had chosen to run off with some guy named Conner instead of telling Amanda what was wrong. Just like Blake had decided to make the biggest decision in his life without even telling her he was thinking about it. When had she become so unnecessary?

"I'll call her and see if she wants me to come," she said, forcing the words around the lump in her throat.

"It was a pleasure meeting you, Miss Amanda. I hope you have a good night." Big E pinched the brim of his hat and made his way down her porch steps.

Amanda said goodbye to her dad and went back inside her house. After shutting the door, she pressed her back against it and let the tears fall.

CHAPTER TWO

IT WASN'T LIKE Amanda to be late. Blake checked his phone for the third time. No messages. No calls. His text asking if everything was okay was still unanswered. His call went to voice mail. Worry began to set in. Once a month they met at the packing facility to oversee the filling of the boxes for Sit, Stay, Play. Amanda was usually the first one here. An uneasy feeling settled in his stomach.

Blake couldn't take it anymore. He had to go looking for her. His imagination was getting the best of him, causing his heart to pound in his chest and his palms to sweat. He dug in his pocket for his keys as he raced out into the parking lot. They slipped out of his hand and skittered across the hot blacktop.

"Where are you going in such a hurry?" Amanda's voice was like a soothing balm on a burn.

Forgetting all about his keys, Blake raced

over and wrapped his arms around her. "Don't do that to me, Harrison," he practically growled into her blond hair, which smelled like Amanda. Other people would call it coconuts. The woman had been using the same shampoo since she was in middle school, making it impossible for Blake to think of anything other than Amanda when he came across something coconut scented.

"Do what? Ask you where you were going?" She stood stiffly with her arms pinned to her sides.

He let her go. "Be late. Not answer your phone. Ignore my texts. Make me think you were dead on the side of the road somewhere. Take your pick and please never do it again."

She scrunched up her face in that adorable way she always did when she messed up unintentionally. "Did I not tell you I was going to drop my phone off to get the screen fixed before I swung by here?"

"No, you did not."

She went around him and bent over to pick up his keys. Hitching her bag strap higher on her shoulder, she held them out for him. "Sorry about that. Yesterday was such a fiasco, I must have forgotten to text you."

Blake froze. Yesterday was a fiasco? Yesterday, he had got engaged. Yesterday had been the biggest day of his life so far.

"What happened yesterday? Is that why you sounded so weird on the phone when I told you about me and Nadia? Is it Lily? Your dad?"

Amanda winced. "I didn't mean to sound weird when you called with your news. I'm super happy for you and Nadia," she said, not sounding the least bit super happy.

"You didn't answer my question," he said, taking his keys. "What happened yesterday that made it such a fiasco?"

"Don't worry about me." She put on her happy face, the one that she wore when she was anything but. "Let's go in and check the boxes so we can go ring shopping."

He snagged her by the arm as she turned to go inside. "Nice try. Tell me what's going on. Your phone screen cracked, but that can't be the worst of it. What's going on?"

Her fake smile fell and her shoulders slumped. "Fine. My father showed up yesterday with the man claiming to be my long-lost grandfather. Only he isn't just claiming to be related. According to the DNA test I sent in, he's most definitely related."

Blake knew she had been hoping to learn

something different, but that was unlikely given the fact that her dad had confirmed it was true the day the wedding got called off. "I know you didn't want it to be true, but look at it this way—now you have *more* family. More people to love you and be there for you. You are so lucky. You know how much I would give for a big extended family."

Being the only child of two only children made extended family hard to come by. Blake had always wished for a big family like Amanda's. He couldn't understand why she saw this as such a bad thing.

"I worry about what all this is doing to the family I currently have. We're all mad at Peyton because she knew. My father thinks he needs to go travel the world with Elias Blackwell to go find our quote unquote real dad. Fiona is freaking out because she's the biggest daddy's girl of all of us. Lily is at some ranch in the middle of Montana, bonding with these cousins of ours, and is coping with all of her emotions about this by giving up her company, moving to this ranch and planning a second wedding to someone she just met. And…" She stopped and shook her head as if scolding herself for saying something else.

"And what?"

She blinked and threw her hands out. "And it's so obviously a recipe for disaster!"

Blake placed his hands on her shoulders and dipped his head so he could look her right in the eyes, which were beginning to well with tears. "It's going to be okay."

"What if it's not?"

"Then we'll figure it out." He ran his hand down her arm and threaded his fingers through hers. "That's what you and I do when things go wrong."

He watched as she bit the inside of her cheek. She was holding something back. There was no way she could argue with him about this, though. They had been through some terrible things. She had been there for him when an injury stole his college athletic scholarship away from him. He had been there for her when her mother died. There was nothing the two of them couldn't get through as long as they had each other.

She took a breath and forced that smile back on her face. "You're right. Everything will be fine. Let's go inside."

There was nothing more frustrating than

when Amanda kept secrets from him. "You know I hate that."

She attempted to act like she had no idea what he was talking about. "What?"

"When you push your feelings aside and pretend you're fine when you aren't. Your sisters might let you get away with it, but you know I won't."

She pulled her hand away. "I am fine. You just told me everything will be okay, and I'm agreeing with you. I'm going to check on this month's boxes, help you pick out a ring for Nadia, and then I'm going to drive to Montana to help my sister. Everything will be okay."

"Whoa. What do you mean you're driving to Montana?"

"Lily needs me, so I'm going."

Typical Amanda. She would drop everything and anything to rescue Lily. Her loyalty was one of the things he most admired about her. He just wasn't certain that Lily needed to be rescued this time.

"She needs you for what? Didn't you already help her plan one wedding? Do you really need to help her plan the second one?"

Amanda's gaze dropped to her feet. "Not

exactly. This ranch she's staying at is supposedly some amazing wedding destination, and she's got all these people helping her plan her new wedding. What she does need from me is to empty her apartment and drive her car and all of her things to Montana. My dad even suggested that I take a road trip."

"Your dad suggested you take a road trip to Montana by yourself? Your overprotective dad, who added an extra dead bolt to your front door when you moved into your own place and gives you a new can of pepper spray for Christmas every year, told you to get in your sister's car and drive to Montana alone?"

She shrugged and brushed some of her hair out of her face.

"That's got to be a two-day drive," he reminded her. "You can barely stand to drive to Santa Barbara to visit Fiona. Montana would be like driving there and back five times in a row."

"Okay, well, maybe he said I should bring you," she said with a sigh.

That was much more believable. Mr. Harrison always made a point of thanking Blake for looking out for Amanda. Not that she needed it much. Amanda was cautious and thoughtful. She didn't take a lot of risks.

"I can come with you," he said.

She shook her head. "You just got engaged. I don't think your fiancée would want you to go running off with me for who knows how long. I could be gone a couple weeks."

"Weeks?" What would he do without Amanda for weeks? Of course, if he went with, he'd be away from Nadia for weeks. They'd only been together a little more than two months. She definitely could not come with them because her job with the district attorney's office wouldn't allow for it. It really wasn't much of a dilemma— help his best friend and lose a little time with his fiancée or stay with his fiancée and abandon his best friend during this really difficult time in her life. Amanda needed him more than Nadia did.

Thankfully, Nadia was also sweet and understanding. She thought Amanda was the best and wouldn't be too upset about him leaving if he explained everything that was going on with Amanda's family.

"Maybe a few weeks, maybe less. Who knows? I wasn't going to buy a plane ticket home just in case I convince my sister to come home. I'm struggling to believe that moving to

Montana is the right thing for Lily to do. I may have to stay awhile to get her to see the light."

Amanda was the most loving person Blake knew, but she had never really *been* in love. She had dated guys over the years, but no one had ever caused her to fall head over heels. She had no idea how being in love could make people do things that others might think were foolish. Or how love could change someone's perspective about life.

"Let me talk to Nadia." He would need to be there for Amanda if or, more likely, when Lily let her sister know she most definitely wouldn't be coming back to San Diego. "Might be fun to check out your family's ranch."

Her expression hardened. "Don't call it my family's ranch."

"Come on, Harrison. Let's take a road trip and see if wc really need to rescue your sister from this Blackwell *cult*."

That earned him a genuine smile. "Fine. Can we please go inside and make sure the boxes are filled with the right stuff now?"

"After you, partner." He motioned for her to lead the way. Amanda had barely survived the loss of her mom, was struggling to deal with the revelation that her father was not her biological father, and now faced losing her sister. This wasn't going to be easy.

"WHAT DO YOU mean you want to go to Montana?"

Nadia wasn't taking the road-trip idea as well as Blake had hoped. She stood in her kitchen with her hands on her hips and one of her jet-black eyebrows raised.

"Amanda needs to check on her sister. She's on this ranch. Look at the pictures of this place. It's pretty amazing." Blake held out his phone. He'd searched the Blackwell Ranch on the internet and found out it was much fancier than he'd expected.

Nadia folded her arms across her chest. With her dark hair slicked back in a bun and dressed in a slim-fitting burgundy top and a tight black pencil skirt, she looked like a hot but angry teacher ready to send him to the principal's office.

"I've already seen the website. I researched all about it when Amanda's sister turned up there."

"You did?"

"She's related to Chance Blackwell. Once I went down the internet rabbit hole on him, I ended up learning a lot about the Blackwells."

Chance Blackwell, the famous singer. Nadia was a fan.

"I could go with Amanda and get Chance's autograph for you," he offered.

"Well, the ranch is quite the premier wedding destination. You could check it out and bring back lots of good information for me," she said to his surprise.

Blake scrubbed his face with his hand. "You want me to check out wedding venues without you?"

"I can see if I can move some things around and maybe we all could go together," she suggested.

This wasn't going the way he'd expected. "Amanda is going through some really tough stuff right now. Her mom died this year, only to then find out six months later her dad is not her biological dad. The sister she's closest to ran off and didn't come back. And now she finds out she's got this huge extended family in Montana. I feel like I need to be there for her because her family can't be. Wedding planning might take away from that."

Nadia's face softened. She wrapped her arms around his neck. "This…this is why I love you. You are such a good man, Blake Collins." She gave him a little peck on the lips. "Amanda is lucky to have a best friend like you."

Amanda had been his best friend since they were thirteen years old. He wouldn't be the man he was today if it weren't for her. "So you're cool with me taking her out there?" He hugged her back.

"You should be there for your friend. I really do think this ranch could be a unique place to get married, though. Maybe you could take a few pictures for me or bring back some brochures. I love horses, and there are sure to be lots of them on a ranch..."

"You do love horses," he agreed.

"Plus, you'd look quite handsome in a cowboy hat."

"Me?" Blake was much more comfortable on a surfboard than he was a horse. He also preferred flip-flops over cowboy boots. Amanda often joked that he was part merman. When they were in high school, they used to practically live at the beach during the summer.

Nadia nodded. "Put on some jeans and a plaid flannel shirt and you'd be a cowboy right out of my dreams."

Amanda would get a good laugh when he told her about that. "Any chance you dream about cowboys who wear swim trunks and tank tops?"

"Maybe being in Montana will inspire you to give up your beach-bum ways. Surfer boys are just that—boys. Cowboys are men," she said with a wink. She spun out of his arms and headed back to the bedroom. "I'm going to change and then you can take me to dinner."

Cowboys were men…pfft. *Boy* was literally in the word. Anyone could ride a horse. Not everyone could ride a wave. Montana didn't really belong on their list of potential places to get married. Mexico and a beach was more his style. He'd indulge his bride-to-be so he could take this trip. He'd get Amanda to her sister, and he'd be there to pick up the pieces if Lily had gone and fallen in love with one of those ridiculous cowboys.

CHAPTER THREE

"Dog food?"

"Check."

"Laptop?"

"Check."

"Sunglasses?"

"They're on your head, Harrison." Blake plucked her glasses off her head and handed them to her. His smile was relaxed and thankfully not patronizing. "It's all packed. All of Lily's things are in the trailer, and everything you need to survive a couple of weeks in Montana is in the trunk. Let's hit the road."

Amanda stared at the trailer Blake had hooked up to Lily's SUV. Everything Lily owned was in there. This was really happening. Her sister was moving to Montana. She had no qualms about leaving Amanda alone in San Diego. She couldn't fret about that. Pushing her feeling aside, she tried to stay focused. "I don't want to forget something important."

"Well, unless Lily had things hiding somewhere other than her condo, there's no way we forgot anything that belongs to her. And I'm pretty sure that we can get anything we might have forgotten in Montana. They have stores there. Stores that sell the things you may have forgotten but haven't because you've checked a thousand times."

His impatience was building. Amanda slid her sunglasses on. "Okay, let's go."

"All right, that's what I like to hear." Blake jumped into the driver's seat and buckled himself in.

Amanda did her best to smile. She would hold on to the hope that she would be able to convince Lily not to jump into this new relationship without thinking things through. Amanda would persuade her sister to come back home and get some clarity before making any more major life decisions.

"It's going to be a million times easier for Lily to plan this wedding since you literally just helped her plan one," Blake said as he pulled out onto the road.

"Stop!"

Blake was careful not to hit the brakes so Clancy didn't go flying through the windshield. He pulled over. "What's the matter?"

"I forgot the book." How could she have forgotten the book?

Blake made a quick U-turn. "The book?"

"The planner that I spent forever putting together for the last wedding. I need her to think I am there to seriously help her plan the next one."

Blake quirked a brow. "You forgot the book that you plan to use as a prop in your scheme to make your sister believe you aren't there to convince her to leave the man she's fallen in love with?"

"Don't judge me. Just take me back so I can grab it." Lily probably didn't want any reminders of the wedding she had run away from, but maybe that was a good reason to bring the book. Amanda could share it with the staff at the Blackwell Ranch so they knew what *not* to do. Lily wouldn't want anything from the first wedding to make it into the second one.

The book was right there on her kitchen table where she had left it. She snatched it up and ran back to the car. Blake had her phone in his hand. "Here she is." He held it out for her. "It rang as soon as you jumped out. Caller ID said it was a doctor, so I answered it."

Amanda felt panicked. She grabbed the phone from him and climbed back out of the car. There was no way she would be having a conversation with a doctor in front of him.

"Hello?"

"Amanda Harrison?" the voice on the other end of the line asked.

"This is Amanda."

"This is Farrah from Dr. Waters's office. She wanted me to give you a call to see if you wanted to schedule your surgery."

Amanda's legs almost gave out. This was not what she needed today. Could she schedule her hysterectomy and then get in a car with Blake for two days? She could already feel the tears pricking at the corner of her eyes.

She cleared her throat and stepped farther away from the car. She didn't want Blake to hear anything. "I'm going to be gone possibly the rest of this month. I'm not sure I'm prepared to schedule anything right now."

"Oh, that's okay. We actually don't have anything available this month. Dr. Waters's schedule fills up so fast we wanted to give you a chance to get something on the calendar if you wanted to get this done before the end of the year. Right now, we have an opening in the morning on the third Tuesday in October or the first Thursday in November."

Amanda pressed her hand against her stomach, a stomach that would never be swollen with a baby. It was a reality she had to accept. "Let's do the third Tuesday," she forced out.

"All right. I will put you down for Tuesday, October 20. We will contact you again as it gets closer to give you some instructions."

"Thank you." Amanda hung up and cringed. Had she really just thanked the woman who'd called her to schedule one of the worst days of her life? She had, and it made her want to throw up her breakfast.

Composing herself wasn't as easy as she needed it to be, but she had to do it. She kept the phone to her ear so he wouldn't know she was no longer on the call. Telling Blake what was going on wasn't an option. She didn't want him to know how defective she was. She couldn't deal with the way he would look at her once the truth was out. The pity and the discomfort would kill her.

Amanda knew Blake as well as she knew herself. As soon as he found out she couldn't have children, it would make him self-conscious about mentioning wanting kids or sharing with her when he was going to have kids. It would ruin their friendship because what he wanted more than anything was the one thing she would never have and that would make him feel terrible.

Amanda never wanted Blake to feel bad about having his own children, so this secret had to be buried. It had to be buried as far down as she could push it.

Three deep breaths and she pretended to end the call. Her heart calmed but was still very much torn in two. She turned and walked back to the car.

Predictably, Blake asked, "What was that about?"

Amanda buckled her seat belt. "Nothing. I need to get a mole removed and they wanted to get something on the calendar."

Instead of pulling back out onto the road, Blake kept the car in Park. "Since when do you have a suspect mole? Where is it? What does it look like? Is it not round? Is it discolored? Let me see it."

So overprotective. He was worse than her dad sometimes. "It's on my back and I'm not undressing in the car so you can look at a mole that I've already had a doctor look at."

"Did they do a biopsy? Why didn't you tell me you had a doctor appointment? When did you go?" His questions came so rapidly that he wasn't even giving her a chance to answer.

"Can we get going? If we're going to make it to the first stop by a reasonable hour, we need to get going. Drive."

Blake was in full panic mode. "You have cancer, don't you? That's why you've been acting weird lately. You have skin cancer, and you didn't tell me because you didn't want me to worry."

"I don't have cancer. I am having a mole removed from my back that is not skin cancer. I swear on my mother's grave that I do not have cancer." Who knew that declaring something completely honest would be the easiest way to get out of this debacle?

"You swear?" He took off his sunglasses and stared at her hard. The way concern emanated from his eyes made the guilt feel a bit heavier.

"I swear. I definitely do not have cancer.

Can we please start driving in the direction of my sister?"

Blake seemed satisfied that she was being truthful, and he put the car in Drive and carefully pulled away from the curb. He placed a gentle hand on her leg and his touch unleashed a swarm of butterflies in her stomach. "Promise me that you won't shut me out if there's anything really wrong. You're always so good at taking care of others but really bad at letting others take care of you."

"I let people take care of me," she tried to argue. "You know how my dad dotes."

He put his sunglasses back on and both of his hands returned to the steering wheel. "Oh, come on. Your dad micromanages all of you girls. He practically shoved Danny down the aisle. Had your grandpa not shown up to help Lily escape, she would have ended up married to someone who wasn't in love with her and who she wasn't really in love with, either."

Amanda had been so jealous of Lily marrying her best friend that Amanda hadn't noticed how unsure her sister had been. But it was something else that Blake had said that struck a major chord. "Don't call Elias Blackwell my grandpa. He's not my grandpa. He was basically a sperm donor. Great-Aunt Pru raised Thomas on her own. Elias didn't even know he had a son."

"Yeah, but it's not his fault he didn't know. As soon as he found out, he went right to work trying to find everyone in his family. He's doing everything he can to find Thomas. Family is clearly important to him. I think that makes him, at the very least, worthy of a chance to be a grandfather to you and your sisters."

Amanda's face felt hot. "If this is your way of supporting me, I think I've changed my mind about letting you come with me on this road trip. Clancy will keep me company and won't try to convince me to let strangers invade my life."

Blake chuckled. "I love it when you get all dramatic. It's actually very entertaining."

"Don't laugh. I mean it. There is a lot on my plate right now. I can only handle one thing at a time, and right now, I want to focus on Lily." Anything other than her impending surgery, the reality that she would never have children of her own, the sad fact that the man she was in love with was getting married to someone else. She couldn't confess that to him, however. "I'm not ready to figure out where Elias Blackwell fits into my life. And I'm really not ready to process that there's some other man out there who's my biological father. Please don't push me."

He reached over and took her by the hand. The butterflies were too mad to react this time. "I'm sorry, Harrison. I don't want to stress you out. I know this isn't easy for you and I don't mean to make fun."

His sincerity may have triggered a few of those butterflies. "There is one way you can make it up to me," she said, knowing that she should take full advantage of this time they had together. Once he and Nadia said "I do," there would be little chance for Amanda and Blake to do things that weren't work related.

"What would that be?"

Amanda's lips curled up in a devious grin. She turned up the radio, and, based on his grimace, he immediately knew where this was headed. "Road-trip karaoke, of course!"

Blake groaned and Clancy poked his head in between the two front seats to see what was going on. "Please don't make me."

Road-trip karaoke was something that Amanda and her sisters had done growing up anytime they were forced to spend hours together in a car for a family vacation. Everyone got a chance to search through the available stations for a song they were familiar enough with to sing along to. Blake had been subjected to a few rounds over the years, like when he joined Amanda and Lily on their first trip to Vegas, and the time he went with Amanda, Lily and Fiona to Florida for spring break when her baby sister was a senior in college.

"You know it's my favorite. And you are here to keep me sane during this very long trip."

"But don't you want to wait until we at least get out of San Diego?"

"Nope. Me first." She scanned through the stations. Amanda loved Lily's SUV because she had satellite radio. That meant so many more songs and genres to choose from. She settled on the Beach Boys channel. They were her dad's favorite band. He played them all the time when he was home and they had backyard barbecues.

"Good Vibrations" was on, and she belted it out like she was one of the boys. Blake shook his head, surely rolling his eyes behind those sunglasses. By the end of the song, he was definitely bopping along with the beat. It was impossible not to.

When it was over, it was Blake's turn. "Start searching. I bet there's a Lady Gaga channel for you. We both know you know every word to her songs," Amanda teased.

"You're *so* funny. But if you are going to make me do road-trip karaoke, I will be torturing you with your favorite genre of music."

Amanda's curiosity was piqued. His sarcasm was clear, but what it was that he thought she would loathe was less. Blake scanned through the channels using the buttons on the steering wheel. When he took the ramp to get on Route 163, he stopped the radio on an unfamiliar channel. "Oh, this one is perfect," he said.

On the screen it was described as the best of folk past and present. There was no way Blake would know the words to any of these songs. He was bluffing. He tapped his fingers on the wheel to the beat, but he didn't sing a word.

"The karaoke part means that you have to sing along. If you don't know the song, we have to move on." She attempted to start scanning again.

He stopped her. "Wait. I want to see what's on next. I might know it. My mom used to play James Taylor songs all the time. And I would say Mumford and Sons is kind of folksy. I like them."

Sure… How long would they have to wait for one of those songs to come on? "If you don't know the next song, you have to move on. That's the rules."

They both suffered through the end of some song neither one of them had ever heard before. The next song was introduced by the DJ. "One of my favorite songs of all time is 'Butterfly Blue' and this new one by Chance Blackwell is equally as good, if not better, in my opinion. Give 'Sounds Like Home' a listen and let me know what you think."

"Don't be mad, but Nadia has been listening to this song on repeat ever since she figured it out." Blake cranked up the volume.

In the distance he sees what he never saw. Laughter ringing like wind chimes in a summer storm. Across rocky tipped

horizons and cloudless skies. And just
like that he knows…the sounds of home.

Amanda used her hands to cover her ears.
Nadia had been the one to make the family connection. Chance Blackwell was Elias
Blackwell's grandson. That made the singer/
songwriter Amanda's cousin. Blake thought it
was "so awesome" to have a famous relative.
Of course he did. He found all blood relatives
fascinating, thanks to his lack of them.

"You're the one who forced me to play this
game. Don't look so salty," he said when the
song was over.

"Of all the songs in the world, that's what
you had to sing?" Amanda couldn't escape
this new connection to the Blackwells even
if she tried.

"Harrison, you need to work on changing
your mindset. These could be good people.
People you'll be fortunate to know. You love
your dad. No one is asking you to not love
him anymore just because he isn't your biological dad. Liking the Blackwells doesn't
mean you can't be a Harrison."

He was right. It was so hard, though. "Lily
says that all the Blackwell cousins and their

wives are good people. I just can't imagine how any of them think this isn't incredibly weird. How can they open their arms to Lily without any reservations? One month ago, she was no one to them, and suddenly she's part of the family. Not just related but living on the ranch and helping train horses. Like she's been some kind of cowgirl her whole life."

Blake laughed. "Lily as a cowgirl. I still have to see this with my own eyes. Lily does yoga on a paddleboard. Lily likes mountain towns where she can ski and drink expensive coffee. Montana? A ranch? Cowboy boots? Horses? So not Lily."

"Exactly!" It felt so good to hear someone say what she had been feeling from the beginning. Her sister loved the beach. She wasn't a huge fan of red meat. She liked fresh fish that didn't have to be shipped across multiple state lines. She also didn't fall in love with guys she'd known for a little over a week. Lily had been an adventure seeker, but she wasn't out-of-her-mind reckless.

"Are you nervous the Blackwells won't like you as much as they like Lily?"

"What? No." Amanda couldn't believe he would ask such a question. She didn't care what the Blackwells thought about her. She wasn't going to Montana to win over the hearts of some cousins she didn't even want. She was going to convince her sister to come back to San Diego so they could have lunches at Casa Bonita and go Rollerblading along the boardwalk by Mission Beach. It wasn't the Blackwells she wanted to love her. "Maybe I'm worried Lily will love them more than she loves me."

Blake turned his gaze on her. "Stop right there. Don't even think it. You and your sister have something no one else can compete with. I know that if the three of us were on a sinking ship and you could only save one of us, you'd save Lily."

He was right. Sort of. "I'd make you save her and sacrifice myself. I truly couldn't bear to live in a world without either one of you." The pain in her chest was back because that felt like what was happening. Blake would get married and start his family with Nadia, leaving Amanda behind. Lily, on the other hand, was already starting her life with Conner in Montana. She had people named Hadley and Katie looking after her. She didn't need Amanda anymore.

"Actually, let's not kid ourselves. If the ship was sinking, I would simply have to save both of you gorgeous Harrison ladies and be the ultimate hero of the story."

Blake had always been the hero in Amanda's life story. That was why she was madly in love with him. Nadia was the luckiest woman in the entire world. She was getting the very best man the world had to offer, and it made Amanda want to cry.

CHAPTER FOUR

THE LITTLE TOWN just south of Salt Lake City where they spent the night was not the most interesting town in the United States, but it did have one of the cleanest hotels that accepted pets Blake had ever stayed at. Their continental breakfast wasn't too bad, either.

Always the early riser, he had gone down to grab something to tide himself over until they stopped for lunch and some coffee for Amanda, who had been blissfully snuggling with her dog when he got up.

"You ready to hit the road again?" he asked his sleepy-eyed companion upon his return to the room. She was up and dressed but had dark circles under her eyes. After ten and a half hours in the car yesterday, Amanda looked like the last thing she wanted to do was get back in that SUV.

"Let me take Clancy for a quick walk and then I'll be ready to go."

"I can come with you," he said, handing her the coffee he had gone down to the lobby to get for her.

She smiled. It was slight, but it was something. Her eyes closed as she inhaled the aroma. "Thank you for this, and we would love if you joined us."

He waited for her to slip on her shoes and grab Clancy's leash. Just as they were walking out the door, his phone rang. Nadia was calling. He had cut things short last night when they had been driving only because it had felt a little weird having a conversation over the car's Bluetooth with Amanda sitting right next to him.

"Nadia?" Amanda guessed. "You talk to her—I'll walk the dog." She smiled, but it was strained. He'd been noticing it more and more lately. He didn't like it. The more he tried to encourage her to get to know Nadia, the less the two of them seemed to make it work. He needed the two of them to be friends because Amanda was always going to be his person.

"Good morning, sweetheart," he said as he answered the phone.

"Good morning. Are you guys back on the road? Am I on Bluetooth again?"

"We haven't left yet, so it's just you and me right now. Amanda took Clancy for a walk."

"Thank goodness," she replied with a sigh.

"What's wrong?"

"It's silly." She had clearly switched him to speaker. She went on and on about what a busy day she had yesterday and how she was looking forward to the same thing today. "It doesn't help that I didn't sleep very well, thanks to you."

"Thanks to me? How did I ruin your sleep?"

"I made the mistake of telling my mother that you were on this trip with Amanda, and thanks to all of her feedback, I proceeded to have the worst nightmare."

"Worse than the one I had about Amanda's driving? She is a terrible driver, but don't tell her that I said that. Did you have a nightmare about her driving me off a mountain like I did? I promise I will offer to be the only one behind the wheel today. We'll be safe."

"I'm glad you'll be safe," she said with a hint of unease. "My mother's fears have nothing to do with you getting into a car accident, however. She's beside herself that I could be such a fool for having no qualms about your need to run off on vacation with your best friend. Your *female* best friend."

This was a conversation Blake had had at some point during every single one of his relationships. People didn't believe that a man and woman could be friends without there being the constant temptation of romance. He had to inform those who asked that he and Amanda had agreed long ago not to cross that line with each other.

Of course, what he didn't tell everyone he ever dated was that if Amanda ever changed her mind about that, he wouldn't need any time to also change his. When they were younger, he truly only thought of her as a friend. As they got older, though, some of the feelings got a little muddled. There were times he was sure the love he felt for her was a bit more intense than friendship, but after that fateful night a year ago, the one that led to The Incident, there was no chance.

The Incident was something they swore to never speak of again, and the takeaway from that evening was Amanda wanted to be only friends. She had made herself very clear, and

Blake respected her too much to ever think about crossing the line again. Being solidly in the friend zone meant Nadia had nothing to worry about.

"First, this isn't a vacation. We're moving her sister's stuff. Secondly, did you tell your mother that Amanda is basically like my sister? Would she be worried about me going on a trip with my sister?"

"I didn't think to describe her like that," Nadia replied sheepishly.

"Amanda and I are like family. You can sleep soundly, my dear."

"It would help if she was a little less attractive. Maybe she could not be so sweet all the time, too. Tell me she chews with her mouth open or something equally annoying."

Blake chuckled because Amanda would be shocked that she could make someone like Nadia feel so insecure. His best friend did not see herself the same way the rest of the world did. Amanda was perfect. She was the whole package—smart, funny, compassionate almost to a fault. Beautiful. It had taken some time to come to terms with the fact that some lucky guy would do what Blake had been unable to accomplish—sweep Amanda off her feet and win her heart.

He stood up and went to the window. The sun was shining, and there were no signs that fall was on its way yet. The air conditioner was on full blast since both he and Amanda liked to sleep in an icebox. They were so perfect together that maybe the most annoying thing about Amanda was that she didn't want to spend her life with him. "She's super annoying," he said. "In fact, Amanda is probably the most annoying person I know."

It was Nadia's turn to laugh. "I know you don't mean that, but thank you for trying."

The click of the door closing captured his attention. The crestfallen way Amanda looked at him made him want to punch himself in the face. He could tell she had heard what he'd said. "I have to go. I'll text you when we get to the ranch." He ended his call. "Nadia had a nightmare that you invited me on this trip to seduce me," he explained to Amanda. "She begged me to tell her you're annoying so she can sleep tonight."

Amanda stepped farther in the room and began to gather up her things. She didn't say a word.

"Her mom gave her a hard time about 'letting' me go on this trip with my *female* best friend. It's so funny that people can't accept that some men and women just have platonic relationships."

"Are you ready to go, or do you want to give me the keys so I put the dog and my bag in the car?"

"Harrison," he said, taking a step in her direction. "I was trying to make Nadia feel better. It was a joke. Why is it that she didn't believe a word coming out of my mouth, but you do?"

She turned her head and made eye contact. He could see the hurt there in her sapphire-blue eyes. That fake smile spread across her face. "I know. It's fine. Are you ready or not?"

"It's not fine and I'm sorry." He reached for her hand, but she pulled away. "Would I have entered into business with you or stayed your friend for this long if I thought you were annoying?"

"I shouldn't have walked in when I knew you were on a private call. You don't have to make things up to try to make me feel better about something I was never meant to hear." She didn't bother to wait for him to offer her the keys. She spotted them on the dresser and took them, instead. "We'll be waiting in the car."

She had successfully made him feel like the biggest jerk in the whole wide world. Maybe he deserved it. She left with her dog, her bag and his heart. She just metaphorically ripped that sucker right out of his chest.

"The part I didn't want you to hear was when I called you a terrible driver because that is true. And you're only annoying because you won't let me love you," he said to the ceiling after he flopped down on the unmade bed he had slept on last night. Amanda's bed looked as if no one had slept in it. She made her bed even in a hotel. That was Amanda. No one was allowed to take care of her. She did the caring and asked for nothing in return. Practically demanded it. That was also sort of annoying.

Blake scrubbed his face. She would forgive him because she always did. Deep down she had to know that she was stuck with him, no matter what. He'd make this up to her by helping her get Lily to come back to San Diego.

When he got to the car, she was sitting in the back seat with Clancy. That was not happening.

"Now you really are annoying me," he said as he got in the car. "Please come sit in the front with me. I can't handle you being mad at me for the next six-plus hours."

"I'm not mad at you," she lied.

"You're mad at me. You think I said you were annoying."

"Super annoying. The most annoying person you know, actually. And I don't *think* you said it. I *heard* you say it."

He twisted in his seat to look at her. "My fiancée thinks you're going to steal me away while we're on this trip. You know this drill. Everyone I date does this. They get jealous of you. It happens every time."

Amanda folded her arms across her chest. "Your fiancée? The gorgeous, brilliant, successful lawyer who looks like she should be a supermodel instead of a prosecutor? That fiancée is jealous of me?"

She never saw it coming no matter how many times this kind of thing happened. "Yes, Harrison. She is jealous of you. Just like Rebecca and Ariel were. Just like Kira was, too. She's not at the completely paranoid level of Dana. She's definitely not foolish enough to try it's-her-or-me like Veronica, because she's as smart as you think she is." Nadia knew that an ultimatum like that would be the end of their relationship like it was for his and Veronica's. Amanda trumped everyone. Period. "But she worries that one-on-one time with you will lead me to realize there's no other woman I want in my life as much as I want you."

As soon as he said it, he felt it. Darn it, these feelings! His cheeks warmed and he shifted to face forward. If she knew how he felt about her, things would forever be awkward. Amanda didn't feel that way about him. She loved him but was not *in* love with him.

The back door opened and shut. The passenger door opened and Amanda climbed in next to him. "It was sweet of you to tell her I'm annoying, then. That probably made her feel a little better about things."

"It made her laugh, at least." He quickly glanced in her direction. She was much more relaxed than she had been a moment ago.

"I'll never understand why people don't get that sometimes a guy and a girl are just friends. It's not that weird, right?"

"I don't think so," he replied, starting the car.

Amanda cleared her throat. "I love our

friendship. It means everything to me. I hope you know that."

Blake reached over and took her hand. How he wished it could be more. He gently rubbed his thumb across her knuckles. "Same here, Harrison. Glad we're on the same page about that. Should we go get your sister?"

"Please."

They got on the road again. The highway wasn't very congested. There were a few truckers and a few people on their way from here to there. Hopefully, things would stay this way so they could get to the Blackwell Ranch before dark. He was excited to see the ranch, and it would be hard to get a feel for it at night.

Amanda turned up the radio, and he could sense where that was headed.

"For the record, I'm not singing or playing any games that have to do with the alphabet, license plates or I Spy. You need to come up with a different way to entertain yourself."

"Wow. Aren't you a party pooper?" She pulled out her phone. "Well then, I'm going to do work, and you can sit over there not singing, ignoring license plates and refusing to look for anything I might spy."

"You forgot that I also won't be thinking of words in alphabetical order."

"You're *hilarious*." She reclined her seat and received a friendly lick from Clancy in the back. She got busy making some calls and answering emails. The best decision he had ever made was going into business with Amanda. Her work ethic was second to none, and she cared so deeply about doing what was best for animals that it was easy to earn the trust of investors and customers alike.

For two hours, they drove and talked business. A quick stop in Idaho for lunch gave them time to take Clancy for a walk.

"You sure you don't want to play a little bit of road-trip karaoke?" Amanda asked when they got back on the road.

"Positive."

"What else is there to do in a car for the last four hours? If you don't play something with me, I'm just going to go to sleep and you'll be so bored," she threatened.

Few things were worse than having a sleeping passenger. When there was no one to talk to, even short drives felt endless, but he was not singing the rest of this trip.

"I'm not in the mood for games, but we could talk about what I need to do to get you to become friends with Nadia." His eyes left the road for a second to catch her reaction, which was…unreadable.

"We are friends," she said, fidgeting in her seat.

"You're nice to one another, but you're not friends. Yet." He desperately wanted them to get along. If they were friends, it would make it so much easier for him to keep Amanda close. Not that he'd ever let anything or anyone come between them.

"I don't know what you want me to do. I plan to continue being nice to her. Isn't that how to be friends with someone?"

"It would be cool if you two spent some time together even if I wasn't around. Or if you texted her, offered to help with the wedding." Nadia worked so much that she had already hinted that she needed some help. She had one sister, who lived in Boston. They weren't as close as Amanda was with her sisters. In fact, Nadia didn't talk much about her sister. Her parents were also across the country in New York.

Amanda had her head turned, staring out the window. It was a beautiful view with the mountains in the distance and the big blue sky. The closer they got to Montana, the more he understood why it was called Big Sky Country. Still, her silence made him uneasy. What was it about Nadia that she didn't like? Nadia was a good person. She and Amanda weren't *that* different.

"You don't want to help us with the wedding?" he asked.

She snapped out of whatever spell she was under. That fake smile was back and more concerning than ever. "Of course. I will do whatever you want. I'll also try harder to reach out to Nadia. I want us to be close."

"Okay, so that's what you know I want you to say. Now, tell me what you were really thinking about while you were staring out the window."

"That's it. Why wouldn't I want to be close to the person you're in love with?"

"That's why I'm asking. I feel like the last week or so you've been off. Putting walls up. I can't tell if it's what's going on in your family or if it's that Nadia and I are getting married. Or is it that mole?"

Her forehead creased. "Mole?"

"The mole you're having removed when we get back to San Diego." He had a sinking feeling that she was not being completely honest about what was going on. "The one you swore wasn't cancer."

"Oh, right." She made direct eye contact. "I do not have cancer. I wasn't lying."

There was something she wasn't telling him about that mole, but as long as it wasn't going to kill her, he had to let it go for the time being. "Okay, so what's the issue? Ever since I told you I was engaged, you've been weird."

"Wow. Thanks."

"You know what I mean."

"There is a lot going on, Blake. So much that it makes my head hurt. If I'm not acting like myself, maybe it's because I recently learned I'm not who I thought I was."

He felt bad for being so self-centered and assuming the issue was his engagement. Amanda had much bigger issues on her mind. "Being a Blackwell doesn't mean you aren't still you. You'll always be a Harrison. Until you get married, I guess. Even then, I'll probably still call you Harrison."

"When I get married, right," she said as if there wasn't a chance. As if Amanda couldn't have any guy she wanted. The only reason she wasn't already married was that she had very high standards, which made Blake very happy. She didn't let the wrong guys stick around for very long. Sooner or later, she would find Mr. Right.

"I did it again. I am supposed to be here to keep you upbeat and I am failing miserably. Let's play a game. I'll play anything you want."

"Nope. I am not choosing. It made you miserable yesterday, apparently."

"Fine. I'll choose. Let's play Would You Rather."

She wrinkled her nose in the most adorable way. "Fine, but not the gross version."

"You mean like would you rather eat your boogers or mine?" he asked with a smirk.

"You are such a child sometimes," she replied with a shake of her head. He didn't mind the insult because he had made her smile.

"Okay, would you rather have animals understand everything you say or be able to understand what they're saying?"

This was right up her alley. She loved animals and had always wanted to be able to communicate with them. He was interested in which she would choose. She took a deep breath through her nose and let it out nice and slow as she thought over her answer.

"This is an impossible question. I can't choose between these two things." She held her head in her hands. "Imagine if Clancy could tell me what he wants and needs. Oh, my gosh, I could go to the zoo and know for sure if the animals are being treated well or not." Amanda had a love/hate relationship with zoos. Her passion for all animals made it one of her favorite places, but she also worried that certain animals shouldn't be confined. "But what if I could communicate with animals? I could explain when things don't make sense to them. Clancy wouldn't sit at home, worried I'm never coming back when I leave the house. I really need both. I need to know what they're thinking, and I need to be able to tell them things, as well."

This was more entertaining than he had

thought it was going to be. Blake shook his head. "You are really bad at this game."

"It's not me—it's you! You're the one who came up with the impossible question."

"It's called Would You Rather. The purpose of the game is to choose between two things that feel impossible to choose between."

"Fine. I'll choose." She clasped her hands behind her head and resumed fretting over how difficult it was to pick only one.

"At this rate, we're going to make it all the way to the ranch before I get an answer," Blake teased.

"Shush!" She reached over and covered his mouth with her hand. "I would choose to be understood by the animals. No! Wait! I would choose to understand the animals. I think I need to know what they think more than the other way around. I'm going to trust they read my body language well enough that they get the gist of what I say."

"Is that your final answer?"

"I think so. Wait—I don't know."

Blake couldn't help but laugh. "You are really overthinking this."

"Fine," she said with a self-aware grin. "I would rather understand animals. Your turn.

Would you rather…eat everything with a fork or eat everything with a spoon?"

"Spoon," he answered without a second thought.

Amanda's mouth fell open. "You didn't even think about it. You need to at least consider both options before answering."

"It was too easy. Obviously, there are things that you eat with a spoon that can't be eaten with a fork, but everything you eat with a fork can be eaten with a spoon. There's nothing to really think about."

"I stink at this game," she said with a pout. "New game."

"No quitters. Use your phone to look up better questions. Right after you answer this one. Would you rather be able to teleport anywhere you want to go or be able to read minds?"

She dropped her head and groaned. Clearly he had picked another one she'd have to debate for much longer than she could handle. She often talked about how she wished she could read people's minds because she was just nosy enough for that to be intriguing. She also hated traveling and would give anything to snap her fingers and be somewhere instantly.

"Right now, I want to teleport out of this car because I hate you."

"Is that your final answer?" he asked, knowing it wasn't.

"No! I mean, I want to teleport, but I would obviously not need to use that as often as I would want to read people's minds. But I need to know if I can turn it off."

"Turn off what?"

"Do I have to read everyone's mind all the time or can I choose to read someone's mind only when I want to?"

"I don't know. Does it matter?"

"Yes, it matters. If I had to hear everyone's thoughts all the time, it would be so overwhelming. I also don't want to know what some people are thinking because…ew. Some people are gross."

This was why he loved her. Amanda didn't make the mistake of rushing into anything. It made her an excellent business partner, and she had also kept him out of trouble a time or two because sometimes she forced him to be more cautious.

"You make some excellent points. Let's say you can choose whose mind you invade."

"Great, you made it sound creepy. Now I don't know which one to pick anymore." She frowned and turned her head. He was about to tell her she wasn't a creep because he would love to be able to read her mind, when she shouted, "Watch out!"

CHAPTER FIVE

THE CAR IN front of them had slammed on the brakes, definitely hit something and proceeded to keep on going. Amanda was sick. How could someone show such little regard for an animal's life?

Blake carefully maneuvered to the side of the road without hurting Clancy in the back seat. Amanda didn't hesitate to jump out of the car. The animal that had been struck by the other car was lying on its side motionless. She didn't have to get very close to know that the gray wolf had not survived.

"Be careful," Blake said, coming to her side.

"Poor thing. What is a wolf doing out here by the highway in the middle of the afternoon?"

"I don't know." Blake surveilled the area. "But we both know that wolves run in packs.

It's most likely not alone. We should go back to the car and call the police."

The police would contact the proper local authorities to come and remove the deceased animal. Amanda hated the thought of any animal in pain, but wolves were so much like dogs that this seemed all the more tragic. This wolf would be missed by another wolf tonight. The thought got her choked up. That was when she heard the little yelp from the long grass on the side of the road. Blake must have heard it, too, because he was already moving in that direction.

Not too far off the road, two playful gray wolf pups were wrestling with each other. "Oh no," Amanda said. "Do you think that was their mom?"

Blake shrugged. "Probably. I can't imagine they would be this far away from their den with anyone other than their mother. The rest of the pack can't be too far. One of the adults will find them and take them back."

"What if they don't?" Her heart pounded in her chest. "These two aren't very old. They won't be able to survive out here by themselves. And what if they wander out into the road like their mother? We can't leave them here, Blake. We can't."

"Let's call the police and we'll tell them there are pups."

"Or we can take the pups and find a sanctuary for them once we get to the ranch."

"Amanda, we can't take these two wild animals with us. Clancy will go nuts."

Thankfully, Amanda had been prepared with the perfect solution. Since it was possible she might have to fly home with Clancy, she had brought along his travel crate. "We can put them in Clancy's crate in the back to protect them and us. We can't leave them here. They could get hurt this close to the road. After what happened to their mother, it's way too dangerous."

Blake was a sucker for animals just as much as she was. The only option was to rescue them or wait for hours for someone from animal control to come out, because Amanda was not leaving these two alone.

"I'll set up the crate, but remember wolves aren't as people friendly as dogs, Harrison. Good luck getting them to come to you."

Amanda had been so focused on getting Blake to agree with her plan that she hadn't considered how difficult it might be to convince the little pups that coming with her was the best option. She knelt down near where they played.

One of them took notice of her before the other. He or she stared at her with clear distrust. The other one, who was still a bit oblivious, took its sibling's distractibility as an open invitation to pounce. The two of them rolled around until the second one also realized there was a stranger in their midst. They both got to their feet and stared her down.

"Hello there. I know I'm probably a little bit scary." This was one of those moments when she wished that she really did have the ability to speak to animals. It would make this a whole lot easier. How in the world would she convince them that she meant them no harm?

As if they not only could understand her but also read her mind, the two pups stumbled over to her completely unafraid. They sniffed her and let her run a hand across their backs. She picked them both up, one in each hand, and carried them over to the car, where Blake was on the phone and the trunk was open with the crate all set up.

Blake finished his call and shook his head. "Seriously? They just came to you, didn't they?"

Amanda shrugged. "Maybe animals can understand what I say."

"You've always had the magic touch, that's for sure. Someone from animal control will come and take care of their mom. You better hope that someone at the Blackwell Ranch knows what to do with two baby wolves. They are not coming back to San Diego with us."

There was no worry about that. Lily had told Amanda all about the Blackwell cousins. One of them was a vet. Ethan Blackwell supposedly ran a clinic right out of the ranch. He would at least know how to care for them until Amanda found a place that would be able to return them to the wild.

Clancy was quite interested in their new travel companions. The wolfhound wanted nothing more than to be friends with the wolves. Amanda chose to sit in the back seat with him to keep him from trying to climb into the third row with the pups. The wolves, however, were not big fans of cages or riding in cars. They started howling about an hour into the drive and didn't stop even when they drove under the Blackwell Family Guest Ranch arch.

Amanda craned her neck to take in all the sights. She wasn't sure what she'd expected this place to be. She'd never been to a guest ranch or even a regular ranch. She had looked at pictures of it online, and it seemed more like a mountain resort than anything else. Whoever put their website together did a very good at making it look like an upscale retreat.

"Did you text Lily to let her know that we have Clancy and two wolf pups with us?" Blake asked as he pulled into the parking lot marked for guests. "Maybe she should come out here and meet us. Along with whoever is going to take these howlers."

Amanda texted Lily and hooked on Clancy's leash. "Can you take Clancy for a bathroom break? I'll handle the pups."

"You made it!" Lily came running from the direction of one of the barns nearby. Hearing her voice put a lump in Amanda's throat. It had been over a month since she'd seen her sister, a month when Amanda had needed her the most.

All of her frustration with her sister evaporated as soon as Lily wrapped her arms around her. "I'm glad to see you're really alive and well."

"I am alive and very well. Never been better, actually," Lily replied. She let Amanda go and took a good look at her sister. "How was the drive? How are you?"

"Drive was long and I am happy to see you. I have been really worried about you."

"No reason to be worried, sis. I am happier than I've ever been and I cannot wait for you to meet Conner."

"What about me? Are you excited for me to meet Conner, too, Lily Pad?" Blake asked. Clancy, who was probably excited to simply be out of the car, nearly yanked Blake's arm off trying to get to Lily.

"Clancy!" The Irish wolfhound almost knocked her over. "Good to see you, too, big boy." Amanda took the leash from Blake and settled Clancy down. Lily opened her arms. "Mr. Collins, I hear congratulations are in order."

"I guess I could say the same." Blake embraced Lily, and Amanda felt the faint tug of possessiveness that always appeared when Blake and any of her sisters interacted. Growing up in a family of five girls only a few years apart in age meant never really having anything that could be called their own. The girls shared everything from hairbrushes and makeup to shoes and clothes. Blake, however, was hers.

"Yeah, congratulations. You two have successfully stressed me out."

Blake took a step back but threw his arm around Lily's shoulders. "Oh, Harrison. You love that the two of us keep things interesting. Without us, your life would be so boring."

That was true and why it was so painful that their marriages were going to change things between them.

"You do not have to stress over me. I have more than enough people here to help me with this wedding. You get to come back in December and just enjoy the party," Lily said.

"We're flying back in December," Blake said, stretching his arms above his head. "I cannot deal with your sister's need to play road-trip karaoke."

"How about her ability to attract animals in need?" Lily dipped her head to peek through the window at the rambunctious wolves. "Ethan—that's the Blackwell who's the vet—

said you really should have left them where they were, but he's got a friend who can take care of them."

"Well, Ethan wasn't there, and he didn't see how close they were to the highway. They would have ended up like their mother if we hadn't rescued them."

"Wolves run in pretty tight-knit packs. The adults in the pack look out for the young, even if they aren't the parents." A man in jeans and a plaid button-down seemed to have come out of nowhere. He tipped back his cowboy hat and showed off one heck of a chiseled jaw and some soulful brown eyes.

"You must be Ethan Blackwell," Blake said.

The guy shook his head. "No, sir. I would be Conner Hannah. You must be Blake and Amanda."

Conner. *The* Conner.

"Well, if it isn't the man who stole our Lily Pad's heart." Blake held out his hand. "Good to finally meet you."

"Lily Pad?" Conner raised a brow.

Lily rolled her eyes. "Blake is fond of nicknames. Some are better than others."

Conner nodded and turned his attention toward Amanda. "Welcome to Falcon Creek." He stepped in her direction. "Boy, you sure do look like your sister."

The awkwardness jumped up five notches. Should she hug him? Shake hands? He seemed just as unsure of how to proceed. If he was going to be her brother-in-law in a couple of months, she probably should hug him. Of course, the first thing he'd said to her was that she was an idiot for rescuing the wolf pups. Handshake it was.

Amanda stuck out her hand just as he went in for the hug. "Nice to meet you, Conner. We get that a lot. Seems people don't expect identical twins to look identical for some reason."

He shook her hand and then shoved his hands in his pockets. "I grew up with the Blackwell twins—Ben and Ethan, that is. They also look freakishly alike. Tyler and Chance are fraternal. They look like brothers but not the same. I guess I never know what to expect when someone says they have a twin."

Freakish? Had he just called Amanda and Lily freakish? Amanda was not going to leave her sister in Montana with someone who thought they were freaks.

"Not that I think you guys look freakish,"

he backpedaled, clearly reading her horrified expression. "I didn't mean it like that."

"Hey, we also have a fraternal triplet, Georgie. We kind of *are* freaks," Lily said, trying to make it better for him.

"I am usually much better at making a first impression than this, but I think I am really nervous. I'm sure that you have a lot of questions and want to make sure your sister is making the right decision by settling down with me. Lily and I are moving at light speed. That probably raises a bunch of red flags."

At least he wasn't oblivious to how their rash behavior might appear to those on the outside of their little love bubble.

"I'm making the right decision. There's no doubt," Lily said, entwining her fingers with his and kissing him on the cheek. Amanda didn't miss the way Lily looked at him with pure adoration.

"Well, I know you feel that way, sweetheart, but it would be nice if we had your family's blessing."

"Amanda doesn't need convincing. She's always been the one who knows me best. It won't take her longer than two seconds to see that you are the very best and I am the luckiest girl in the world that Big E asked you to be my chaperone."

They shared another kiss that lingered. It was almost too much. The way they smiled at each other made Amanda uncomfortable. It was like they had known each other forever. Both of them were completely smitten. No one had ever looked at Amanda that way—like no one could or would ever compare.

"Right, sis?" Lily asked, putting her on the spot.

Before she could respond, Clancy caught sight of a couple approaching and pulled Amanda across the parking lot to make their acquaintance. The blonde woman was visibly pregnant and the dark-haired man was quick to step in between her and the overeager monster dog coming their way.

"He's friendly. Maybe too friendly," Amanda assured them as she tried to hold her ground. "Clancy, chill."

"He's beautiful. What kind of dog is he?" the woman asked. She knelt down and gave Clancy a good rubdown. She was now his favorite person here.

"Irish wolfhound. He's huge, but don't let his size fool you. He's a lover."

"You must be Lily's sister," the man said. "I wouldn't be able to tell you two apart if it wasn't for the fact that my ranch hand and your sister are always attached at the hip instead of, oh, I don't know, working."

"Hey, now. Are you calling me a slacker?" Conner asked with his hands on his hips. "Because I have been working my butt off. Hadley can attest to that."

"He has. Be nice, Tyler." Hadley Blackwell stood back up and nudged her husband. Lily had mentioned her to Amanda a bunch whenever they spoke on the phone. Hadley and Tyler ran the guest ranch, and Hadley was also helping Lily plan the big wedding. "We want to help Conner make a *good* impression. Hi, I'm Hadley. We are so excited that you're here. Lily talks about you all the time."

"That's funny. She talks about you all the time, too."

"That's so sweet. It's been fun getting to know each other. It's nice not being the newest member of the family anymore. I mean, Katie was actually the last one to marry into the family, but she's practically been an honorary member of the Blackwells since she was a kid. Being a Blackwell can be a little overwhelming, so don't be afraid to come talk to me if they get to be too much."

Amanda stiffened. She was not a Blackwell. She would never be a Blackwell. That wasn't why she was here.

"Hey, Harrison. You gonna introduce me or do I have to do it myself?" Blake asked, coming up alongside her. He clearly noticed her visceral reaction to what Hadley had said. His use of her last name was exactly what she needed. She was a Harrison. She always would be.

"This is my friend Blake. He's about as shy as the dog."

Blake shook hands with Tyler and Hadley. "This is quite the place. I told my fiancée that I would have to check things out and see if you guys live up to your reputation of being the premier wedding destination. Nadia loves horses."

"We've got those," Tyler said with a grin. "And my wife and I have worked very hard over the last year to earn all the accolades. If you are looking for the dream wedding experience, you came to the right place."

"My husband should have mentioned that his brother also helped put us on the map,"

Hadley said as another man joined them. "Speak of the devil. Ethan, come meet Lily's sister."

Ethan Blackwell was tall and lean. He had the same gorgeous blue eyes as his brother but wasn't as polished as Tyler. The sleeves of his shirt were rolled up to the elbows and his jeans were covered in dust. "The sister who has a thing for rescuing wolf pups?"

"Guilty as charged. I know we probably should have waited for animal control, but they were so close to the highway, I didn't want to leave them there and risk them suffering the same fate as their mother."

"Amanda is the ultimate softy when it comes to anything with four legs. She might love animals more than you do, Ethan," Lily said.

"That doesn't surprise me, coz. Does she have the magic touch with horses like you?"

"No one has the magic touch like my fiancée," Conner replied, giving Lily a squeeze.

What kind of alternate universe had Amanda landed in? Did Ethan call Lily *coz*? Why did she suddenly feel like a complete outsider? These Blackwells had sucked Lily in faster than Amanda could imagine.

"Looks like she brought her own horse," Ethan said with a laugh as he greeted Clancy, who was happy to get some more attention. "Who is this big guy?"

"This is Clancy. I hope it's okay that I brought my dog. I hate leaving him in a kennel, and with my dad gone on this trip with Mr. Blackwell, and Blake here with me, I didn't have my usual pet sitters to stay with him."

"Big E would hate being called Mr. Blackwell," Ethan said with a snicker.

"No worries," Hadley assured her, pulling some keys out of her pocket and handing them to Amanda. "I don't know if Lily told you, but we set you guys up in one of the two-bedroom guest cottages instead of the lodge. We figured you would prefer to have some privacy and a little more room, as well. Clancy is more than welcome in the cottage."

"I've been staying in the one right next door." Lily linked arms with her sister. "We'll be neighbors."

Amanda had to control her facial expression as she stared down at the key chain labeled Green Forest. She had to hide the shock that the plan was for Amanda and Blake to share a cottage. She had assumed that the sisters would be roommates not neighbors. How was she going to convince Lily to come back to San Diego if they couldn't have their late-night heart-to-hearts as they were drifting off to sleep? That was when Lily was her most honest and her least defensive.

"Here comes my wolf guy," Ethan announced as a blue van pulled into the parking lot. Meadow Brook Animal Sanctuary was painted on the side. At least the wolf siblings would stay together. There would be no handsome stranger wolf that would come in between them. No soon-to-be-mama wolf who would make them sleep in separate dens.

There was suddenly a flurry of activity. The sanctuary guy and Ethan transferred the wolves into the van. Conner and Blake worked on detaching the trailer full of Lily's things from Lily's SUV and connecting it to Conner's pickup truck. Hadley and Lily were talking about dinner plans with the rest of the Blackwell gang. Tyler got a phone call that led to him pacing around arguing with someone about the shortage of licensed aestheticians in Montana. Amanda just stood there trying to process how difficult it was going to be to get Lily back from these people.

"Shall we go check out our fancy cabin and drop off our bags before we get a tour of this place?" Blake placed his hand on her lower back, and his touch snapped her out of her stupor. "Conner said he'd take us out on horses."

"Isn't that so sweet of him," she replied. Blake's wide eyes communicated that she hadn't masked her sarcasm.

"Conner and I will go saddle up the horses," Lily said. "Maybe Tyler can show them where the cabin is because Hadley needs to go back to the guest lodge and rest for a little bit. You've been on your feet all day. Your ankles are going to hate you."

"You are so sweet. Thanks for looking out for me." Hadley gave Lily a hug.

Hugging? Lily was not the hugging type, but there she was, getting hugged by a practical stranger. What had these Blackwells done to her sister?

Tyler got off his call and rubbed the back of his neck. "This spa is going to be the death of me, Hadley. I know you're going to say there are worse problems than having a super popular spa that's constantly booked, but if we don't find at least one more licensed worker, we're going to start getting reviews online that say we can't accommodate an entire bridal party."

"We'll find someone. Don't you worry about any bad reviews. They aren't happening on my watch." Hadley smiled at Tyler the same way Lily and Conner looked at each other.

Amanda was surrounded by people blissfully in love. Other people might have found it sweet and endearing, but it made Amanda feel lonely. And ugly jealous. She needed to be alone before she started bawling in front of all of these people.

Tyler kissed Hadley softly on the lips, both of them still smiling. His hand rested on the side of her bulging belly. "I felt her kick. Did you feel that?" he asked.

"Did I feel it?" Hadley laughed. "She kicks me, babe. I always feel it."

"If you guys just point us in the direction of the Green Forest cabin, I bet we can find it," Amanda said, wishing for that power to teleport.

"I'll take you there," Tyler offered. He gave

his wife another peck on the cheek. Amanda hurried to the SUV and got Clancy settled in.

"I'll come get you once we have the horses ready for a ride," Lily said as Amanda climbed in the back. Amanda gave her a thumbs-up.

Tyler directed Blake where to go and they pulled up in front of their home away from home. "This is one of our two-bedroom, two-bath cabins," Tyler said. "It has great views of the Rockies and the grazing pasture. You'll want to sit out on the porch and take in at least one sunset while you're here. It's a gorgeous sight."

Amanda clutched Clancy's leash and led him inside. The dog immediately set off to investigate these new digs.

Blake set their bags down. "I'm going to give Tyler a lift back to the lodge. No picking rooms until I get back, Harrison."

"You got it," she choked out. Once she was alone, Amanda locked herself in one of the bathrooms and let herself fall apart. Sitting on the floor with her knees pulled to her chest, she allowed herself to feel the pain she was so good at shoving down and hiding from the world.

CHAPTER SIX

BLAKE WAS BEGINNING to wish he was a long-lost Blackwell. This place was amazing. Not only was it a dream for cowboy wannabes, but Tyler had shared that there was a sand volleyball court, a cool bar where they could try ax throwing, and every Thursday, they had food trucks come and serve everything from barbecue to cupcakes.

Amanda wasn't going to be happy, because it was clear why Lily wanted to stay. She was going to need him to make it okay when they left without her sister. The only worry Blake had was that Amanda could fall in love with this place and want to stay, as well. That would *not* be okay. He needed her to come back to San Diego with him. Amanda could live without Lily, but he could not live without Amanda.

"I said no choosing rooms until I got back!" he shouted when he returned to the cabin and found Clancy alone on the leather couch in the sitting room. He had seen pictures of this cabin online when he researched the ranch, and the real thing was just as impressive as the staged marketing photos. Exposed wood beams ran across the vaulted ceiling. The stone fireplace on the one wall was going to come in handy if it got a little chilly at night. A painting of a Rocky Mountain sunset hung on the wall near the small café table and chairs. If that was a fair representation of what they might see on the porch, Blake understood why Tyler suggested making time to watch one.

He poked his head in both bedrooms, looking for Amanda. "Harrison, where are you?"

The lock popped on the door of the bathroom inside the larger bedroom and Amanda stepped out. "You need the king-size bed in here. I'll take the other room. I feel like I need to lie down for a few minutes." She tried to slip past him, but that was not happening.

Blake snagged her by the arm and pulled her against him. He wrapped his arms around her and waited for her to sink into this hug. It didn't take more than a couple of seconds for her to squeeze him back.

"Well, if Lily's goal was to shove her perfect new life in your face the minute you got here, she succeeded. There was a lot going on in that parking lot and I could see it was taking its toll on you."

"I'm fine," she said with her face pressed against his chest, muffling the words.

"You're not fine, and that's okay. In this cabin, you get to be not fine. You get to be mad, sad, annoyed. Whatever you feel, you get to feel when it's just you and me." He could give her that much. Amanda didn't give herself permission to be emotional very often. She was always the levelheaded one, the Harrison sister who made sure she was there to support whoever else was overwhelmed by their feelings.

"They're all very nice. If she stays here and marries Conner, she'll be happy."

"I think that's true. If she stays, she should be happy. Isn't that what we want for her?" he asked.

Amanda nodded against his chest.

"But she's the last one," Blake acknowledged.

Amanda nodded again.

Georgie, Fiona and Peyton had all moved

out of San Diego. Amanda hadn't been happy when any of them left, but she still had her dad, her home and business, and, of course...

"You still have me. I'm not going anywhere," he said, hoping to console her.

She held on to him a bit tighter. "Unless Nadia wants to move someday."

"Nadia has a successful career in San Diego. Our business is based out of San Diego. My parents are in San Diego." Not to mention that he would never go somewhere Amanda wouldn't be. He couldn't imagine not seeing her all the time. "I am not going anywhere. I mean, our kids have to go to the same school and be best friends. Can't do that if we don't live by each other."

Her body seemed to tense up and she held her breath. Even though he knew she wanted that, too, her reaction concerned him. Did she not trust him? Was she worried he would run off like Lily had when love took over? Or was she thinking she wouldn't stay in San Diego if the rest of her family was gone?

A loud knocking on the front door kept him from getting inside her head. Clancy's barking made it hard enough to hear his own thoughts. He gave her one more squeeze.

"Let's go ride some horses and see the sights. Nadia is going to want a picture of me on a horse. Can I count on your photography skills?"

Amanda pulled away and brushed her hair out of her face. She still looked so sad. "You'll be Instagram-worthy, I promise."

Lily didn't bother to knock again; she just let herself in. "What's going on in here?" she asked as she walked into the bedroom. "Did you forget this guy is almost a married man? You two can't share a room."

"We're not sharing a room." Amanda slipped past her sister and called Clancy to follow her. "I need to get Clancy some water before we go."

"Is she okay?" Lily whispered.

Blake shrugged. "Depends on your definition of *okay*."

"She's still mad at me, isn't she?" In general, it took a lot to get Amanda mad, but Blake was well aware that everything Lily had done in the last month had made her sister beyond infuriated.

"You two have a lot to talk about, and you need to make amends for leaving and not coming back."

Lily frowned and let out a sad sigh. "I didn't know I was going to fall in love with Conner. If that hadn't happened, I would have come home once I figured things out with Danny."

"You don't need to explain it to me. I'm not the one whose heart is breaking."

"Did she say that? Did she say I'm breaking her heart?"

Blake put his hands on her shoulders and spun her around so she faced the door. "You're going to have to talk to her." He gave her a little push in that direction.

Lily spun back around. "I hate when she's mad at me."

No one understood that better than Blake. The worst thing in the world was disappointing Amanda. She was just so *good*. To the core. She did everything she could to do no harm, put others' needs above her own and brighten the world around her. People like her were rare. When you were someone she loved, you wanted to be good, too.

"Are you guys coming or not?" Amanda stood in the doorway with her hands on her hips.

"We're coming. Lily was just chastising

me for not giving you the bigger bedroom because you should have the private bathroom. She's not wrong. I'll take the other room."

"He's almost seven inches taller than me," Amanda said to Lily. "It makes more sense for him to take the king-size bed." This was why he hadn't argued with her when she offered, because no matter what reasons he came up with for why she should have the bigger room, she would say the reasons she shouldn't were more important. "Isn't your fiancé waiting for us? Let's go so we can see this place while there's still daylight."

Blake shrugged. Lily gave a quick nod and led the way.

"I'm really happy you're here. I wanted you to see that I'm going to be okay. This place is good for me."

Amanda flinched ever so slightly that Lily probably didn't notice, but Blake saw it. Lily's happiness was both a blessing and a curse for Amanda.

"All I want is for you to be happy. Danny wasn't the right person for you and I knew it, but I didn't want to burst your bubble. I hope that you are sure this time."

"I'm sure. I'm so sure. Let's go on this ride,

and you'll see how great he is when he's in his element."

The sisters linked arms and headed out. Cowboy Conner wasn't going to be able to win Amanda over. He was in a lose-lose situation. If he wasn't good enough, that was bad for him, but if he was perfect, it was actually worse for him. *Perfect* meant Lily was never coming back. Amanda would silently resent him forever.

Waiting in the barn was not only Conner but a pregnant redhead, a little girl dressed head to toe in pink and none other than the famous Chance Blackwell.

"Watch out, Rosie," Chance said, his tone full of concern. "Don't get behind the horse. Remember that's dangerous."

"Sorry, Daddy," little Rosie said, following his direction without argument.

"Hey, guys," Lily said. "I'm glad you're here so you can meet my sister."

"I'm going to be a sister!" Rosie hopped up and down.

Lily gave her a high five. "And you're going to be the best big sister. This is my best sister. This is Amanda."

"Hi, I'm Rosie. You look like Lily. I hope

my new baby looks like me and not Daddy. We do not want a boy. I want pink, pink, pink!"

"Whoa. Let's not scare our guests." The woman wrapped her arms around the little girl from behind. "Her pink obsession is her only vice, we promise. Hi, I'm Katie. We've heard so much about you," she said to Amanda.

Lily introduced Blake and Amanda to Chance and Katie. Chance and Tyler were fraternal twins. The Blackwells were all about having more than one kid at a time.

"My fiancée is a big fan," Blake said to Chance. "She's going to be excited to hear I met you on my first day here. She wanted me to tell you that your new album is amazing."

"Well, that's mighty kind of her. Please tell her thanks from me." He placed his arm around his wife. "I had a lot to inspire me."

Katie smiled at him. "Just wait until this little one arrives. Maybe you'll be inspired to write an album of children's songs."

"You sure there's only one baby in there? I hear that Blackwells almost always come in pairs," Blake joked.

Katie placed a hand on her belly. "Oh,

there's only one. We've checked. Honestly, the only Blackwell that's had more than one baby at a time is the one who came out alone. Chance's brother Jon had twin girls with his first wife, and his current wife, Lydia, just had twin boys."

"There are babies everywhere you turn around here!" Amanda sounded a little peeved. "Are you going to ask for his autograph or are we going to get out on these horses?"

Lily stared at her sister through narrowed eyes. "Are you okay?"

"I'm fine. I just don't want to be out there when the sun goes down."

"Well, we're leaving you in good hands," Chance said. "Conner knows this ranch better than I do. He'll be able to show you all the sights. Have a good ride."

"Thanks, boss man," Conner said, giving Chance a fist bump. "And boss woman." He winked at Katie. "I'll take care of the horses when we get back."

"While you're out there, could you check the fencing on the northwest side of the paddock? Someone said there seemed to be some damage that needs repair."

"Will do," he replied with a tip of his hat.

Conner had them all lead their horses out of the barn. Lily showed her new skills by mounting her horse with ease. Conner helped Amanda get on her horse and gave her some basic riding instructions. He showed her how to use the reins and her feet to get the horse to do what she wanted him to do.

"You need any help getting on?" Conner asked Blake.

There was no way Blake was going to let Conner give him a boost. If Lily could get on without help, he should be able to. It couldn't be harder than getting up on a surfboard and riding a giant wave.

"I've got it," he said confidently, putting his foot in the footie thingy.

"Um, Blake…" Conner came up behind him.

"I've got it." He grunted and grabbed the handle on the saddle.

"You're—" Conner wouldn't stop.

Blake pulled himself up and went to swing his leg over the horse. That was when he realized his mistake.

"—going to be facing the wrong way. You need to put your left foot in the stirrup."

Both women were giggling from atop their

horses. Blake shot Amanda a look, but it was good to hear her laugh. "I knew that," he said, stepping down. "I just wanted to provide a little entertainment." He tried again, with the right foot in the stirrup, and mounted the horse without a problem.

Conner went over the same basics, and this time Blake paid attention because riding a horse could be as dangerous as surfing. Horses had minds of their own and could be unpredictable, much like the ocean. Thankfully, his horse followed the rest of them along the trail. As they settled in, Conner led the group on his horse with Lily to his right and just a bit behind him. Amanda and Blake were side by side in the back of the pack.

The Blackwell Ranch continued to impress Blake. The family owned a vast amount of land that butted up to the foothills of the Rockies. The mountain views were breathtaking. There were also acres of prairie grass and herds of cattle and horses. Conner explained that even though the main income came from the guest ranch, the Blackwell Ranch was still a working ranch, which Katie was in charge of running.

One of Conner's main responsibilities on

the ranch was to lead guests on horseback-riding tours, so he was good at narrating their ride. He was full of interesting facts about the wildlife and the changes that came with the seasons. Conner had stories about everything.

"Big E's grandfather arrived here with his family in the early 1900s. They built a little cabin not too far from the creek on the southern border."

"Is it still there?" Blake asked. He loved family history. He had spent a year on one of those genealogy websites trying to trace his family's lineage back several generations. He was the epitome of a family man.

"It's no longer standing, but Big E's dad did take some of the wood from that original homestead and used it to make the sign outside the main barn that says Blackwell Ranch," Conner explained.

Blake adjusted his grip on his reins. "That's a great touch."

Even though Amanda didn't want to be a Blackwell, she seemed interested in hearing about their history.

"Big E's father was the oldest son and therefore he took over the ranch from his father in 1930. His dad's name was Henry, but everyone in Falcon Creek knew him as Dirty Henry because he wasn't a big fan of taking a bath."

"And someone married Dirty Henry and had children with him?" Amanda asked. The woman was a bit of a neat freak. She would never marry anyone named Dirty anything.

"Someone married him all right. A sweet lady named Marjorie. And they had two children, Big E and his sister. I know this may come as a shock to you, but they were not twins."

Lily laughed. "Not going to lie, that's surprising given the way the later generations had kids."

"Marjorie had a series of miscarriages early on, but they were blessed with two healthy kiddos in the end."

Amanda was paying close attention, but didn't say much.

Conner led them along the trail near some cattle grazing in a field. "Big E kept running this place as a working ranch and had planned to leave it to his son, who unfortunately passed away in a tragic accident on the property with his wife."

"That was our cousins' parents, right?" Lily asked.

"It was. The boys were pretty young when it happened. Big E raised them. Most of them took off after high school for college or, in Chance's case, a music career. The only one who stuck around Falcon Creek was Jon."

"But they all came back home, huh?" Amanda asked.

Conner let out a laugh. "Big E made sure of that. The man went to great lengths to reunite his family. I wouldn't put it past him to do the same to you and your sisters."

"Amanda isn't going to move to Montana," Blake replied. He probably shouldn't speak for her, but it came out of his mouth before he had time to think about how it sounded.

"You never know, Blake. This place has a special kind of charm that sucks you in," Lily teased.

"Harrison, tell your sister you have no plans to move to Montana."

"It does have a little more charm than I expected," Amanda replied with a mischievous grin.

Blake didn't find any of it very funny. He turned his head to look at her. "Not happening. Ever." Amanda could come visit Lily whenever she wanted, but California was her home. Their home.

They turned to head back to the barn. Conner complimented everyone on a good ride. "I'm impressed that this is your first time on a horse. You guys are doing really well."

"This isn't nearly as hard as surfing is," Blake said. "The horse really does all the work. I was worried that the horse might go wild, but this guy is so chill. I could shout 'Giddyap!' and—" He was going to say his horse would still keep pace with everyone else, but his horse decided that *giddyap* meant *giddyap*, and he took off like he was trying to win the Kentucky Derby.

Blake tried not to panic even though his heart was racing and his adrenaline was pumping. He tried shouting "Whoa," hoping that would work as well as "Giddyap," but he had no luck. This was like wiping out and being caught in a two-wave hold-down. The fear made it hard to think straight.

The trail began to narrow and trees lined both sides. Blake ducked his head as the horse ran under a low-hanging branch. His knuckles were white from gripping the reins so tightly, but Blake couldn't loosen his hold.

The horse wasn't responding to anything he did or said. This was so different from being on a surfboard. When he surfed, it was the ocean that often threw him a curveball, but at least he had control over what the board did. Here, the horse had all the control and he was literally along for the ride.

The trail widened and they were back in an open field. Blake tried to keep his wits about him. Should he bail? Maybe if he jumped off, he could control how he fell and hopefully reduce the damage to his body. If he stayed on and the horse came to a sudden stop, he could end up being thrown off and suffer some serious harm.

He was sweating and his life was flashing before his eyes. He had a really good life. It was full of love and adventure. He loved his family, but the best times had been with Amanda. He was going to die and she would never know how much he loved her. He couldn't die.

Suddenly, Conner was there beside him and shouting at him to get his feet back in the stirrups. Blake hadn't even realized they were out.

"Relax! And lean forward!" Conner directed. Blake did as he was told. "Pull the reins down and back! Keep it low!"

Blake pulled back on the reins with both hands as Conner maneuvered his horse in front. The combination of the reins and Conner's horse slowing in front of him helped Blake regain control. Blake was out of breath almost as if he had been running alongside his horse instead of riding him.

"Magnus is usually quite mellow," Conner said, falling back. "I think he was trying to show off for you. He must have thought you were getting bored."

All Blake wanted to do was put his feet on the ground and have complete control over where he went and how fast he went there. "Can I get off of him?"

"Yeah. Let me help." Conner dismounted first and stood beside Magnus to keep him still.

Blake carefully got off the horse and wanted to kiss the ground. It took a while for Lily and Amanda to catch up, but as soon as they did,

Amanda climbed down off her horse and ran to him.

"Are you okay? Were you trying to give me a heart attack?" She wrapped her arms around him and his whole body relaxed. His heart rate went back to normal and the knot in his stomach unraveled. She always had the magic touch.

"I didn't fall off."

That earned him a little laugh. "I'm so glad you're all right," she said, resting her cheek against his chest.

"Good thing we don't have to call Nadia and tell her we accidentally killed her fiancé," Lily said. "You still have a way of keeping things interesting."

A near-death experience wasn't exactly how he wanted to cap off the day, but it had made one thing crystal clear. When Blake had been on that horse, afraid he might die, there was only one person he was thinking about. There was only one person he wished he could say *I love you* to, and it wasn't his fiancée.

It was the woman in his arms.

CHAPTER SEVEN

"HE'S GOING TO be hurting in the morning. I grabbed you some ice packs. You're going to want him to sit on these to ease some of the soreness that he's bound to feel tomorrow."

Amanda gratefully took the ice packs from Conner. It was nice of him to think about how Blake would be feeling. He kept racking up the bonus points today. It made her like him and hate him.

"And I brought you guys some dinner from the dining hall." Lily carried in a bag of something that smelled like exactly what Amanda's growling stomach was carrying on about. "They have the best cheeseburgers I've ever had. That's saying a lot since you know how I feel about cheeseburgers."

"You guys are the best. Let me see if Blake is up for eating something."

Blake didn't need Amanda to rouse him. The mention of food did that. "Did someone say cheeseburgers?" he asked, stumbling out of the bedroom.

"The best, according to Lily."

He carefully lowered himself on the couch, wincing all the way. "Well, we know how our Lily Pad feels about cheeseburgers."

"Conner brought you these to sit on." Amanda held up the ice packs. "He says you're going to be really hurting tomorrow. I'll get you a towel."

"Wow. You guys thought of everything," Blake said. "Thank you."

Lily passed out the food while Amanda got Blake situated. Clancy got a little too curious about that delicious smell and was sent to Amanda's bedroom. Today had been a roller coaster of emotion, but at the end of it, Amanda had to admit she was grateful. As much as she wanted to not like Conner, he proved over and over that he was a decent guy. Her sister could do so much worse.

"Thank you for everything, Conner. You really saved Blake's life today."

Conner's gaze dropped to the floor. "You don't have to thank me. You all were my responsibility. I'm sorry that he could have been hurt. That's not how I wanted the ride to end."

"Well, you were pretty amazing," Blake

said. "If you hadn't caught up to me and told me to relax, I probably would be in the hospital right now. I was ready to jump off."

Lily tossed a balled-up napkin at him. "You can't bail off a horse like you do a surfboard."

"Oh, wow. Really? You're an expert now after living here for a month?" He tossed the napkin back at her.

Amanda smiled. She loved the way Blake and Lily got along like brother and sister. All of her sisters treated Blake like he was part of the family. Getting the Harrison girls to agree on anything was a difficult task, so the fact that he had won each of them over was quite a feat.

His phone vibrated on the coffee table in front of him. Nadia's face appeared on the screen, and reality smacked Amanda in the face once again. Blake would never actually be part of the family. He was about to start a family with someone else. Someone who was unlikely to allow Amanda to be a relevant part of it.

Blake leaned forward gingerly and grabbed his phone. "Hey, can I call you back? We just sat down to eat dinner."

Nadia apparently didn't want to wait and

must have said so because Blake dragged himself off the couch and disappeared into his bedroom.

"I guess that's a no." Lily's eyes were wide. "What's this Nadia like? Are we happy he's getting married to her? I'm not sure how to feel because he hasn't been dating her very long, right?"

"Oh, hello, kettle," Amanda quipped. "No offense, Conner."

"None taken. We definitely moved super fast. I don't expect y'all to welcome me with open arms. I don't blame you for any skepticism you might have."

Ugh. He made it so hard to not like him. Understanding and humble? There had to be some flaws underneath all that perfectness.

"She can be as skeptical as she wants to be. I know you're the one. The only one." Lily leaned across the little café table where they sat and gave him a kiss.

Amanda tried to steer the conversation away from how nauseatingly in love they were with each other. She was eating, after all. "I am trying to keep an open mind about everyone, including Nadia."

"So you like her? You guys get along?" Lily asked.

"Of course I like her. She's nice. I haven't spent a ton of time with her, but Blake seems happy." That was all Lily was going to get out of her. She wasn't going to speak badly about Nadia even though she didn't think Blake was making the best decision by marrying her so quickly.

However, Lily wanted more. "This is Blake we're talking about, though. He has a new girlfriend every couple months. What makes this one the one?"

She wasn't wrong. He'd had a lot of girl-friends. He always seemed to find something wrong with whomever he was with and would walk away like it was nothing. She wasn't sure what was different about Nadia. He hadn't shared anything specific.

"You'll have to ask him," Amanda said with a shrug.

"Maybe I will." Lily popped a french fry in her mouth.

Blake limped out of the bedroom. "Every-one say hi to Nadia." He held the phone out— Nadia was on video chat and waved hello.

They all said hi. "All right, I'll talk to you tomorrow," Blake said to his fiancée.

"Love you," she said.

"Love you, too," Blake replied. Amanda set her burger down. It was hard to hear those words when he said them to someone else even though when he said them to her they meant something different. He was in love with Nadia. He loved Amanda like a sister.

Sisters got left behind when people fell in love. Lily was proof of that.

"So…" Lily said once Blake ended his call. "That was Nadia, huh? The woman who finally convinced you to settle down. I need to know how she did it. I never thought it would happen."

"Sometimes we just have to take the leap, right? Isn't that what you're doing?"

"I'm marrying the guy who swept me off my feet and makes me feel like I can do anything."

That was sweet. Amanda wanted that for all of her sisters. She wanted it for herself.

"I don't know if I swept Nadia off her feet, but we get along really well. She wants the same things that I do—a big family and to settle down somewhere near the beach."

Lily's face scrunched up in confusion. "You get along with everyone you've ever dated. None of them wanted a family or to live by the beach? That's what makes her the one?"

Amanda ate her cheeseburger and listened closely for his answer. She had also been wondering what it was that had convinced Blake to settle down.

Blake stopped to think about what Lily asked. "I guess some of the other women I've dated wanted those things, as well." He played with the front of his hair, something he did when he was anxious. "I mean, let's be honest—we're not getting any younger. We're almost thirty. If I want that big family, I need to get started. I've always been good at comparing the women I dated to—" He glanced over at Amanda, who froze. Was he going to say *her*? He looked away and continued, "To my idea of what the perfect woman should be. But that's unrealistic to expect someone to be perfect, right?"

Lily shrugged. "I don't know. I don't think anyone is perfect, but I think that the person you spend the rest of your life with should be perfect for you."

"I think Nadia will make a really good mom. To me, that makes her perfect for me."

Amanda struggled to swallow down her bite of food. Her condition made it impossible for her to be perfect for Blake. That was something she had known all along, but to hear him say it out loud was almost too much to handle. "And you're madly in love," Lily said matter-of-factly as she finished off her fries.

He cleared his throat. "Yeah, of course I am," he croaked.

Lily's eyes snapped up and she fixed her gaze on him. "That's what makes Nadia different, right? Different than Rebecca or Veronica or… What was that one brunette's name? Kendra? Kerry?"

"Kira," Amanda answered.

Lily snapped her fingers. "Kira! That was it."

"I didn't realize you were so invested in my love life." He chuckled, but Amanda sensed his discomfort. "Will you tell your sister that Nadia is not like the others and that she doesn't have to worry about me?" he asked Amanda.

Neither Blake nor Lily realized that this

conversation was killing her, but she had to slip on her mask and make them all believe she was fine. "I told her that Nadia is great."

"Okay, I believe you," Lily said. "I'm happy for you. We've always wondered who would manage to convince you to settle down. I was curious about her, that's all. If Amanda thinks she's the person for you, there's no doubt she is."

The cheeseburger was not sitting well in Amanda's stomach anymore now that all eyes were on her. "If Blake says he's sure, why wouldn't I believe him?"

Blake's jaw ticked. Amanda could tell that Lily was unintentionally making him feel defensive. He said, "I love Nadia more than I have ever loved anyone."

"Whoa. Sorry, Amanda. You have finally been replaced." Lily took a long swig of her drink.

Blake grimaced. "You can't compare how I feel about Amanda with how I feel about Nadia."

"I'm not trying to give you a hard time." Lily tried to backpedal.

"So, Conner, I was so impressed with all your Blackwell family knowledge. Is that part of the regular tour information?" Amanda asked, desperate to change the subject.

Much to her surprise, she had been enthralled by the history of the ranch. She had felt for Marjorie Blackwell, Big E's mother. Today was the first she had ever heard of anyone related to her having issues getting pregnant. There was strong evidence that endometriosis was hereditary, but Amanda had a mother who had got pregnant by just thinking about it. It always made her feel like she didn't belong. Perhaps she wasn't the odd one out.

Conner and Amanda conversed about Blackwell history, and she learned more about his ranch while everyone ate their dinner.

"I need a shower and my bed," Blake said, getting up without finishing his food. "You guys have a good night."

"We should go," Conner said, rising from the table.

"We'll see you tomorrow," Amanda said, walking them to the door. "Thanks again for the food and the ice."

Lily gave her sister a hug and left with Conner. Blake didn't waste any time retreating into his bedroom. He took a shower and came back out to grab the ice packs.

He ran a hand through his damp surfer-boy hair. "I didn't realize your sister was so worried about my love life. Is there something I should know?" he asked.

Amanda's stomach clenched. She couldn't tell him that she understood why Lily was asking those questions. Amanda wondered the same thing. What made Nadia different from everyone else? Why was she going to win the big prize? Was he marrying her for the right reasons?

"I mean, she's going to challenge me about rushing into things when she's doing the same thing? She's going to question if I'm in love enough? How do we know she's really in love like she says?"

Before they had arrived at the ranch, Amanda would have agreed with him. She would have wondered if Lily was truly in love or just infatuated. Now, seeing the two of them together, it was harder to doubt that her sister knew what she was doing. It was the way he held her hand when they walked together and how she talked about how amazing he was to his mom. Lily seemed to be in love with Conner and he seemed in love with her. It was a big reason Amanda was so miserable. The other reason was the possibility that Blake and Nadia were equally in love.

"If you tell me you are in love with Nadia, I believe you. I want you to be happy and have that family you've always wanted. You are going to be an amazing dad."

"Thank you. I appreciate that you have my back." He got up and gathered his garbage. "Your sister also doesn't understand how she's making you feel. I would never leave you behind. Things aren't going to change between you and me when Nadia and I get married. I would never move a thousand miles away from you."

It was sweet of him to say that, but Amanda wasn't so sure. If he really loved Nadia, she came first. What she wanted would always have to be considered. As much as Blake wanted to believe that Nadia had roots in San Diego, there were no guarantees.

"Well, that's good because I could end up a lonely spinster in need of someone to take me in on holidays."

Blake chuckled and shuffled over to her. He tucked some hair that had fallen out of her ponytail behind her ear. "Like you aren't going to get married and be the greatest mom of all time. I already hate the guy who finally wins your heart. He's not worthy."

The pain was so intense. It started in the center of her chest and radiated to every part of her body. This heartache was like nothing she'd ever experienced. When she lost her mom, the pain had been horrible, but this was unbearable. She wasn't sure how she would survive it.

"You're a funny guy." She had to step away from him. "I think I am almost as exhausted as you are. I'm going to take Clancy for a walk, and then it's shower and bed for me."

"I would go on the walk with you—"

"But you told your horse to giddyap and now you need to giddy down on those ice packs." She pointed at his bedroom door. "Go. Lie down."

His smile was electric. It lit up his entire face. "Yes, ma'am."

Amanda got Clancy leashed up and took him outside. The lights were on in the cabin next door—the cabin Lily had made her home until she got married and moved in with Conner. Surprisingly, Conner's truck wasn't parked next to Lily's SUV.

Clancy was a big fan of the ranch. He found everything extremely interesting. It might have been his goal in life to sniff every square inch of it as well as water every tree, bush or tall grass. He started to bark as soon as they made their way back to the house. Lily stood on her porch, holding a mug of something warm.

"Conner went home?"

"He has to get up so early in the morning and work at his ranch before coming here to work."

"He just keeps getting more and more impressive." Amanda climbed the steps to join her sister on the porch. She loosely tied Clancy's leash to the banister. He was tired from their walk and lay down by the steps, looking out at the grazing pasture.

"He also said that I might have offended Blake with all my questions. Did I? I'm sorry if I did. I wasn't trying to upset him. I was honestly curious."

"I don't think I'm the one you need to apologize to," Amanda said, taking a seat on the white wood glider next to the front door.

Lily sat down next to her and they rocked back and forth. "No offense, but he clearly can't admit that maybe he hasn't thought things all the way through. If his only criteria for a wife is that she'd be a good mom, why didn't he ask you to marry him like five ycars ago?"

Amanda wasn't touching that question with a ten-foot pole. "You probably madc him feel defensive, and that made it hard for him to express himself clearly. I also suggest not calling him *stubborn* when you apologize tomorrow."

"I will do my best, I promise. It still makes me wonder. We both know that the man has commitment issues. The only woman he's ever been faithful to is you."

Amanda rubbed her sternum, hoping to ease that pain that was back with a vengeance. "Well, friendships aren't the same as romantic relationships."

"I don't know what you'd call it, but what you two have is not just friendship. He tends to break up with women when they start to get jealous of you two. He's always chosen you. What happens when Nadia asks him to choose?"

Lily had no idea that the answer to that question was what had been giving Amanda nightmares. There was always going to be a day when someone else would overthrow her in his life. "What happened when Conner asked you to move here instead of coming back to San Diego to be with me and Dad?"

"He wasn't asking me to choose him over you. You will always be my sister no matter where I live. That is never going to change. Georgie, Peyton and Fiona are still our sisters even though they live somewhere else."

"I know that. It doesn't make not having you around any less sad for me, though. Plus, have you thought about how it makes Dad feel that you went full Blackwell after finding out the truth?" Lately, it felt like all Amanda did was lose the people she loved. Her father had to be feeling the same way.

Lily rested her head on Amanda's shoulder. "Dad," she said with a sigh. "I'm not trying to be a Blackwell. I'm trying to be Lily. The Lily who doesn't need her dad to micromanage her life. The Lily who actually loves what she's doing with her life and feels in control of things for once. Back in San Diego, it was Danny who ran the business, not me. Here,

I've found something I'm good at, that I can do with or without Conner. It feels good."

"I didn't realize you felt that way in San Diego. I mean, I know Dad likes to look after things, but I didn't know you didn't feel in charge of your life."

"I'm in charge now. I know what I'm doing and I am the one making the decisions. I love Conner."

"I love you. Does that matter?"

"Do you know why it doesn't surprise me that you rescued those wolf pups?"

Sometimes Lily came at her from left field and made it impossible to figure out where she was going. "Because I love animals?"

"Yes, you love animals, and you want to take care of them, and you don't trust that anyone else can take care of them as well as you can. You brought those pups here because you didn't believe that the other adult pups would take care of them after their mother died."

"True. So what?"

"Sometimes I feel like those pups. Like someone you think you need to rescue. But I need you to trust that I have other people capable of having my back. I have Conner. I have the Blackwells. Not to mention I'm not a pup. I'm a grown woman capable of taking care of myself. I promise."

Amanda closed her eyes and prayed that the tears wouldn't leak out. Lily wasn't ever going to come back to San Diego except to visit.

Clancy stood up and started barking at the darkness. Amanda opened her eyes to see what had caught his attention. "Shh, Clancy. There's nothing out there." Nothing she could see, at least.

He kept on barking, and before Amanda could get up to grab his leash, he took off down the step. The loose knot she had made didn't hold, and there was nothing to keep him from running toward whatever he thought he heard out there.

"Clancy! Stop! Come here, boy!" Amanda called after him. But, just like everyone else in her life, he had better places to be.

CHAPTER EIGHT

"HE'LL COME BACK," Blake assured her. Man, he really hoped that dog came back. Preferably this second.

Lily ended her call. "Tyler said that we could take one of the ATVs out and look for him, but that there's so much land to cover, our best bet is to stay put and wait for Clancy to find his way back. If we're moving and he's moving, we might never cross paths."

Amanda paced back and forth across the cabin's front porch and chewed on her thumbnail. Clancy had already been missing for over an hour. They had walked around the cabin area and down to the lodge and back, but had no luck finding him. They needed to widen their search.

"I can't just sit here. He's in an unfamiliar place. There are wild animals all around. Did you listen to what your fiancé said on our tour today?"

"I'll go out with you if you want to go," Blake offered. He would do whatever she wanted. He knew she'd be a wreck if the dog didn't come home tonight.

"I think she needs to go with someone who knows the land," Lily said. "You two could easily get lost out there."

"Clancy! Come on, boy!" Amanda shouted into the night. "You want a treat? Come get a treat!"

Bribery was always a solid strategy when trying to lure a pup home. The reality was they were on a ranch with a whole lot going on, however. Clancy could easily be too wrapped up in the new sights and smells to want to come back for a boring treat.

"Do you want me to ask one of our cousins to come help?"

Blake could tell that Amanda wanted to say, *Please don't call them "our cousins."* She opted for, "I don't want to bother any of the Blackwells. I'll just take a walk and call for him. He'll come to me."

She started for the stairs, but Blake snagged her arm. "Whoa. You are not walking around in the dark."

"Well, I'm not going to sit here and leave

him out there, hoping he'll show up eventually. He could be attacked by some other animal. He could be hurt."

"Then I'm coming with you. We'll use Tyler's ATV."

"Oh, my gosh, you two!" Lily let out an exasperated sigh and pulled her phone back out. "How are you going to find your way around in the dark? I'm going to ask Tyler to come help."

"I don't need the help from the Blackwells," Amanda protested.

"Why not? They're family. They're more than happy to help."

Blake braced himself for Amanda's reaction to the "family" comment. Her concern for her dog's safety was fraying the edges of her patience. There were only so many negative feelings she could repress.

"They aren't my family, Lily! They aren't your family, either. They are strangers whose grandfather forced us on them because he's decided he wants us in his life regardless of how any of us feel about it. I'm sure deep down they're annoyed that we are here."

Anxiety and fear—the ultimate truth serum.

Lily gasped and was rendered speechless.

Conner's truck pulled into their little cul-de-sac. Blake feared what might come out of Amanda's mouth with him here. How could he warn the poor man to run?

"Somebody looking for this big guy?" Conner said as he got out of his truck. A panting Irish wolfhound followed him out, looking a little worse for wear.

Amanda went from ornery to elated in an instant. "Clancy! Where have you been, big boy?" He was as happy to see her as she was him. He bounded in her direction and put two muddy paws smack in the middle of her chest, almost knocking her over.

Lily turned to Conner just as quickly. "I can't believe you found him. Ty said he'd look."

"I figured the least I could do was check out a couple places I imagined would interest a dog and got lucky almost right away. He had found the pond like I feared."

Amanda clearly didn't care how dirty her dog was—she was too relieved to have him back. "Thank you so much, Conner. I can't thank you enough. I don't know what I would have done if I hadn't gotten him back tonight."

Thank goodness none of them had to find out. Conner was the hero of the day. With this rescue, he made it impossible for Amanda to hold a grudge. It would be interesting how she would handle things now that Conner couldn't be simply the bad guy trying to steal her sister away.

"I was happy to help. Y'all have a good night."

Amanda gave Clancy a shower since there was no bathtub in the cabin. It was quite comical to watch her bathe a dog the size of a small horse in the tiny bathroom. He shook what seemed like a few gallons all over the two of them and the sitting room when they tried to towel him off. Clancy slurped down two bowls of water and then followed Amanda into her bedroom, where he promptly fell fast asleep on her bed.

"Leave it to the dog to keep this evening from being boring," Blake said, scratching Clancy behind his ear.

Amanda had changed into her pajamas and was taking out her earrings. "Leave it to Conner to save the day. He makes it impossible to not like him. It's so infuriating."

Blake laughed. "I think we both have to

admit that Lily isn't going to find a better guy than that one. We might have to welcome him into our exclusive club." Her humored grin made his heart happy.

"We have an exclusive club?"

"Of course we do. You and I have a very small circle. We don't let just anyone in."

"Is Lily still in?"

"I know she didn't mean to make me feel bad. Plus, to forgive and forget is my motto. Especially since Conner is the reason you are going to be able to sleep soundly tonight."

"I'm going to really try to be happy for the two of them. I need to do that. He deserves it and she does, too," Amanda said, eyeing the sliver of bed that was left for her thanks to the enormous dog sprawled sideways.

"Then I will, too." Blake nodded. "Get some sleep, Harrison. We have a busy day ahead of us tomorrow. Wedding planning, meeting more Blackwells, and I'm going to destroy you in sand volleyball."

Amanda's laughter filled the room. "You're not even going to be able to walk tomorrow. I will bury you on that court."

"Oh, we'll see about that." He was bluffing because his backside was already sorer than it had ever been in his life. He kissed her on the forehead. It was an innocent gesture until he locked eyes with her afterward. Her big blue eyes were always his weakness. They were what had sucked him in the night of The Incident.

"Good night, Blake."

He cleared his throat and took a step back, then left the room. He could never repeat the mistake he had made that one night. Not if he wanted to keep Amanda in his life. Being in love with his best friend was never easy. It was like walking into a candy store and having no money in your pocket. Being close to something so sweet would have to be good enough.

"Good night, Harrison."

"This is our brand-new wedding barn. It can accommodate up to three hundred guests. We completely remodeled it last spring, and it has been the number one most requested spot on the ranch since then." Hadley slid one side of the barn doors open. Beyond that were chiffon drapes tied back with rope. "We close these curtains once all the guests have arrived and then the bride gets to make a real grand

entrance. For those who get married just before sunset, the photographers can capture the
silhouette of the bride and her dad behind the
curtains before she walks down the aisle, and
the pictures are incredible."

Amanda was both wide-eyed and open-
mouthed. "This is so beautiful," Amanda
said, spinning around to take in the whole
room. The entire barn had been gutted. There
were strings of globe lights running along the
ceiling's wood beams, and sheer white fabric
draped up there, as well. The shiplap walls
were whitewashed and the floor was polished
concrete. Wooden folding chairs were set up
in rows on either side of the center aisle.

"This is what it looks like for the ceremony,
and then we move everyone back outside so
we can set it up for the reception. On the north
side of the barn, we have a patio where there's
a bar. In the warmer months, the guests can
mingle while the wedding party takes some
pictures. While that's going on, we transform
this space into the reception area. We have
round tables for the guests and a long farm
table for the bridal party. Over there, we make
room for a dance floor."

"What about in the winter?" Amanda

asked. She winced and lifted her foot to adjust her shoe. They had done more walking around than they had expected to and Amanda had worn the wrong shoes for that.

"In the winter, we have these dividers that we bring in to separate the room. Guests mingle on one side while we set up the other."

"I love this," Lily said. "Why didn't Pepper get married in here?"

"Who's Pepper?" Blake asked.

"Our cousin who got married when I first got here," Lily answered. "She rode a horse down the aisle and had her reception in the guest lodge dining room."

"After yesterday, I do not want to ride horses down the aisle. This barn with the outside bar seems much more up my alley." Blake didn't want anything to do with horses ever again.

"We've been working hard to provide a variety of options for our brides. Since Dorothy wanted to give Pepper her dream Western-style wedding and have the whole bridal party on horses, we had her ceremony outside," Hadley explained.

"I think Nadia would love this place," Amanda said. "It's really magical. You said she loves those shows about remodeling houses in Texas. That means she likes the farmhouse style. You should send her some pictures."

Blake was impressed that Amanda thought about Nadia and what Nadia would like. Part of the reason he had been so upset last night when Lily was grilling him was because he feared Amanda wouldn't accept Nadia. Making sure they were good friends was his number one priority before he and Nadia tied the knot.

Blake snapped a few pictures and texted them to his bride-to-be. He should have thought to do that. Thank goodness for Amanda.

"I kind of like the idea of having horses involved in the ceremony," Lily said. "I don't want to ride them down the aisle like Pepper did, but is there a way to include them? Horses are what helped bring me and Conner together."

Hadley pulled out her phone. "Since you're thinking about getting married at Christmastime, we could do a horse-drawn sleigh that brings you and the bridesmaids to the barn. We did it last year. Let me find the pictures."

She scrolled through her photos until she found what she was looking for.

"So perfect," Lily said. She squeezed Amanda's hand. "Couldn't you picture all of us on the sleigh? Fiona would love it."

"She would," Amanda agreed.

"If we go back to my office, I can show you my scrapbook of weddings so you get an idea of what we've already done. Would you like to see the patio first?"

Blake followed Hadley back outside while Lily and Amanda took some pictures of their own to send to the other sisters. Amanda and Georgie had already been texting all morning about Blake's behind. Georgie recommended a soak in a hot tub to relieve his soreness from that horse race yesterday. That quickly turned into Georgie asking a million questions about the ranch and the wedding and Conner.

A woman carrying a black leather portfolio jumped out of an ATV. "Oh good, you are here," she said, looking a bit frazzled in her jeans and flannel shirt. Her hair was in a loose ponytail. "I need your signature on this." She held out the portfolio for Hadley.

"Sorry," Hadley said. "I looked for you this morning, but you weren't in the office."

"I'm having a day. We have a sick baby boy at home, and Ethan said he needed to be here early because he had to check on one of the horses that's been recovering from some treatment he's being doing. I had to wait until Sarah Ashley could come and help me out."

"Oh, Grace, I'm so sorry. Poor Eli. Let me know if there's anything I can do to help."

Grace put her hand on Hadley's shoulder and looked at Blake. "If you were having any doubts, this is why you should let her plan your wedding here. This woman is amazing and will go above and beyond for you."

"She is doing a great job of winning me over," Blake said.

"Grace, this is Blake Collins. He's here with Amanda, Lily's sister." Hadley waved a hand in Amanda's direction. Lily exited the barn behind Amanda and waved hello.

"Oh, Lily! Hi! I didn't realize you were the ones taking the tour."

"Grace is Ethan's wife," Lily explained to Amanda.

Blake watched as Amanda acted pleased to meet another Blackwell. She was good at putting on a happy face. She would be an expert by the end of this trip.

"Will we see you at dinner?" Lily asked Grace. They were supposed to go to Jon Blackwell's house tonight for dinner so they could meet all of the Blackwell cousins and their families. Blake knew Amanda was dreading it.

"I have to send Ethan solo. The last thing my sisters-in-law will want is for Eli to pass his illness on to the rest of the cousins."

"Good thinking," Hadley said.

Grace took the portfolio from Hadley and smiled in Amanda's direction. "Well, at least I got to meet you. Lily has told us so much about you and your sisters. We've all been looking forward to meeting everyone. How long are you guys here for?"

"We planned for a couple weeks. I wanted to help Lily with some of the wedding planning, but I didn't realize she had a Hadley to do all the work."

"Everyone needs a Hadley in their life," Grace said. "I seriously don't know what we're going to do when she goes on maternity leave. Which you should think about, Lily. You have until the end of the year or you are going to have to wait until spring."

"Conner and I were thinking a Christmas

wedding, so we're cutting it close but still under the wire."

"Oh, we're good at Christmas weddings," Grace said. "I have to head back to the lodge and finish up some business so I can get back home to my little guy. I'll see you all around, I'm sure."

"It was nice to meet you," Amanda said. "I hope Eli is feeling better soon."

Grace got back on her ATV, and Hadley led the rest of them to the patio to finish their tour. As nice as this all was, something still felt off. Blake couldn't put his finger on it. Amanda was right about Nadia loving it. She texted back that it was gorgeous. She added lots of exclamation points. Still, when he imagined his wedding day, he couldn't see himself standing in the wedding barn.

As the ladies talked about themes and centerpieces, Blake closed his eyes and tried to picture his wedding day. When he really thought about what he wanted, he saw himself standing by the ocean. He could almost smell the salt water in the air and feel the sunshine on his skin. His feet would be bare and so would his bride's. When he looked down the aisle she was there walking toward him dressed in white with her blond hair in an updo so the sun could kiss her tan shoulders. She would smile at him with the smile that made his heart beat faster, and those blue eyes would lock with his.

Amanda.

Blake's eyes snapped open as the panic set in.

Lily nudged him with her elbow. "You all right there, big guy?"

No one could read minds. There was no way any of them had a clue what had just happened inside his head.

"Are you okay for real?" Amanda stood in front of him and placed a hand on his cheek. "Your face just got real pale. Do you need to sit down for a second?"

Her touch sent electric currents through his body. He never felt this way with anyone other than Amanda. He held her face in his hands. What he wouldn't do to be able to kiss those lips and tell her how he truly felt. She stared at him with a mixture of concern and confusion in her eyes.

What terrible thing could happen if he kissed her? How could she deny this magnetic pull that existed between them? If he was honest, maybe she would be, too. All he had to do was put his lips on hers.

Snap!

Nothing like fingers snapped right in front of the face to wake a person up. Blake let her go instantly.

"What was that for?"

"I don't know. You were in a weird trance or something," Amanda said, stepping away from him. "Are you okay? You're freaking me out."

Hadley had brought a chair outside. "Sit down for a minute."

Blake didn't want to sit. His backside was still hurting from the runaway horse yesterday.

"Sit," Lily insisted.

He cautiously took a seat. What had come over him? This was much too much like the night of The Incident. He needed to remember how very clear Amanda had been that they could only be friends. Admitting that he was in love with her would be the end of their friendship. She would not be able to be around him knowing how strong his feelings were when hers were not.

"Here, drink this," Hadley said, handing

him a bottle of water. "Maybe you're dehydrated. That happens when you're at this elevation. Falcon Creek is a little higher up than San Diego. Your body needs time to adjust."

Blake decided to pretend that she was right. Elevation sickness could easily be the cause of his strange behavior. No one would need to be wise to the fact that he was secretly in love with his best friend and clearly imagined his perfect wedding to be his and hers. He was definitely going to keep that to himself.

With the wedding barn visited and scrapbooks viewed, Amanda and Blake had Hadley book them an appointment at the spa. The Blackwell Ranch had converted an outbuilding into a full-service facility. It was perfect for brides-to-be and their entourages, as well as just right for guests who went a little too hard during the horseback-riding tour.

Hadley made sure they got the works on the house. Full body massage, facial and aromatherapy. Blake loved to be pampered. He played hard and liked his self-care to be just as extreme.

"My whole body feels so relaxed. I'm like Jell-O," Amanda said as she closed her eyes while they finished out their spa time in the hot tub.

"Your sister was so right about me needing to soak in a hot bath. We might be in heaven right now."

The sound of Amanda's giggle was the cherry on top of this happiness sundae. He reached underwater and grabbed Amanda's leg, lifting her foot up onto his knee. Her eyes flew open.

He started to massage her foot. "Don't think I didn't notice you hurting today because of those shoes you put on this morning."

She relaxed and let out a satisfied sigh as he rubbed just under her toes. "Of course you did. You always notice," she said, letting her eyes close again.

"The woman who gave me my massage showed me this trick. You just have to put your elbow into it." He pretended to massage her foot with his elbow. She laughed and squirmed, attempting to pull her foot away. He tugged on it and she slipped off the seat and got dunked in the process. She popped up and wiped the water out of her eyes.

"Dude! Not cool." She splashed him.

Putting his hands in front of his face to protect himself, he begged her to stop. "It was an accident. Stop!"

She lunged at him and wrapped her arms around his neck in an attempt to dunk him. He put his hands on her waist and she stopped. He had to fight the urge to pull her closer, knowing that would be wrong. Why did *wrong* have to feel like the most right thing in his life?

"We should probably get out," she said, pulling away.

"Let's stay a little longer," he begged. "I promise I won't mess with you. Let's just relax."

She sat back down across from him. He had been such a liar the other day when he told Lily he had never loved anyone as much as he loved Nadia. Nothing would ever compare to how he felt about Amanda.

"It seems like your sister is going to be okay out here. How are you doing with that?"

Amanda lifted one of her shoulders. "I think if Mom was still here, I wouldn't be having such a hard time. I'm tired of loss. I can't take much more. I need something that's going to add to my life, not take away."

"When your dad and Big E come back with

Thomas, he could be a positive addition to your life."

She shook her head. "Doubt it. I don't know why they think that even if they find him, he's going to suddenly decide he wants to be part of our lives. He walked out on us. All that revelation has done for me is add to my fear that I'm destined to be alone."

"What?" He moved next to her. "That's not true. You're not going to be alone."

"You don't know that."

Her insecurity confused him. "The only way you would end up alone is if you chose to be. There are plenty of people in your life who want to be in it. Like me, for example."

She pressed her lips together as if she was holding something in. She did that when she was afraid of starting a fight. Why would she argue about that with him? He was having none of it.

"Harrison, you're stuck with me. Not to mention there's some guy out there who is going to marry you and—" *make me jealous* "—you're going to live happily ever after."

"Right," she said, but her tone clearly disagreed.

"Come on. You haven't met Mr. Right yet. That doesn't mean you aren't going to."

"I said you're right. I'm going to get out. I can feel my fingers starting to prune."

All the tension that the massage had worked out of his body seemed to return the second she got out of the hot tub. There was something she wasn't telling him. He was going to find out what it was before they left this ranch. Heaven help him.

CHAPTER NINE

"IS THIS TOO CASUAL?" Amanda stood in front of the mirror. Her hair was flat. Lifeless. Why couldn't she have gorgeous golden locks like Hadley? Hadley had fun hair. She probably rolled out of bed, gave it a quick tousle, and it was perfect. Everything Hadley did was perfect. She was amazing at her job, sweet to everyone around her and would probably have a baby that wouldn't ever fuss or cry.

"I think you look beautiful." Blake smiled at her in the mirror. Dressed in a pale blue button-down and his worn-out jeans, he was the beautiful one. "Are you ready to go? I'm pretty sure I heard Conner's truck pull up."

"I'm not sure I'll ever be ready." She spun around to face him. He also had perfectly tousled hair. It was like he just combed his fingers through it, shook his head and was instantly transformed into a hot surfer dude.

He cocked his head and frowned. "If you go

to dinner tonight, you meet all of the Blackwells in one swoop. If you don't go, you have to spread it out—meet one here, one there. Bump into one in the dining hall, get introduced to another in town. You will be in constant torture."

Blake was handsome and smart. Nadia better appreciate everything he had to offer.

"I would rather get it over all at once. I'm a big fan of ripping the bandage off." She squared her shoulders and took a deep breath. "Let's go meet Lily's new family."

"Would you look at that, ladies and gentlemen," Blake said in his best sports announcer voice. "Harrison is digging her heels in and completely denying the Blackwells are her family, as well. There's no telling how long she'll be able to keep this up, but she seems determined to live in denial forever."

"Just because we have a tiny bit of the same blood in our veins does not make us family. Family is the people you've created memories with, the people who have cared for you and let you care for them. It's the people who are there for you when you need them, the ones who don't run away or leave a wife and five little girls all alone." The more she thought about her biological dad, the more her blood boiled. He'd left when her mom was pregnant with Fiona. Who did that? Not anyone Amanda wanted to be related to.

"These Blackwells don't know Thomas any more than you do. He was never part of their lives. You can't blame them for his bad behavior." He took her hand and tugged her out of the bedroom. "Even if you had been raised by your biological dad, you wouldn't have known about this part of your family until Big E figured it all out. Do you think you'd be more open to them if that had been the case?"

"You're making my head hurt with all your rational thoughts and sensible points of view," she complained with a smirk. He had a way of making things easier. Except for when he made them hard by being so wonderful that she wished she could be with him forever.

"Let's go meet these Blackwells and make them wish they could all move down to San Diego and open some big beach resort where they give wave-runner tours instead of horseback-riding ones. They're going to want to hang out with us all the time because we are so cool."

"*Right*, so cool." She'd try to tell herself that when she was dining with the perfect Blackwells.

Jonathan Blackwell was the oldest Blackwell brother. He did not have a twin like the other four did, but he did have twins. Two sets. He also had his own spread not far from the Blackwell Ranch. Conner parked behind a familiar-looking pickup truck belonging to Tyler and Hadley. Next to it was an Audi Q8, which seemed quite out of place on a Montana ranch.

Four little girls were playing outside with a black-and-white border collie. Their giggles and squeals squeezed Amanda's heart. She was literally walking into the world she wanted more than anything and could never have. The girls ran up to them as soon as they noticed the newcomers were there.

"Are you Lily's sister?" one of the older girls asked Amanda.

"I am."

"You guys are twins like me and Gen."

"Well, kind of. Lily and I are identical, but we actually had one more sister at the same time, making us triplets."

"Three babies at the same time?" Sweet

Rosie's eyes were as big as quarters. "Mama K only has one baby. No fair."

"No fair!" repeated the littlest of the cousin crew. She couldn't have been more than three years old.

"Poppy, you and Rosie can be twins, okay?" Gen said.

"Yay!" The little girl seemed to love the idea that she and her cousin could magically be twins. Rosie, on the other hand, clearly knew that she could not be twins with a three-year-old.

Lily appeared and did the introductions. "I'm going to wow you with my ability to tell you who is who and who their mommies and daddies are. I know Gen and Abby live here. They belong to Jon," she said, placing a hand on the top of each twin's head. "You met Rosie already. And this little one is Poppy, and her mom is Rachel, who is married to Ben."

"Eli is sick. He couldn't come. He's a baby like our babies," Abby explained.

That was a lot of babies with two more on the way. Amanda's soul ached. Sadness and regret crept over her all the faster when surrounded by all of these children.

"Do you have any babies?" Rosie asked. It

was an innocent question but a killer at the same time.

Amanda could only shake her head. If she tried to speak, it was quite possible she would begin to sob.

"No babies in our family yet," Lily answered. "But you guys just wait. In a few years my sisters and I might have a whole bunch of babies like you do."

Conner inhaled. "It smells like someone is grilling up something delicious."

"Daddy is cooking tonight. Mom is super tired because the babies are sucking the life out of her," Gen said.

"You aren't supposed to say that," Abby chastised her.

"But Daddy said it this morning."

Amanda started to second-guess her decision to spend an evening with all of the Blackwells at once. She'd only met four of the children and was feeling overwhelmed.

"Is everyone behaving out here?" A woman Amanda hadn't met yet had opened the front door and poked her head out. "Oh, looks like our guests of honor have arrived."

Blake and Amanda followed Lily and Conner as they made their way to the door. "Hey,

Rachel. Good to see you," Lily said. Rachel was the attorney who was married to the attorney. She had grown up with the Blackwells and with Conner.

She picked up Poppy. "I hope the girls weren't attacking you on your way in."

"They were all very welcoming," Lily assured her. Amanda couldn't disagree. The Blackwells seemed to have welcoming in their blood. Couldn't someone be obnoxious, horrible, mean? It would make it so much easier to not like them if someone would be a little unfriendly.

Rachel raised her eyebrows knowingly. "I'm sure they were. Everyone is excited to meet Amanda. Hi, I'm Rachel."

"Ben's wife, right?"

"Guilty. Please don't hold anything he says tonight against me, though. I love him, but sometimes he opens his mouth and I want to have a judge order him to keep it closed. *Forever*."

Oh boy, she was nice and had a good sense of humor? It was like anyone who married into the Blackwell family was pure awesomeness. Maybe Lydia would be the bad apple. Of course, she was someone who had managed to put on this dinner for all of these people while taking care of two sets of twins. She was clearly the martyr of the group.

"Come on in. The guys were told they couldn't eat until you got here. They're really going to be thrilled to see you." Rachel led the way, calling the kids to follow.

Amanda could hear the chatter in the main room when they stepped inside. There was laughter and then, "I just don't understand why we let Big E drop random family members in our lap. Why are we stuck entertaining them while he's off traipsing across the country again?"

"Benjamin Blackwell!" someone said. She sounded like an older woman. Their grandmother was supposed to be invited.

"What? I'm just saying what everyone else is thinking but is too afraid to say out loud."

Rachel froze and her face contorted into a grimace. "Remember when I said that thing about my husband? This would be one of those times I beg you not to hold his words against the rest of us."

Finally, a Blackwell who got how ridiculous this was. "He's not totally wrong, right?"

Rachel shook her head. "No one else feels

like you've been dumped on us." She grabbed Lily by the hand. "We are so happy for you and Conner. He's needed a good woman for as long as I've known him." She winked at Conner.

Conner did not appear amused. "He better watch himself or else he's going to have something else dropped on him."

"I don't blame you." Rachel's embarrassment colored her cheeks. "Come, meet everyone. Besides Ben, they're all very nice." She led them toward the great room. "Leave it to my husband to stick his foot in his mouth the second our guests arrive."

Amanda entered the room and found a mixture of familiar and unfamiliar faces. The great room was open to the kitchen, and the whole family was spread out throughout the two rooms.

"You guys made it!" A dark-haired woman wearing an apron crossed the room to welcome them. "I am so happy you are here. And I know Jon feels the same way. He would have told Ben to stuff it had he been in here instead of outside at the grill."

Amanda and Blake were introduced to Lydia, Grandma Dorothy and Ben, who didn't look the least bit ashamed for speaking his mind. Ethan was there, as well as Chance and Katie.

Dorothy Blackwell had a thoughtful disposition. She made sure Amanda and Blake were settling in at the ranch and suggested they have Tyler show them where the pond was on the property. Amanda had admittedly been curious about it since Clancy went there on his runaway adventure. It was a perfect place to have a picnic, Dorothy said.

Amanda had been most nervous to meet her. She had every reason to side with Ben in the argument that it was a little weird for them to be hosting Big E's secret family, but she was totally gracious. Thankfully, Big E hadn't been a cheater. He and Great-Aunt Prudence—who was really Grandma Prudence—had a relationship before Dorothy was even in the picture. Still, it had to be strange.

Tyler and Hadley were seated on the couch, each holding one of Jon and Lydia's babies in their arms. They were letting them snack on cereal puffs. Dorothy insisted Amanda take a seat next to Hadley.

"This is Marshall," Hadley said, tickling

the baby on his chubby sides and making him giggle. "And Brendan's snacking with Tyler."

While Hadley looked like a professional managing Marshall in her arms, Tyler seemed so uncomfortable. Brendan was wiggling all over the place and Tyler looked like someone trying to hold on to a slippery fish. "Why did you give me the one that can't sit still?" he asked his wife.

"Would you relax? Wrap one arm around him like this. Hold the snack cup and let him take the puff out himself." She tried to help him readjust.

"You need to learn how to do that, brother. It's not going to be long before you have your own," Chance said.

Blake stepped up. "Can I help?"

Amanda couldn't believe he asked, and she felt her heart stutter when Tyler placed that baby in his arms. Unlike Tyler, Blake was at complete ease. Brendan needed no more than two seconds to know that he was in good hands. He smiled at Blake and reached out to touch his face.

Blake used his softest voice to chat little Brendan up. They shared cereal puffs and Brendan gave Blake several high fives.

"Well, aren't you a natural," Lydia said. "You better hang on to this one, Amanda. He's cute and good with babies. Men like that aren't easy to find."

"Oh, we're not… Blake and I are…just friends," Amanda stammered.

"Just friends?" Blake looked offended. Amanda's face felt hot. What else would he call them? "We're business partners, aren't we?"

She should have known that was what he was going to say. She quickly tried to back-pedal. "Right. We are business partners, but he's here with me because we're friends. We've been friends since we were kids."

Lydia grimaced. "Oh, I'm sorry. I didn't mean to assume."

"It's funny that you thought that," Lily interjected. "When we were thirteen and these two became friends, it was the biggest shocker at White Oaks Middle School."

"Why was it such a shocker? Weren't girls and boys friends at your middle school?" Hadley asked.

"It was because Blake was the hottest guy at school and super popular, and Amanda was—"

"Do not finish that sentence," Amanda warned. As if it wasn't bad enough that she had to explain they weren't a couple, her sister had decided it was a good idea to discuss her awkward adolescence.

"Amanda may not have been super popular, but that was what I liked about her. The popular girls were so self-absorbed. Amanda cared about animals and the environment. I thought she was mature and very cool."

His compliments made her even more embarrassed. She would rather talk about anything other than herself and the reasons Blake liked her.

"You thought Blake was the hottest guy in middle school?" Conner asked Lily.

"Everybody did," Lily replied unabashedly.

Ben, Ethan, Tyler and Chance all howled with laughter. Conner gave Ethan a shove since he was standing close enough to reach.

"Conner's just jealous because we all know I was the hottest one in our middle school," Ben said.

"If you were the hottest, then I was also the hottest," Ethan argued since they were identical twins.

"Being hot is more than this face. It's also my amazing personality."

Tyler and Chance exchanged looks and then doubled over with laughter again.

"What?" Ben challenged. "We all know it wasn't either of you two. You were both chumps in middle school."

"Chumps?" Chance folded his arms across his chest.

"Don't even take that bait," Tyler said. "Ben's ego has blinded him his entire life."

"My ego? This from the guy who had to bring a fake fiancée home with him because he couldn't bear to be the only brother in town without one?"

"Well, sounds like my brothers are doing what they do best in front of new people. Can you four not do this right now?" Jon Blackwell stood in the kitchen with a giant platter full of steaks, burgers and chicken.

"Ben started it," Tyler said.

"Doesn't he always?" Rachel said with a sigh.

Dorothy stood up and patted Rachel's back. "It's a good thing he's got a heart of gold under all that nonsense. So much like his grandfather, I tell you."

Lily was beaming, completely entertained by the bickering. "You guys remind me so much of my family, I can't even tell you."

Dinner made things a bit more tolerable. With food in their mouths, no one could say anything that made Amanda want to run out the door. Blake kept his tabs on her, making sure she was okay. The way her stomach flipped every time he put his hand on her knee might have been the reason her foolish imagination kept running wild.

What if things had been different? What if she could have children like Blake wanted? What if she was brave and told Blake how she really felt about him and he felt the same? What if he was here with her because they were in love and getting married like Lily and Conner? What a different trip this would have been.

Jon and Lydia had a huge farmhouse-style table in their dining room. All the adults were squeezed in there while the kids were set up at the kitchen table. Everyone helped make sure the children had what they needed. The Blackwells might argue about who was better looking, but the group as a whole was a well-oiled machine.

As dinner wound down, the conversation picked back up. "So how is the wedding planning going?" Rachel asked Lily.

"Having it at the ranch makes things so easy. We looked through Hadley's scrapbooks, and there are so many beautiful examples of what they can do there, the hardest part will be deciding what *not* to have."

Perfect, perfect, perfect. It was all so perfect. Lily wouldn't need Amanda to do a thing. She wasn't even sure why she was still there. Maybe she should pack up and head home. She certainly didn't have a place here.

Lily continued, "It's been so great, I think I even convinced Blake to get married here, too. He's been texting his fiancée a ton of pictures."

"You're planning a wedding, too?" Dorothy asked, looking surprised by that.

"Well, I'm using this as an opportunity to check things out. I couldn't make a decision without my fiancée seeing it first."

"Smart man," Chance said from across the table.

"You two have always just been friends? Never tried dating each other or anything like that?" Dorothy seemed perplexed.

Amanda shook her head. "No, ma'am. We have always been friends only. There was never a good reason to risk our friendship for romance."

Blake contradicted her. "Well, it's not like we never thought about it. There have been a few moments in time when we almost did."

Was he really going to talk about the times that had almost been? What next? Would he talk about The Incident?

"Shut up," Lily said, setting down her fork. "You two thought about getting together? When? How do I not know about this?"

Amanda needed to do some damage control. "We did not get together. We thought about it. Two very different things. There's talking about something and agreeing it was a bad idea, and there's dating."

"So you've never kissed?" Hadley asked, as if it was totally normal to talk about one's private business in front of practical strangers at their first meal together.

"Nope."

"Yeah, of course," Blake said at the same time.

Amanda could feel her whole body flush red with embarrassment. "No, we haven't."

"We…" He must have noticed the look in her eye. The one telling him to be quiet. To not go there in front of these people. "We kiss like friends, I mean. You know." He leaned over and placed a chaste kiss on her cheek. "I thought when you asked if we kissed, you meant any kind of kiss. Not *kiss* kissing. We don't make out. We've never made out." His voice cracked over the *never* part of that sentence because it was the biggest of the lies.

They had made out. A year ago they had crossed lines that were not to be crossed. Ones they had sworn not to ever speak of again. She had been so foolish that night. For a brief moment, wanting to be loved by him had become more important than what was best for him in the long run. Amanda knew she couldn't be with him, so that one moment of weakness was swept under the rug.

"I tried being just friends with Rachel and we all know how that turned out," Ben said.

"Ditto for me and Grace. I didn't last long," Ethan said.

Tyler raised his glass. "I was never happier than when I married my best friend."

Hadley placed her hand over her heart and leaned in for a kiss. "You are so sweet."

"What about you?" Katie asked Chance. "Did you kiss your female friends or did you keep things platonic?"

Chance looked uncertain about how to answer. "I don't make out with friends."

"So, I'm not your best friend? What am I if I'm not your best friend? Just your wife? Your baby-making machine?"

"Uh-oh, another hysterical pregnant woman," Ben teased, earning him a swat on the shoulder from his wife.

Chance and Katie both glared at him.

"What? What did I say?" Ben held his hands up in surrender.

"Honey." Chance cleared his throat. "You are the best friend I could ever ask for. I figured you already knew I couldn't resist kissing you. Surely that baby is proof of that."

Katie leaned into him and he pressed his lips against her temple. Amanda had to look away but caught Lily staring at her with a suspicious glint in her eye. Lily suspected there was a story to be told, and it was unlikely she wouldn't bring it up again when they were alone.

Hadley set down her drinking glass and had the same look of suspicion on her face.

Only she was staring at Ben. "What did you mean when you said *another* hysterical pregnant woman? I know you weren't talking about me."

Ben and Rachel exchanged glances. "He was talking about me," Rachel confessed as the whole table erupted in congratulations. "We're twelve weeks and I know this will come as a shock to some of you. It's twins."

The deafening uproar that ensued was something Amanda had never experienced before, and she had grown up in a home with five girls only a few years apart in age. Another Blackwell, two more babies at once. Amanda wanted to magically transport herself far, far away. Instead, she put on her game face and congratulated the happy, expectant couple. Their lives were so full.

Would Amanda ever feel the same about her own?

CHAPTER TEN

"I'M SORRY" WAS the only thing Blake had said when they got back to the cabin after dinner with the family. He'd decided not to talk to her about some of the other things on his mind until the morning. She was mad at him and afraid that Lily was going to start asking questions. The other person he needed to talk to this morning was Lily.

Blake poked his head into Amanda's room. "I'm going to take Clancy for a walk. You can sleep in."

Clancy only needed to hear the word *walk* and he was all over it. Montana mornings on the ranch were pretty peaceful. Blake loved the view of the mountains. This time of year they were green and gold with a dusting of snow on the highest peaks. The squawking of falcons made it obvious how the town got its name. Blake missed the ocean, though. As nice as this place was for a vacation getaway, he couldn't imagine being here long-term.

Clancy, on the other hand, was a big fan. He was right at home running along the trails around the cabins. When they got back, Blake decided to knock on Lily's door before checking on Amanda.

"Well, good morning," Lily said as Clancy came bounding in for a hello head scratch. "Everything okay? Where's Amanda?"

"Still in bed. I thought maybe you and I could have a little chat before we start our day."

Her brows pinched together. "Chat about what exactly?"

"Can we get him some water and sit down for a minute?"

The cabins didn't have fully functional kitchens—just a sink, minifridge and microwave. Lily got creative and dumped the decorative ceramic balls out of the bowl that sat on the coffee table and filled it with water. Her cabin had a small front room and a bedroom with an attached bathroom in the back. A dirty sweatshirt was tossed on the floor. Three pairs of shoes were piled up by the door. The brochures Hadley had given her were scattered over the counter in the tiny kitchenette.

"So, what would you like to chat about, Mr. Collins?" she asked, sitting down on the wing chair and curling her legs underneath her. "Are you here to confess that you've made out with my sister? Because I could tell you were lying. You always do that thing with your voice. It's totally your tell."

This was what he had wanted to avoid happening when Amanda was awake. "I came to tell you that you need to drop it. For your sister's sake, you need to drop it. She's already struggling with a lot of negative emotions and she doesn't need you giving her a hard time about me and her."

"So you're confirming there was a you-and-her at some point in this friendship?"

Blake's shoulders tensed. "Listen, Lily Pad, what I'm trying to tell you is that your sister is putting on a brave face, but all she talked about last night when we got back to the cabin was how we should pack up and leave today because there was no reason for her to stay."

"What does that mean? Everyone was so nice to her. I thought that the Blackwells welcomed her with open arms. She got to see that Conner fits in so well with them, proving I have made a good choice. And we have to talk to Hadley about colors, and maybe we can even do the cake-tasting part while you guys are here. That was her favorite part of planning my last wedding."

Blake tried to explain. "That's just it. The last wedding—she helped you plan the whole thing. There was no Hadley. Amanda got to be the one to wow you with your options. She's feeling a little pointless during this one. She brought the book and hasn't even given it to you because why would you need that when you have Hadley's scrapbooks. She feels a little lost not being the one to help you out."

"I hadn't thought of that." Lily shifted in her seat, placing both feet on the ground. She took a deep breath. "I know that since Mom died, she's been struggling. I also know that since we found out that my dad Rudy isn't who she thought he was, she's been questioning everything. I get that, but I also need to make sure she understands that I'm here because it's what's best for me. I have to find my own way to handle everything that's happened in the past year."

Blake rested his elbows on his knees and folded his hands together. "And your sister supports you one hundred percent. She would never ask you to choose her over Conner. She will smile and tell you that she is happy for you. I'm just asking you not to assume that it's easy for her to do that."

"I won't. I will try to be more aware of how I come across to her."

Blake stood up. That was all he needed to hear. "Thank you."

Lily got to her feet to follow him to the door. "I should thank you. You're always looking out for her."

He grabbed Clancy's leash and attached it to his collar. "She's my best friend."

"And you're hers. You should probably remember to take your own advice, though."

"Oh?"

Lily opened the door, keeping her hand on the doorknob. "I think she's just as sad about you getting married as she is about me moving away."

"Nothing is going to change between us because I get married. It's not the same as you moving here."

"Ha!" She leaned against the doorjamb.

"Things have to change. You might think they won't, but they will. They have to if you want to have a successful marriage to someone who isn't Amanda."

"Nadia understands that Amanda and I have a special relationship. You're wrong." He needed Lily to be wrong because he needed Amanda in his life.

"Nadia hasn't ever expressed feeling a little jealous of Amanda? A little worried about how close you are?"

"Not really," he lied.

"Interesting." She sounded skeptical. "Everyone you have ever dated ends up taking issue with how close you are to Amanda. Nadia will, too—it's human nature. You'll put her needs before Amanda's because you'll want to be the best husband you can be. It's inevitable that my sister is going to be the one with the broken heart, because if you get married and want to stay married, you won't choose her."

Blake shook his head. She did not know what she was talking about. She didn't know Nadia and she was severely underestimating him. Blake was more than able to care for a wife and family and have a best friend. It wasn't going to be that hard.

"Amanda and Nadia are going to be friends. As close as family. Just like me and Amanda."

"I hope so. If that would make Amanda happy, I would want that for her. All I'm saying is…before you remind me to consider Amanda's feelings, maybe you should consider how you make her feel."

Clancy lost his patience waiting in front of an open door and tried to pull Blake with him. Blake could only manage a curt nod, finding it hard to acknowledge the possible truth of what Lily had said.

He left her cabin and headed back to his. Amanda was sitting on the couch with a cup of coffee. "Can we go into town for some breakfast?" she asked. "I don't want to see any Blackwells first thing this morning."

"Yeah, whatever you want. I'll ask Lily if we can take her car." He let go of Clancy, who made a beeline for Amanda. That dog loved her more than anything in the world. Blake knew the feeling. Her hair was up in a messy bun and she had on her plaid pajama pants and one of his college T-shirts. She had slowly stolen all of his San Diego State shirts over the years, claiming she was only borrowing them. "You gonna go like that?"

She stood up and spun around. "What? Are you saying this doesn't look like breakfast-in-town attire?"

He laughed. "In San Diego, no. In Falcon Creek? Why the heck not?"

She shook her head and snickered right back. Handing him her coffee cup, she made her way to her room. "Because I'm not wearing a bra. Duh."

Blake pretended that he hadn't heard that. Friends didn't think about friends not wearing a bra.

"I'LL HAVE A bear claw, and I need one of those raised doughnuts with the vanilla frosting and sprinkles." The Maple Bear Bakery was a quaint little shop in downtown Falcon Creek. There were a couple of café tables inside and a huge display case filled with deliciousness. Blake wanted to eat one of everything.

"And for your lovely lady?" the woman behind the counter asked.

Amanda and Blake were no strangers to having strangers assume they were a couple. It usually didn't faze them, but after his conversation with Lily this morning, it made him feel more awkward than normal.

"I am thinking I need that chocolate cake doughnut and one of those blueberry glazed," Amanda told her.

"I'm going to warn you now," the woman said. "Once you eat one of our chocolate cake doughnuts, you will never want to eat any other doughnut again. They're so addictive that people call them Chocolate Junkies."

Amanda gave Blake the what-the-heck-is-she-talking-about look while the woman was busy grabbing doughnuts. "I will make sure to eat the blueberry one first."

"Okay, trade the vanilla one for one of those Chocolate Junkies," Blake said. He turned to Amanda. "I mean, I need to try it for myself, and we know you won't let me have a bite of yours."

The only thing Blake was a junkie for was that smile on Amanda's face. "No, I will not," she said. "Good call."

The woman behind the counter placed the four doughnuts in the bag. "There's only one more Chocolate Junkie left. I'll throw it in for free since I have a feeling you two have no idea what you're getting yourselves into," she said with a wink.

"That's so kind of you," Amanda replied.

"I also need a coffee with cream and sugar."
Amanda grabbed some napkins and reached
in her purse for her wallet.

"I got this, Harrison. You can buy me lunch
later."

She put her money away, knowing he wouldn't
change his mind. She took a seat and waited patiently for her breakfast. It was moments like
these that made Blake the happiest. When it was
the two of them, relaxing, enjoying good food
and not trying to solve the world's problems.

"We should play some volleyball today and
then have Tyler show us the spot by the pond
that Dorothy mentioned yesterday," Blake suggested. He wanted to keep today light and fun.
That meant limiting how many Blackwells they
ran into and not focusing on anyone's wedding,
especially his since Lily was so sure that his
impending nuptials were making Amanda sad.

She was not listening because she had made
a fatal mistake. Instead of taking a bite of her
blueberry doughnut, she had bitten into the
chocolate cake one. She closed her eyes and
savored every moment it was in her mouth.

"She wasn't wrong. Doughnuts have been
ruined for me forever. This is... There are no
words for how yummy this is. It's the best

thing I have ever eaten." She took another bite and moaned loud enough for the man at the counter to glance in their direction.

"Chocolate Junkie," Blake explained.

The guy nodded as if he knew all about the power of those doughnuts.

Blake wasn't going to be so foolish, and he started with his bear claw. It was good, which made him wonder how amazing the doughnut could be. Amanda skipped her blueberry altogether and went right for that third chocolate doughnut.

"Hey, now. You only get to eat half of that. Cut it right now before you get carried away."

"I will pay you one hundred dollars to let me eat this whole thing," she said with chocolate frosting on the corner of her mouth. She was a literal junkie after one. Blake had to know what they tasted like.

He snatched up his chocolate cake doughnut and took an enormous bite out of it. The fudginess of the frosting mixed with the soft, tender cake was pure magic. There was no way she was getting that whole doughnut.

He shook his head and she looked like she was about to cry. "Come on. Two hundred," she begged.

Money was not going to change his mind. He shook his head again and grabbed her wrist before she took a bite. "Cut it in half, Harrison."

"I will give you sixty percent of the company," she said.

He shook his head again. She tried to take a bite, leaving him with no other option. He bit out of the other side at the same time. Both of them were so eager that they had frosting smeared all over their top lips. She looked ridiculous with her chocolate mustache. He must have as well because Amanda cracked up.

"Okay, okay, I'll cut it."

He let go of her wrist but watched her closely. She stood up and walked backward toward the counter with the napkins and plastic cutlery so she could keep an eye on that doughnut. Blake sat on his hands to prove he was trustworthy. If she didn't hurry, however, he had no qualms about eating off the table without picking it up. If Clancy could eat that way, why couldn't he?

She returned with a plastic knife and carefully found the exact center of the doughnut. He stopped her twice to make sure both sides were even. He nodded when he was content that they would both get an even amount.

"We need to come here every day until we leave," she said when she finished. She gave her belly a rub.

Blake reached over and wiped the glob of fudge from the corner of her mouth with his thumb. Their eyes locked and there was that look again. She mesmerized him more than these doughnuts ever could. One of the reasons he was so sure he'd never not be there for her was because he couldn't be without her.

"Does that mean we're going to stay a little longer? I know your sister wants your help picking out a cake and probably a dress. We know how much you love cake and dresses. The only thing that would make it perfect was if Lily needed your help picking out a rescue dog. Then all your favorites would be covered."

"You think she still needs me?"

"She'll always need you for love and support. That's what families are for, right?" Just like he would.

Amanda's gaze fell to the table and she fidgeted with the napkin in her hands. "We can stay a little longer. At least until Nadia calls and begs you to come back home."

Nadia. Blake didn't want to upset her, but what if Amanda wasn't ready to go back and Nadia begged him to come home? Could he convince her he needed more time without making her think he was choosing Amanda's needs over hers? There had to be a way for him to keep both of them happy. He would find a way.

"Don't worry about Nadia." As soon as her name came out his mouth, his phone rang and her picture appeared on his screen. "Hey, good morning. Aren't you at work already?"

"I am, but I don't have to be in court until ten today. How are you?"

Blake smiled at Amanda and motioned to give him a minute. He got up from the table and stepped outside. "I'm good. How are you?"

"I miss you. Have you booked a flight home yet?"

He paced back and forth along the sidewalk in front of the bakery. "We haven't picked a day yet. I'm thinking sometime next week. It all depends on what Lily needs Amanda's help with."

"You said there were amazing wedding planners there at the ranch. What does she need Amanda to do?"

"Well, she values Amanda's opinion above everyone else's. You know how sisters can be." Nadia wasn't very close to her sister, but maybe there was a little bit of her that could relate.

"O-kay. Well, I miss you. I feel like you've been gone for weeks and it's only been a couple days."

Blake glanced up when he heard the bells above the bakery door ring. Amanda stood on the tiny stoop, holding the bag of doughnuts and a carrier with their coffees.

"I promise we won't be gone forever. I miss the ocean breeze and my surfboard. And you, of course." He cringed at how that must have sounded.

"Hmm, glad I rank up there with your surfboard." Her tone confirmed it sounded terrible.

"You are what I miss the most. I was saving the best for last."

"What's on the agenda for today? No more horseback riding for you?"

"No more horseback riding. We were going

to play some sand volleyball, maybe check out some more of the property. Tonight, we're going to this bar to do some ax throwing."

"Ax throwing? What will you be throwing them at?"

"Targets on the wall, I hope. I'll be sure to send you some pictures."

Amanda joined him on the sidewalk and shuffled things around, placing the doughnut bag on top of the coffee. She held out her hand. *Keys?* she mouthed.

Blake dug in his pocket and got her the car keys. She started for Lily's SUV and he followed.

"Okay, well, have fun. Not too much fun. I mean, I want you to still miss me like crazy."

"I do. Don't worry—I'm missing you. I wish you were here so you could see how nice this place is."

"Amanda could always fly back to San Diego on her own if you wanted to leave before she did, right?"

He stopped dead in his tracks. It was like someone was testing him. "She probably could, but she's counting on me to be here for her."

"It's just a thought. If I can't take it any longer, you would leave her there and come home to me, wouldn't you?"

Blake's heart beat faster and his mouth went dry. He didn't want to lie, but Lily's words were screaming at him in his head. *Everyone you have ever dated ends up taking issue with how close you are to Amanda. Nadia will, too—it's human nature. You'll put her needs before Amanda's...* Why did she have to be right?

"I'd do whatever was best," he replied, hoping that she didn't realize he hadn't really answered her question.

"Making your fiancée happy is always what's best, sweetheart. You know that. I have to go. Duty calls. Love you," she said before hanging up. He didn't have time to return the farewell.

Blake climbed in the car and avoided looking at Amanda. He pulled on his seat belt and clicked it in place.

"Everything okay back home?" she asked.

"Everything's fine. Nadia says hi. She hopes you're enjoying your time with your sister." Suddenly the lies just kept coming. "She really wishes you two will be close like that someday."

"Sounded like she was telling you to fly

home without me," Amanda said, starting the car.

"I would never do that. She knows that," he said. Lily's words played in his head on a loop. *My sister is going to be the one with the broken heart, because if you get married and want to stay married, you won't choose her.* He would, he wanted to scream back. He would.

CHAPTER ELEVEN

"HAVE YOU EVER thrown an ax before?"

Amanda had never even held an ax before, let alone thrown one. "I have not," she replied. "But I am assuming it can't be too hard if they let people in a bar throw them."

Conner chuckled. "Good point. Although, if you have been enjoying yourself at the bar too long, they will not let you come over here and throw any of these."

Amanda had given up trying to find something wrong with Conner. He was a decent human. She couldn't find a reason to hate him, so she was going to try to like him and hate the fact that her sister would not be coming back to California. After listening to Blake on the phone with Nadia this morning, she wasn't sure she wanted to rush back to San Diego, either.

"So I heard we have a couple first-timers!" Chad was their throwing instructor. He was there to make sure they knew what they were doing and to lead them in some games.

"We're waiting on two more people," Lily said.

"We are?" Amanda thought it was just the four of them tonight. Which Blackwell was Lily going to force them to hang out with tonight?

"We invited Conner's friend Logan and Logan's brother, Evan, to join us. It's more fun when the teams are a little bigger."

Amanda glanced at Blake, who seemed just as surprised as she was. She wondered if Conner felt like he needed backup. Tonight she needed to put him at ease. She wasn't here to quiz them about their engagement anymore. It was clear that what they had was different from what she had expected, and Lily was clear that Conner was it for her.

All around the bar were flat-screen televisions with country music videos playing on a constant loop. People gathered in small groups in the bar while other people congregated near the throwing lanes. Amanda couldn't decide if Battle Axes was a bar where guests could do ax throwing or an ax-throwing place with a bar.

"So what did you guys do all day?" Conner asked Amanda.

"We spent some time in downtown. Came back to the ranch and played some volleyball. We thought about finding that pond Dorothy was talking about last night, but we got sidelined at the petting zoo. Have you seen the bunnies they have in there?" Amanda wasn't sure how the petting zoo hadn't been their very first stop when they arrived on the ranch. It was an animal lover's dream.

"The bunnies were cute, but you know I'm smuggling that baby goat out when we head home," Blake said, joining the conversation.

"Scotty? He did fall in love with you."

"Kids love me. The human and goat kind. What can I say?"

It wasn't hard to do. Everyone fell in love with Blake. Two cowboys came strolling in and Conner's face lit up. He waved them over and shook hands with each of them.

"Y'all made it. We were about to get started."

Lily hugged the one introduced to Amanda and Blake as Logan Hill. The Hill brothers got themselves a drink at the bar and were ready to throw. Chad was back in charge. He had them divide into two teams. Lily suggested they do California versus Montana. Lily would go against Conner, Amanda was paired against Logan, and Blake took on Evan.

"All right, the first game we're going to play is the numbers game. As you can see on the bull's-eye, the different rings are worth different points. And up here—" Chad pointed to the two blue dots at the top in the corners "—are the kill shots. These are worth the most points. Even more than a bull's-eye."

Chad drew on a whiteboard hanging on the side of their throwing alley. He wrote six ones, four threes, two fives and one seven under each group's name. The objective was to be the first team to clear the board by hitting those numbers.

Lily and Conner were up first. Chad gave a quick group lesson on how to hold the ax and showed them the best form for getting the ax to stick in the board. Amanda watched Lily clench and unclench her fists before choosing an ax. Lily had unreliable fingers. They didn't always work the way she wanted them to, and sometimes her struggles with fine motor skills made her self-conscious.

"Just hit the board, Lily Pad. Knock off

any of the numbers. You can do it," Blake said, cheering her on from the safety zone. Amanda sat down on one of the stools and rested her elbows on the counter that separated the throwing area from the safety zone.

"You got this, Lily."

Chad gave them the okay to throw and they both let their axes fly. Conner threw his and landed smack in the center bull's-eye. Lily's ax bounced right off the wall and onto the floor. Maybe Amanda should have put some cowboys on her team. This was harder than it looked.

She and Logan were up next. Amanda picked an ax with a black handle and went through the motions without releasing her ax.

"Am I doing it right?" she asked Chad, who was quick to help her adjust her footwork.

Blake clapped loudly. "You can do it, Harrison. Don't let us down." He was quite the competitive monster when he wanted to be. He'd played lacrosse all through high school and got a scholarship to San Diego State. An injury his junior year had totally devastated him.

Logan adjusted his cowboy hat before he

got in position. "I've only done this once before, so don't make me look too silly."

Chad gave them the okay to throw and Amanda tried to do what had been suggested. She got her ax to stick and knocked off one of the ones. Logan hit the kill shot.

"Why do I get the feeling this isn't really your second time?" she said as they both went to retrieve their axes.

"I swear that was a lucky throw. I was actually aiming for the center bull's-eye." Logan had dark hair and brown eyes that were framed in thick lashes. He had a square jaw and a nice smile. He was a picture-perfect Montana cowboy, the right mixture of rugged and handsome.

Blake gave Amanda a high five as she left the throwing area and he entered. He had a determined look on his face. "You better hit something good," she said.

"Logan here is an auctioneer," Lily said when they rejoined the group in the safety zone. "You may think you have met fast talkers in your lifetime, but I will guarantee that Logan talks faster than anyone we know."

"That's actually really cool." Amanda had never met anyone in that profession. "I'm going to need you to narrate Lily and Conner's next throw in your auctioneer voice."

"You're gonna have to outscore me when we battle if you want me to show off for you, Miss Amanda," he said with a wink.

He was fun. "Oh, it's on."

"Where are my cheerleaders?" Blake asked as he yanked his ax from the kill shot spot. "Are you two even paying attention over there?"

"Sorry! Good job. Of course you're awesome at this," Amanda said. Lily switched places with him.

Blake threw his arm over her shoulder. "So what's going on out here that's more interesting than me?"

"We were just making a friendly wager. If I score higher on our next throw, Logan here will show off his auctioneer skills for me."

"Well, it's not a bet unless you put something on the table if I outscore you," Logan said. "Again, by the way."

Lily got a one and was cheering for herself even though Conner had hit the bull's-eye. Amanda had to come up with something. Buy him a drink? She didn't have any talents to show off like he did.

Blake gave Amanda's shoulders a rub. "Let's go, Harrison. You're up."

If anyone could come up with a good bet, it was Lily.

"If Logan has to fast-talk for me, what should I do if he beats me?" Amanda asked her as she high-fived her.

Lily pursed her lips and tapped her chin with her finger. "You got any pets, Logan?"

"I got a golden named Honey."

"Amanda owns a pet supply subscription box company. If you win, she sends Honey a box."

"I've never heard of a pet supply subscription box. Exactly what is that?"

"Every month we send out a box full of fun toys and treats for your pet. Sometimes we get samples of new products from companies we trust, and other times we put in things that we love or our pets love. It's something new every month. It's fun."

"Well, Honey loves treats and toys, so I guess I better hit the bull's-eye."

"Let's go, Amanda! You can do it!" Blake was yelling at her like she was miles away instead of feet.

She glanced at him over her shoulder. What

was that about? She grabbed an ax and squared herself to the target. There was no way she had the skill to beat Logan, so she was going to have to hope for luck. She closed her eyes and let the ax go.

"Yes!" Blake screamed.

Amanda opened her eyes to see her ax stuck in the center bull's-eye while Logan got a solid three. She threw her hands up in victory.

"You better get ready to run that mouth of yours."

"Honey is going to be so disappointed in me."

She placed a hand on his arm. "Impress me and maybe Honey will still get a little something in the mail from me."

"You have to go back to the safety zone," Blake said, placing his hands on her hips and turning her toward the exit.

"I have to get my ax," she said, pulling away from him. It wasn't unusual for him to touch her, hold her, be there for her, but he was acting extra. She retrieved her ax and went behind the counter.

It was highly amusing to hear Logan pretend to be at the auction before Lily's and Conner's throws.

"Can he get a one, one, one, one, now three, can he get a three, I said we need a three, can we get a three, three, hit a three, three, can he get a five, I need a five, five, five, five, now five, how about a seven, looking for a seven, seven, now seven, seven," he said at record speed. Conner threw and hit the bull's-eye. "Sold for five!" Lily got ready to throw and Logan continued, "Can she beat a five, five, five, five, will she get a three, three, no one, we want a one."

Lily threw the ax and it bounced off the wall and to the ground.

"We have a boomerang situation here. No sale, no sale."

Amanda's stomach hurt from laughing so much. "That was amazing. Even though I beat you to win that, I'm sending Honey six months' worth of boxes."

Logan's face lit up. "That's sweet of you. I feel like I won just seeing the smile on your face when you hit that bull's-eye and listening to your laugh."

He was sweet. Blake was seething. What had happened?

"Are you two going to stand there smiling at each other or are you going to play? It's your turn," he snapped.

The game went on, and in the end the Montana folks won. They moved on to King of the Hill. It was all fun and games until it was Logan versus Blake. *Serious* was their middle name. They both hit the bull's-eye four times in a row. That was when the trash-talking began. They both hit threes, and finally Logan hit the kill shot while Blake only got a one.

"Montana wins again," Evan gloated.

Blake rolled his eyes and grabbed his beer. Amanda walked over, giving him a pat on the back. "You did awesome. None of us even got close to beating him."

"I hate losing," he said, making her smile. He was being honest, and it was sad and kind of cute.

"We'll get them next time, champ," Lily said before turning to Chad. "What's next?"

They didn't. Three more games and three more losses. San Diego could not compete with the guys from Falcon Creek. Lily offered to buy the next round of drinks, and Amanda went with her to the bar.

"This was fun. Even though we lost, I had a good time," Amanda admitted.

Lily tucked her hair behind her ear. "I'm glad. That was why I wanted to do it. I know that being here hasn't been exactly a blast so far."

"What are you talking about? It's been fine," Amanda lied.

"Nice try. I know that you're disappointed that I'm not coming home with you guys when you go. If you go."

Amanda could feel her eyebrows pinch together. "If I go?"

"Logan seems nice, huh?" Lily's coy smile made everything clear.

Amanda's eyes went wide. "What did you do? Did you seriously invite those guys to try to hook me up with Logan?" Her devilish sister shrugged her shoulders and smirked. "Lily! What are you thinking?"

"I don't think you're going to fall in love in a week like I did, but I believe that you should consider making a change like I did. Just think about it. You can do your work from anywhere. You guys don't even have an office." Before Amanda could say anything, she continued, "I'm only asking you to keep an open mind. Blake is getting married. Married. He's going to start his family, and then what do you have tying you to California? Nothing."

"Um, my house, Dad, Fiona, Peyton. Two of our sisters aren't very far from San Diego. And just because Blake is getting married doesn't mean that we aren't going to be close. We're like family."

"I'm your family. The Blackwells could be your family if you let them. I'm not saying you have to welcome them into your life with open arms. I'm asking you to consider what being here with me could do. It could offer you a place to have your own family."

Her own family? That was a joke. Amanda couldn't have a family. Logan probably wanted a big family, too. She couldn't marry anyone around here. They all seemed to have a ton of kids, usually more than one at once. At least, that was the Blackwell way. She would be such a disappointment to this extended family that had kids on demand, it seemed.

Why would Lily want her to think about leaving her life in San Diego and coming to Montana like she had? That was a terrible idea. She would never be able to leave Blake on his own. He needed her.

She glanced over at where he was standing. He had his phone out and was texting. He was probably texting Nadia.

Nadia.

She remembered their phone call this morning and her dread returned. She had overheard only his side of the conversation, but that was all she had to hear to know that Nadia was asking if he would come home even if it meant leaving Amanda behind. He hadn't said yes, but he also hadn't said no.

He wasn't going to be alone in San Diego. He would have his wife and soon his own children. The only one who would be alone in California was Amanda.

What did Falcon Creek have for her? Lily, who was going to have a new husband and her own family someday. Amanda would be "extended family," someone they would visit with every now and then. Of course, things wouldn't be much different in San Diego, where she'd be Auntie Amanda to Blake and Nadia's kids. She would be the outsider no matter what. Which happy family would be more painful to be around? Amanda didn't have to think too hard to answer that.

Conner and Logan came over to help them with the drinks. Amanda waited for her glass of chardonnay. Conner and Lily headed back to the throwing area.

"Why the long face?" Logan sidled up next to her. "I hope that losing didn't ruin your evening."

"You guys were the real deal. You totally deserved to win. There are no hard feelings."

He turned and leaned back against the bar. "Well, that's good. Truth be told, my buddy over there is super worried about making a good impression. I was supposed to show you that he's friends with decent people. I don't want you to think we're super competitive jerks."

She had been right about Conner's motives. "I don't have any qualms about what kind of guy Conner is. It's clear that he's a good man. Trust me, I've tried and tried to find some massive flaws, and I keep coming up empty-handed."

"He'll be happy to hear that, but I wonder why it makes you look so sad."

Amanda shook her head. "That doesn't

make me sad. I'm sad because my sister is going to live far away. We've been kind of attached since before we were born."

"Makes sense. I don't know what it's like to be a twin, but my brother and I are close, and it would be weird to not have him around. It's nice that family means something to you."

The bartender came over with her wine. She tipped him and took a sip. "Family is important. That's why I hate to see mine growing apart. I have four sisters, and now the closest one will be hours away from where I live."

"You have a lot of family here."

"Now you sound like my sister. Are you sure you're here to talk up Conner and not to lure me into staying in Falcon Creek?"

Logan pushed up the brim of his hat. "Would anything I say really influence you to stay around here a little longer?"

"After knowing you for a little over an hour?"

He laughed. "Probably not, huh?"

A giggle bubbled out of her, as well. "You're very charming, but probably not."

"Harrison, you coming to play some more

or are you going to nurse that chardonnay all night?" Blake called from across the bar.

"That's the most jealous not-your-boyfriend I've ever met," Logan said, pushing off the bar.

"What? Blake? He's not jealous. We've been friends forever."

"If you say so." Logan took a long pull of his beer.

Pushing away the unexpectedly warm and fuzzy feelings that crept over her at the thought of Blake being jealous about her talking to another man, she needed to set the record straight. After dinner at the Blackwells' and everyone thinking they must have been together as more than friends, this was a rumor that couldn't spread. Blake was marrying someone else.

"He's only a couple months older than me, but he acts like he's my protective older brother. People confuse that for jealousy." Her included. But she knew better. Blake definitely saw her like a sister.

Logan glanced over at their throwing area. "If you say so," he said again, smirking.

Amanda checked to see what he thought was so amusing. Blake was staring and motioned for her to come over there. This was probably more about the fact that they had lost all of the games and the competitiveness inside him needed a rematch. He was marrying Nadia. Why would he be jealous of Amanda talking to Logan? It wasn't like she was going to marry him and move to Montana.

"I think he wants another try at beating you guys. He was never a very good loser."

"What are you doing tomorrow?" Logan asked.

Taken aback at his question, her brain froze and she couldn't even remember what she was supposed to be doing right now. "I don't know. We love The Maple Bear Bakery. I plan to go there every day I'm here."

"You got one of their bear claws?"

"No, the—"

"Chocolate Junkie doughnuts," he finished for her. "I should have guessed that first. Didn't they warn you before you bought one of those?"

Amanda smiled down at her feet, embarrassed by her addiction. "They did, but I never imagined they could be that good."

"Maybe we could go grab some doughnuts and coffee together."

"Together?" Her eyes latched on to his. What was happening right now?

"I would prefer to go together since the point would be to spend some time with you since you seem pretty cool." He shifted his weight from one foot to the other. "And maybe you'll want to stick around longer if you know me for more than an hour."

"That's… I…you…we…" Amanda couldn't put a sentence together.

Blake appeared and tugged at her arm. "We're starting a new game. Let's go, you two. No more consorting with the enemy, Harrison."

Without answering Logan, Amanda followed Blake back to their throwing spot. The second round of games ended much like the first, except that Blake managed to win King of the Hill. Amanda tried to remind him that if he'd had different teammates, he might have been able to win all the games. The Harrison girls were not going to be signing up to be in any professional ax-throwing competitions anytime soon. Amanda was better at hitting the target than Lily was, but not as good as Logan.

Lily had no issues with losing, which wasn't

like her. Apparently, love changed people. She was slow dancing with Conner while the rest of the group finished off their last round of drinks.

"Can I see your phone?" Logan asked Amanda as she was sending pictures to Fiona of her and Lily holding axes in front of the target.

"Sure," she replied hesitantly. Blake had gone to the bathroom, so there was no worry about him being the overprotective brother.

Logan tapped on the screen and handed it back. "If you change your mind about getting breakfast tomorrow or any day while you're still in town, I just texted myself from your phone. Now you've got my number. It was nice meeting you, Amanda."

Evan and Logan said their goodbyes. Blake was anxious to call it a night, as well. Lily and Conner wanted to hang out some more, so they were left behind. Blake was quiet during their walk back to the cabin.

"You're not still mad about losing, are you?" she asked as they strolled past the guest lodge. It was late and there wasn't anyone else outside.

"I'm not mad about losing," he said. Amanda

had to stifle a laugh. "Okay, maybe I'm a little mad about that."

"I had fun tonight. I thought Conner's friends were nice. It makes me feel good about the life Lily will have here."

"They were okay. A little bit overcompetitive, if you ask me."

She bit her tongue and nodded. He was hilarious. "Well, I think I got asked out on a date."

Blake stopped in his tracks. "What?"

"Logan asked me to go out for breakfast."

He started walking again, and this time much faster. Amanda had to jog to catch up. "Why would he try to date someone who is just here visiting?"

Amanda wasn't sure why he'd do that, either. He might have been swayed by her sister. "I can only guess that Lily put him up to it."

Blake rubbed the back of his neck. "Why would your sister tell him to ask you out on a date?"

"It's silly, but I think she's trying to convince me to move out here with her."

He came to a dead stop, causing Amanda to run into him. "Are you kidding me?"

CHAPTER TWELVE

LILY WANTED AMANDA to stay in Montana? Blake loved Lily, but if that was true, she was forgetting that Amanda belonged in San Diego. "You're not moving to Montana."

"Wow. Okay, *Dad*." Amanda laughed. "Any other rules I should know about? Am I allowed to stay up past ten on weekdays? Do I need permission to talk to boys?"

Blake didn't mean to come off as controlling, but he also couldn't have her even consider moving away. "I meant you wouldn't want to move to Montana, right? It's silly that your sister thought it."

"So you were asking me, not telling me?"

"I'm asking you because I know you have no interest in being here."

"And if I did?"

"You don't." The way she stared at him gave him the chills. "Do you?"

She marched ahead of him without answering. Blake chased after her. "You know I would never tell you what to do. I respect you and your decisions because you have excellent judgment."

Amanda slowed. "You say that but don't always show it."

"What? I ask for your advice all the time. You're my person."

She let out a sharp laugh. "Right. Except for the important stuff, like should you ask someone to marry you? You didn't seek my advice on that one."

Blake had no idea where that came from. Since when was she mad at him about proposing? He had told her it had been spontaneous and he had thought she understood. Wasn't she happy for him?

Amanda climbed the steps to their cabin and unlocked the door. He didn't want to fight with her. She had to understand that all he meant by what he'd said was he absolutely did not want her to move to Montana.

"I should have said, please don't move to Montana. Obviously, it would be your decision. I just want you to know that having you around matters to me. Even though I get caught up in my emotions and do things like propose to my girlfriend without talking to you first."

"I have to take Clancy out," she said, grabbing his leash.

"I'll come with you." He held the door open for her.

She brushed past him. "You don't have to."

"I want to because I hate when you're mad at me. Can you stop being mad at me?"

"I'm not mad. I just think that maybe I've spent too much of my life worrying about what you and my sister want. And for what? You're both getting married. Neither one of you bothered to tell me you were thinking about getting engaged before you did so. You both don't really care where I'm going to fit in your lives once you get married. And, honestly, I'm not sure I fit anywhere anymore."

"What are you talking about? You fit exactly where you have always fit in my life. That's why I don't want you to move here. Just because Lily decided to uproot her life doesn't mean she should bring you with her. That's not fair."

"Not fair to who? Me? Or you?" she asked, head cocked ever so slightly.

Honestly, the desperation he felt meant he

was taking it more personally than he should. He couldn't admit that, though. "To you. Why should you give up everything you have in San Diego to move here? Your life is in California. I feel like she forgot that."

"What do I have in San Diego, really? I could do my work for Sit, Stay, Play wherever. My family is all gone except maybe my dad, who is off trying to find my other dad. Who knows how long that will take."

Blake was sure he was having a heart attack. His chest was tight and it was hard to breathe. "You have me. What about our monthly visits to the packing facility? You can't do that from wherever."

"Come on, Clancy." She tugged on his leash to get his attention away from the bush he was currently sniffing. "We both know that the 'we' you want me to hold on to isn't going to exist after you get married. It's changing already."

"How is it changing? I'm here, aren't I? When you need me, I'm always there." His pain began to turn into anger. The only one acting like she wasn't going to be the friend she'd always been was her. "Are you planning on not being there for me?"

Her shoulders fell and she started back toward the cabin. "You act like you're going to need me. Nadia is going to be your person, Blake. She has to be."

Blake's breaths were heavy, as if he had taken Clancy for a run instead of a quick bathroom break. He wanted to shout that he didn't want Nadia to be his person. Amanda would always be his person. If she would give him a chance, he would be her husband. Again, the only one who wanted to keep them from being together forever was her.

She went back inside with the dog. He stayed outside, needing to pull himself together. If he told her how he really felt, she would probably move to Montana to get away from him. It felt a bit like a no-win situation. If he married Nadia, she would leave because there would always be another person in their relationship. If he didn't marry Nadia because he was in love with Amanda, she would leave because she didn't want to be a couple.

They were both going to have to accept less than they wanted. That was the way it had to be if she didn't want more than friendship. What did she want from him? How was he supposed to make her happy? Not get married? Ever. She knew how important it was to him to have a family. Wasn't she planning to get married someday?

He kicked at the dirt, sending a rock skittering across the walking path in front of the cabin. Given the way he felt tonight simply watching her flirt with someone else, he would most definitely spend his entire life jealous of whoever married Amanda. It was the way he had felt about all of her boyfriends, which was thankfully not many men. Amanda spent more time rescuing animals than she did searching dating apps for a boyfriend.

The sound of the cabin door closing got his attention. Amanda stood on the porch with her arms wrapped around herself. "Are you going to stay out here all night?"

Blake sighed and climbed up the steps. They'd had such a nice day together. They had laughed harder and been playful with each other in a way they hadn't since he'd started dating Nadia. It made the way it ended more of a bummer.

The desire to tell her how he really felt and to let the chips fall as they may was strong. The fear of losing her forever was stronger.

"I'm sorry you feel like things are changing. I guess I believe that our friendship will survive any of life's changes. I mean, it survived high school and college. We stuck together through all the good times and the bad. Why would the next phase of life be any different?"

She gripped the railing and stared out into the starry night. "I don't know. It feels different."

Blake wished there was a way to reassure her. "Can we try something?" he asked, coming up beside her.

"What?"

"Can we pretend while we're here that nothing is going to change? We aren't going to talk about my wedding. We aren't going to think about whether or not you should move to Montana. Let's just be us. We can deal with everything else when we get back to San Diego."

Amanda turned to face him. "And when Nadia calls and wants you to come back ASAP?"

"I'll tell her that there's no way for me to get to Bozeman."

Those blue eyes of hers got wide. "You

would lie to Nadia in order to spend time with me?"

Lying was probably not the right thing to do. If he was going to marry Nadia, he should be nothing but honest. But if he wanted to figure out a way to fix things between him and Amanda, he needed to have this time with her.

"I'm willing to do what I have to so we can have a little bit of drama-free friendship."

Amanda bit down on her bottom lip. She was trying to decide if this was a good idea or a bad one. Clearly, she was going to say it was a terrible idea, because she had better judgment than he did.

"Fine," she said, stepping away from the railing. "Just you and me until we get back to San Diego."

Blake didn't move right away. Maybe this wasn't such a bad idea. Maybe this was what they needed to keep their friendship intact after all the changes came their way.

"ONE PICNIC LUNCH." Tyler handed Blake the bag of food. "There are two turkey avocado club sandwiches, a container of some fresh fruit, two bags of potato chips—one barbecue and one salt and vinegar, two fresh-baked chocolate chip cookies, and two bottles of water in there. If there's anything else you need, just text me."

"I think I've got everything else. You drew me a map, let me borrow your ATV and had someone make us lunch. I really appreciate it."

"Well, Grandma Dot said you guys should picnic by the pond, so I needed to make that happen. She and I have the same love of this land. The pond is one of my favorite spots. It's where Hadley and I tied the knot, actually."

"You have weddings out there?"

"One wedding. Just me. It's my special spot. We built this arched bridge across one of the inlets. It was a beautiful ceremony. If you guys weren't family, you would never know it existed. If you tell anyone else about it, I'll have to ban you from the property permanently."

Blake waited for him to say he was kidding, but he got the sense he wasn't when Tyler just stood there with his hands on his hips.

"We will take this location to our graves. You have my word."

"Great." Tyler punched him on the shoulder. "Have fun."

Blake could only hope. The plan was to enjoy the day with his best friend. They had gone back to The Maple Bear Bakery and got a half-dozen Chocolate Junkies to share. They went shopping in the little downtown area. Amanda bought a pair of boots she swore she would wear back home. Blake would bet a million dollars she wouldn't. He found himself a cowboy hat that he most likely would never wear again except maybe as part of a Halloween costume. It didn't matter, though, because Amanda had been smiling all day.

The next stop was to have a picnic by the pond and relax with nature. Blake jumped onto the borrowed ATV and headed back to the cabin to pick up Amanda. She sat on the bench on their front porch, wearing his new cowboy hat and her new boots.

"You look like a real cowgirl," he said, stopping in front of the cabin.

Dressed in jeans and a dark purple sweater, she stood up, smiling from ear to ear. Purple was a good color on her. It made her blue eyes look violet. She grabbed a blanket off the bench and came down the steps. "I would hope so considering how much I paid for these things. Thank goodness you got us a ride, because I'm pretty sure if I walk around in these I am going to have the worst blisters."

"I think you and I were made for flip-flops. Get in."

"We're going to have to take Clancy on a long walk later to make up for leaving him behind," she said, taking a seat.

"We'll make it up to him. Tyler said there was no way we could walk there. He only goes by horse. I am finally able to sit without cringing, so there was no way we were going any way other than by ATV. Either way, Clancy couldn't come along on this particular adventure."

The ride to the pond was filled with beautiful sights. There were horses grazing in the fields and towering pine trees peppering the hills that bordered the property. The sky was bright blue with a few clouds drifting by in slow motion. Blake almost regretted bringing Amanda out here because scenery like this could tempt her to stay.

Blake took the turn off the trail where Tyler had marked it on the map. Another mile or so and they arrived. Tyler had drawn the pond in the shape of a splat with three fingerlike inlets. Blake noticed the bridge on the east side right away. The sky made the water look turquoise blue. It was smooth as glass. The trees and mountains around it were also reflected on its surface.

"I can see why this is his favorite spot on the property," Amanda said, shaking out the blanket.

"It's not La Jolla Beach and the ocean, but it's nice." That was their favorite place to go and the best beach to catch some waves back home. He didn't want her to forget everything she loved about California.

Amanda sat down on the blanket and patted her belly. "Feed me."

"Yes, ma'am." He set the picnic bag down in front of her before taking his own seat. "I got your favorite sandwich and salt-and-vinegar chips."

She dug in and handed him his sandwich. "It's surprising that I can eat after that breakfast, which truly should have put us both in a sugar coma. If I stay here any longer, I'm going to weigh a ton."

Blake shouldn't have encouraged going back to that bakery. It was another lure for her to stay here, but he liked that she saw the positive as a potential negative. He could work with that. "I feel like they've challenged us to find a better doughnut back home. I will not rest until I find one that can compete."

Amanda's laugh made him want to kiss her until she promised to never leave his side. That was wholly inappropriate, so he took a bite of his sandwich instead. Anything to keep his mouth occupied.

"I don't think we will ever find anything that tastes as good. Who would have thought Falcon Creek, Montana, would be home of the best doughnut? This place hasn't been anything like I thought it would be," she said.

"What did you think it was going to be like?" Blake took a bite of his sandwich. Of course it was delicious. Were these people bad at anything?

"I don't know. I couldn't figure out how Lily could fit in here so quickly. I assumed the cowboy lifestyle was the complete opposite of ours in California. But Lily doesn't seem out of place even a little bit. It's so annoying."

She made him smile so hard his face hurt. "I know what you mean."

"Fitting in has never been very hard for her, though. She didn't have the same hang-ups that I did. It was always confusing to me that people could say it was so freaky that we looked so alike, but at the same time she was always considered the pretty one."

"No, she wasn't. What are you talking about?"

"Oh, come on. Tell me you didn't think Lily was prettier than me and Georgie, especially when we were in high school."

Blake fell back, pretending to faint at the absurdity of that question. "All three of you are pretty. You've always been pretty."

"But I have always been a little quieter, a little more reserved. Lily, on the other hand, has always seemed fearless. Stronger. Funnier. And all of that made her stand out. She's someone people want to be around."

He sat back up. "People want to be around you." He wanted to be around her all the time. She didn't need to be bigger than life to be important and so beautiful.

She pulled a piece of crust off her sandwich. "I think that's why I love animals so much. They love, and all they ask for in return is to be loved back. So easy."

So easy. Hearing her say that was like she had stabbed him in the heart. He loved her and all he wanted was for her to love him back, but she wouldn't do it. Even though it would be so easy.

"You don't even realize that you make it so hard."

"What is that supposed to mean?"

Maybe this wasn't the best time, or maybe she needed to hear this. It was a complete toss-up. He was in the barrel of the wave and he needed to ride it until the end. He'd either kick out without a problem or hc'd wipe out. There was no telling.

He stared her right in those ocean-blue eyes. "You are the most loving person I know. You love to love those you love. You take care of the ones you love. You put those you love before yourself."

She shook her head and let out a soft huff. "Are we still talking about animals?"

"I'm talking about your family and your friends. When it comes to the people in your life, you do not let everybody love you back the same way. You put up…roadblocks."

"No, I don't."

"Yes, you do. Like when you lie to your

sisters about how you feel about things if you think your feelings will make them feel bad. You like to do things for others, but sometimes you refuse to let them return the favor. You're so easy to love and impossible to love at the same time."

Her lips fell in a straight line and her expression was hard to read. Blake wasn't sure if he was going to be swallowing a bunch of salt water or celebrating a perfect ten.

"So you're telling me that my sisters don't love me?"

Wipeout. "No, your sisters adore you, but you don't always let them be there. You don't give them the chance to put you first sometimes."

"Put me first? I would never feel right about asking them to do that. They're busy. They have other—"

"What about me?"

"What about you?" She never did see it. No matter how obvious he tried to be.

"Why don't you let me? What's my fatal flaw that makes me unworthy?"

"You are the only one who picks me up when I fall. You're the only one I let see me cry. For the last dozen years, you've always put me first." Her face fell. "I think that's why I'm having a hard time with your impending wedding."

They weren't supposed to talk about the wedding, but it always found its way into their conversations these days.

"I'm sorry," he said. Sorry he kept moving forward with his life. Sorry he wasn't enough for her to be in love with. Sorry things were inevitably going to change, like Lily had said.

They finished eating their lunch in silence. It meant something that she acknowledged that he cared about her like no one else. He had to admit that she did let him in more than she let anyone else. Did he love Nadia enough to risk losing that?

"You want to go exploring before we head back to the cabin?" he asked, getting to his feet. He held out his hand to help her up. She took it and let him pull her to her feet.

"Let's go check out that bridge," she said. The view was spectacular from the bridge. The mountain range seemed to stretch on forever in both directions. "This is totally an Insta-worthy picture." She pulled out her phone and got a couple of photos of the scenery. She flipped the camera and put her arm around him. "Smile," she said before taking a selfie.

"You want me to take a picture of you on this bridge from over there?" Blake pointed to the shoreline.

"Yes, please. It's a cool bridge. I need a shot of the whole thing. Fiona will love it."

"I'm on it." He crossed the bridge and followed the edge of the pond until he was directly in front of it. "She's really going to love you in that hat."

"She's going to want one. Or three."

"Definitely three," he said with a laugh. Fiona was the free spirit of the family, the youngest, who saw everything through rose-colored glasses.

Amanda posed with one hand on her hip and the other on his hat. "We gotta get the boots in the photo." She hopped up on the railing and his heart skipped a beat.

"Jeez, be careful, Harrison."

"I'm fine," she said. Sitting on the railing, she brought one foot up and rested her elbow on her bended knee.

She was gorgeous. More breathtaking than anything else in the picture. He zoomed in on her. How wild it was that she didn't think she was the pretty one.

"You got it?" she asked. She dropped her leg and tried to readjust her position, but she lost her balance and went tumbling backward and straight into the water below.

Blake covered his mouth with his hand to cover up his laughter. She was going to be so mad. He put her phone in his pocket and started walking back around toward one end of the bridge, waiting for her to pop up furious and soaking wet.

Only when she resurfaced, she screamed out in pain, not frustration. The sound caused his heart to race faster than that horse he'd ridden earlier in the week. Without thinking twice, he ran into the pond and dived in after her.

CHAPTER THIRTEEN

COUGHING UP WATER was uncomfortable. Cutting her shoulder open on the rocks below the surface of the water under the bridge had been painful. Riding on an ATV being driven like it was a race car by a very panicked best friend was nauseating.

"Can you slow down? I think I'm going to be sick."

Blake slammed on the brake and Amanda lurched forward. Without a seat belt, she was lucky she didn't fly out of the passenger seat. She only had one hand to brace herself. The T-shirt in her right hand was wet with pond water and a lot of blood. Blake had stripped down and given it to her to stop the bleeding.

"Sorry. What do you need? What can I do? I feel like we have to keep going. We need to get you to a doctor." He sounded frantic, which wasn't helping her calm her own nerves. She didn't have the ability to take care of him and herself at the moment, and for once she was going to put herself first.

"I need you to get us back to the guest lodge but not at lightning speed." Her teeth were chattering. She was freezing, another reason the high-speed racing wasn't helping. The rush of cold air sent shivers through her body. The picnic blanket that Blake had wrapped around her was just as wet as her clothes at this point.

"Right. I'm sorry. I'll be more careful. I wish you had been more careful." His voice was shaky. Maybe it was because he had to be just as frozen as she was. All he had on were his jeans and sweatshirt, both of which were soaking wet. "Please keep pressure on that wound. Okay?"

She held the shirt to her shoulder and he started driving again. This time, he managed to move at a more reasonable speed. When they got to the lodge, Amanda's whole arm was throbbing. Ethan happened to be standing outside, talking with some guests.

"Can someone help us?" Blake said, quickly getting his attention.

Before she knew it, Amanda was in Ethan's truck and headed to the hospital. Blake sat in the back with her and held tight to her free hand. He didn't let go until she was placed on a gurney and wheeled into a room in the ER.

Seven stitches and one dose of painkillers later, Amanda was feeling much better. They'd had her change out of her wet clothes and into a hospital gown. Blake had been given some surgical scrubs.

"It's not fair that you got pants and I didn't," she joked, trying to ease some of the tension.

"Ethan said he would tell Lily to stop at the cabin and grab you a change of clothes. If my phone wasn't waterlogged, I would call her to find out how long she'll be. What is taking her so long?" He stepped out of the room to scan the hall. "You made it. Did you get her some dry clothes?"

"Yes. And I fed and let out Clancy. How's our patient?" Lily walked into the room with a small duffel bag. "What were you doing out there? How did you fall in the water?"

"I blame social media," Amanda replied. "Thank you for the clothes." She gratefully took the bag.

"Let me see your scar," Lily said, trying to sneak a peek.

Amanda pulled the gown over her wound. "It's all bandaged up. You can't see it."

"Is it bad? How big is it?"

Amanda showed her approximately how long the scar was with her fingers.

"Can she go home?" Lily asked Blake. "Do they need to do anything else?"

"They were finishing up her paperwork and we were waiting on you with some clothes."

"Okay." Lily smiled. "Let's get you out of here."

Amanda shooed them out of the room so she could change into her dry clothes. The nurse gave her the final instructions for how to care for her stitches and they released her.

"I can't believe you broke my sister, Blake," Lily teased when they got in her car.

Blake was still too wound up to take it as playful. "I didn't break her. It's this town. She never once got so much as a scratch in San Diego and she's been in the ocean hundreds of times."

"Please don't feel bad. It was an accident, you guys. It could have happened anywhere."

The two of them were quiet the rest of the ride. All Amanda wanted to do was climb in her bed and take a nap. She wanted to get under the covers, be warm and not think about anything for a couple of hours. Clancy was happy to see her and followed her into the bedroom.

"Do you need anything?" Lily asked.

"Just my bed." Amanda kicked off her shoes and pulled back the covers. Her bed was calling her. She climbed in and lay down on her belly since the wound was on the back of her shoulder.

"Okay. I'll see you for dinner?"

Amanda's stomach roiled at the thought of food. "Maybe."

"We're supposed to go dress shopping tomorrow. Are you going to make it or should I reschedule? I would say I could text you pictures, but Blake's phone and your phone both drowned."

Amanda didn't want to throw a wrench in any of the plans. "Hopefully, I'll feel better tomorrow. Don't change anything yet."

"The nurse suggested we stick our phones in rice," Blake said. "Do you think we can get some dry rice from the lodge?"

"I'll get you some. I'll leave you my phone while I do that because you need to call all of our sisters and Rudy and let them know you're okay."

"You called Dad?"

"If you don't think that Big E would have found out about this by the end of the day, you underestimate our grandfather. Do you know how Rudy would have felt if Big E found out about your accident before he did?"

Dad would have been devastated. She would text her sisters and call her father. "You're right. That was a good call."

Lily handed her phone over to Amanda and gave her the passcode. "You can use it, too, Blake. I'm sure your fiancée is going to be bothered when she can't get ahold of you."

"Thanks."

Lily left and Blake lay next to Amanda on the bed. She was under the covers and he was on top. Clancy climbed up and curled into a ball by their feet.

"Why don't you call Nadia first and let her know she'll have to call the cabin's phone until we either fix your phone or buy you a new one." She held out Lily's phone, but he didn't take it. "What?"

"Honestly, I don't know her number," he confessed.

"You don't know your fiancée's phone number?"

"She gave me her number, I put it in my phone, and I never had to learn it. No one knows anyone's number anymore. We all tell our phones to call whoever."

He wasn't totally wrong. Phones made it easy to not bog down your brain with numbers. It wasn't like when they were in middle school. "You know whose number I still have memorized?"

"Who?"

"Besides my parents' number, I could call your parents, Joanie Simpson's parents and the pet hospital. I have all those numbers pointlessly stored in my long-term memory."

Blake chuckled, softly shaking the bed. "I could totally call both of our parents. And you."

"You have my cell phone memorized?"

He tapped his finger against his temple. "I have every number you've ever had memorized." It gave her a warm and fuzzy feeling to know that he knew all of her numbers and not Nadia's. Or maybe it was her pain medication. It was becoming hard to tell. Her eyelids were heavy.

"I have your number memorized, too," she admitted as her eyes fluttered closed.

"You have to call your dad," he reminded her. Amanda groaned. "You still have to call him."

She refused to open her eyes. "Fine. Call him and put it on speaker."

A moment later, the call was going through. "How's your sister?"

"I'm fine, Dad." Amanda knew that wouldn't be good enough for him.

"Amanda. Thank goodness. You gave me quite a scare."

"That makes two of us," Blake chimed in.

Amanda opened one eye to glare at Blake.

"Blake, is that you?"

"Yes, sir, Mr. Harrison."

"Thank you for pulling her out of the water and getting her to the hospital, son. You saved her life."

Amanda closed her eyes again. She hadn't been close to dying, but it was nice to have Blake take care of her.

"How many stitches did she get?" Elias Blackwell could be heard saying in the background. It was unsurprising that he was butting in.

"Seven," Amanda answered.

"She got seven," her dad relayed to him.

"Dorothy and I can't figure out how she could fall into that pond and cut herself up. It's a pond, for goodness' sake! Did she decide to jump in for some reason?"

"Well, Dad, I'm going to let you go. I need to rest in a dark room with complete silence." She didn't want to answer any of Mr. Blackwell's questions.

"Okay, sweetheart. I will call you later. Perhaps when we can have a little *privacy*."

"Privacy? We live in an RV. There is no such thing as privacy. If I have to listen to your snore at night, I also get to listen to your conversation with my granddaughter."

"I'll call you, Dad. My phone didn't survive my accident. I have to get a new one. Love you."

"Love you, too."

She ended the call and noticed Blake staring back at her. His expression was soft and his gaze was intense. She wanted to look away but couldn't.

"I love how none of the stuff that's happened has changed the way you feel about your dad. I'm sure that means the world to him. I've always admired the way your dad was there for you and your sisters. I can't imagine having five daughters. Don't get me wrong, I want a daughter or two, but five would be rough. I need at least one son to go surfing with."

It was a shame that those painkillers she took didn't work on her heart. It felt like he had taken a hammer and pounded it with reckless abandon. What she wouldn't give to be able to dream about future children. To imagine teaching them to do the things she loved. Being there for them when they needed her. Being.

She closed her eyes before the tears welled up and he noticed something was wrong.

"You know that you could teach a daughter to surf. You *better* teach your daughters to surf."

Blake tucked her hair behind her ear and kept his hand on her cheek. "Of course I'll teach my girls to surf. I'm an expert teacher. I taught you, didn't I?"

Amanda loved the water. She loved the ocean. When she had seen Blake surf for the first time, there had been nothing she wanted to do more than learn how to do that.

It had looked fun and terrifying, but she had known that if Blake showed her how to do it, it wouldn't be scary at all.

She'd been wrong. It had been terrible. Wipeout after wipeout. She'd swallowed more salt water than a fish that day. But through it all, Blake had been there patiently coaching and encouraging her not to give up. With his help, she'd managed to stay on her feet and ride out one wave. It had been nothing short of a miracle.

He was going to be an amazing dad. His heart and soul were so good and pure she couldn't imagine him not having a family who would adore him as much as he would love them.

The tears forced their way out even with her eyes closed. She buried her face into the pillow.

"Are you okay? What's wrong?"

The worst part of this was that she needed him. She needed someone's shoulder to cry on, and the only one that would do was his. Yet this was the one thing she couldn't tell him because things would never be the same.

She faced away from him and wiped her

eyes even though they had no intention of stopping. "My shoulder hurts."

"I'm so sorry." He sounded pained. "It's too early to take more pain pills. What can I do? Maybe I should get you some ice?"

"I need to sleep. I'm tired and I don't want to feel anything for a little bit." Lately, she wished she could not feel anything ever again.

Blake gently rubbed her back. "Okay, sleep. I'll be right out there. I'm going to be checking on you every couple hours, okay?"

"You don't have to do that. I don't want you to worry yourself all night."

"You telling me not to worry won't stop it from happening. I'm not taking any chances with you, Harrison." He placed a soft kiss on her good shoulder before leaving her alone to get some rest.

Blake was a man of his word. He watched out for her all evening and through the night. When morning came, Amanda opened her eyes and there he was, out like a light on the pillow next to hers. With him asleep, she could really look at him. He was beautiful for a guy. His skin was always sun kissed but soft, thanks to his very complicated, multi-step skin-care routine. She liked to tease him that he was higher maintenance than all of her sisters combined.

Amanda carefully ran her fingertips down his cheek. He made her heart feel too big for her chest. Yesterday, before she hurt herself, he had accused her of not letting him love her or, at the very least, making it difficult to love her. What she couldn't tell him was that if she didn't love him so much, she would selfishly try to keep him for herself. It was because she loved him that she had to put up those so-called roadblocks. Blake deserved to have everything he wanted. What he wanted the most she couldn't give him.

His eyes fluttered open and a tired smile lifted that soft cheek. "Good morning. How are you feeling?"

"Meds are still working." She had woken up once in the night in some terrible pain, but right now the only thing that hurt was her heart. "Did you ever get our phones to work?"

He rolled over on his back and stretched his arms above his head. "No luck last night. I can go check to see if being in the rice overnight helped."

"Nadia is probably worried sick."

"She won't freak out because of one night.

We will have to buy new phones today if we can't get ours to work. I can't fall off the face of the earth two days in a row."

"You have your laptop here. You could email her," Amanda suggested. If Nadia loved him as much as Amanda did, she deserved to know he was okay.

He sat up. "Good idea, Harrison. You are the smartest." Blake went to check the phones. "Looks like we're going shopping," he said, holding up two phones with black screens.

"I'm sorry you ruined your phone because of me."

"Phones can be replaced." He tossed her phone on the bed. "Best friends cannot," he said with a wink.

Best friends cannot. When Blake got married, she could lose him. She could lose *this* him. The one who slept over to make sure she didn't die after an accident. The one who did not judge her for wanting to go to the bakery for the third day in a row to eat doughnuts. The best friend who could never be replaced by anyone else. His absence would simply be a gaping hole in her life moving forward.

He couldn't marry Nadia. She hadn't been

in their lives long enough for Amanda to know that she was the right person. If Amanda was going to lose her best friend, it had to be to the most deserving woman out there.

She had to tell him. Her near-death experience had changed how she thought about this.

"Blake," she said, coming out of her bedroom, dressed for the day.

He came out of his with his shirt in his hand and not on his body. Her knees went weak and she got light-headed. "Ready to go?"

Amanda tried her best to tear her eyes away from his chest and get words to come out of her mouth, but it was not working. There was a knock at the door and Clancy ran to it, barking to make sure Amanda and Blake were aware that someone was there.

Blake slipped on his T-shirt and the spell was completely broken. Amanda went to the door. Leave it to one of the Blackwells to show up right when Amanda had got up the courage to ask Blake to call off the engagement.

Frustrated, she swung the door open. Only it wasn't a Blackwell on the other side.

Standing on the front porch next to a giant suitcase, in her skintight jeans and a sweater that looked like it was painted on, was Nadia. She clutched her oversize, expensive designer purse. Her dark hair was slicked back in a tight bun and her eyes were shielded by huge white sunglasses.

She whipped her sunglasses off and scowled. "Where is my fiancé?"

CHAPTER FOURTEEN

"NADIA?" BLAKE COULDN'T believe his ears. He joined Amanda at the door. "Nadia! What are you doing here?"

"Well, if you'd answered any of my calls or texts in the last twelve hours, you would know what I was up to. But apparently you've been having too much fun on your vacation with Amanda to be bothered to respond to me."

Clancy barked and tried to get a sniff of the new guest. Nadia recoiled. "Can you please get this dog away from me?"

Amanda grabbed Clancy's collar and tugged him back. She apologized and put him in her bedroom.

He reached for Nadia's suitcase. "My phone died. Like died died. Drowned. I was actually about to go buy a new one. I can't believe you're here. Come on in."

"How did your phone drown on a ranch?"

"It's a long story, but the short version is Amanda fell, cut herself on some rocks, and I had to jump into a pond to save her. I didn't think to take my phone out of my pocket."

Nadia set her purse on the café table and stared hard at Amanda. "How did you fall into a pond?"

"That's the long part of the story. I was messing around on the bridge and fell backward. It was stupid of me, and now I have seven stitches and a nasty scar to remind me not to do dumb things."

Blake needed to put Nadia at ease. He wrapped his arms around her. "I can't believe you're here. You came all this way because you couldn't get through to me last night?"

Nadia pulled back and, instead of answering the question, turned to Amanda. "I'm glad you're okay, Amanda, but could you and your dog go back to your cabin so Blake and I can catch up?"

Amanda's eyes went wide and darted to Blake. He put his hand on Nadia's shoulder. "Sweetheart, Amanda and I are sharing this cabin. It has two bedrooms. Why don't we go talk in my room?"

He could feel the tension in her shoulders.

She was wound up real tight, but followed him into his room without saying anything else to Amanda. As soon as he closed the door, she unleashed.

"I have tried to be understanding throughout this whole thing, but did you really have to share a cabin with her? Staying in the guest lodge in your own room wasn't a viable option? And how did she fall in the water and not be capable of getting out by herself? She grew up by the ocean. Am I supposed to believe she doesn't know how to swim? I have never in my life seen a woman so dependent on a man who isn't her boyfriend or husband. There's something not right about all of this."

"Whoa. Hold on there. First of all, we are staying in this cabin to be close to her sister, who lives right next door. The whole point of being here was for Amanda and Lily to be together."

"So why isn't she staying in her sister's cabin?"

"Because her sister's cabin is a one-bedroom and this is a two-bedroom. How is staying in my own room here any different than staying in my own room in the guest lodge?"

Nadia kept her arms crossed in front of

her, the look of indignation still on her face. "She's up to something. Everyone agrees with me and this injury story confirms it."

Blake shook his head. He could feel the heat of his own anger coloring his tone. Nadia was the one who had suggested he come here with Amanda to look at the ranch as a possible wedding venue. Now she wanted to act like all this was some plot to break them up?

"That's offensive, Nadia. Amanda is not up to anything. I don't know who this 'everyone' is that you've been talking to, but I'm going to guess it's not people who know me, and they certainly don't know Amanda. Do you really think she wanted seven stitches in her shoulder yesterday just to what? Get my attention? Amanda doesn't have to do outrageous things to get my attention. She's my best friend. She has my attention whenever she wants it."

Arms still folded, Nadia sat down on the bed. Her expression softened a bit. "My mom and my friends have been getting in my head. No one believes me when I tell them there's nothing going on between the two of you. They keep telling me that there's no way she's not in love with you."

Blake sat down next to her. He felt bad that she had all these doubts and even worse that he had to admit that Amanda wasn't in love with him. "She loves me like a brother. She's never and will never be in love with me. That's not the kind of relationship she wants from me."

"How could anyone want you to be their brother?" She shifted to face him and put her hand on his cheek. "Does she not see you? Does she not realize what kind of a man you are? That makes no sense."

He placed his hand over hers. He had no answers to those questions. He often wondered what was wrong with him, why wasn't he what Amanda was looking for in a lover as well as a friend. Truthfully, he'd given up trying to answer that after that night when they'd crossed lines Amanda clearly wasn't comfortable crossing.

"It is what it is. Even if she was in love with me, I asked you to marry me, Nadia. Shouldn't that count for something?"

Nadia wrapped her arms around his neck and hugged him tightly. "It does. That's another reason I came. I want to plan this wedding together. The only way I could feel good about it was if I was here with you."

"I wasn't planning the wedding. I was checking out this place while I was here. You and I haven't even set a date or decided on anything yet."

She sat back. "Well, let's do that. Let's set a date. Let's talk to the people here and see what's available. I loved all the pictures you sent me. I think a summer wedding would be perfect."

Blake wasn't sure he was ready to make final decisions. He wasn't even sure the ranch was where he wanted to get married. It was nice, but it didn't feel like the right place for him; however, Nadia was so mad about so many things right now, it didn't seem like the time to fight about more stuff. He could let her talk to Hadley, but they would not sign any contracts.

"It would be great if you met with their wedding planner. We could start making a list of pros and cons to take back with us to San Diego. We can compare it with some of the venues back home."

"I don't want to get married in San Diego," she said, wrinkling her nose as if the idea literally stank. "That's boring. Let's do something no one else we know has done. I want to offer our family and friends an adventure, an experience they'll never forget."

Blake had always thought of a wedding as something a bit more intimate. Something special for the bride and groom. The guests should have a good time, but the focus was on making the commitment. Starting a life together.

"I will see if Hadley has some time for us. Amanda and her sister are dress shopping today, so I wasn't going to see her."

"Oh, I want to go dress shopping. Not that I would buy my dress in some little Podunk town in Montana, but I would love to have some fun with it."

"Ah…" Blake hadn't meant to invite Nadia along for the shopping trip. He wasn't sure how Amanda would feel about that. "I can ask them if we can tag along."

"It's totally weird that I'm here, isn't it? I wish you had gotten my calls."

Honesty was the best policy. At least, he hoped it was. "It's a little weird. I was not expecting you this morning, but there are worse things than having your fiancée want to be with you."

She kissed his cheek. "I do want to be with you."

Those words warmed his heart. Nadia was a good person. She was a *real* person. Even though she was confident and smart, she had her moments of feeling insecure. She sometimes let her imagination get the best of her. She was strong and opinionated, and there was nothing wrong with that. He never wanted his wife to be afraid to tell him what she thought.

He was a lucky man. He had surrounded himself with amazing women. He had the best friend in the world and was going to marry a fantastic woman. As soon as he got Amanda and Nadia to be friends, all would be well.

DRESS SHOPPING. NOT exactly what Blake thought he would be doing today. Had Nadia not shown up in Falcon Creek, he had planned to shadow Conner on the ranch while the sisters did the shopping. Since Nadia was there, he felt like he needed to go with them to act as a go-between while they were getting to know each other.

Lily struggled to find anything she even wanted to try on. They were at some small bridal shop in the town next to Falcon Creek. This place had racks of dresses that the women had to go through on their own. This was beginning to feel like a slow death.

"Maybe we should start with what you want instead of me showing you dresses and you saying all the things you don't like about them," Amanda said.

"What about this one?" Nadia pulled a dress off the rack. "I love the neckline on it."

Lily made that face, the one she'd made every time one of them showed her a dress and complimented something about it. "I don't like all the beading in the front."

"Okay, no beading, no trains, no mermaid-style, no lace, not white. Give me something you do want," Amanda said again.

"Simple. I want the opposite of what I thought I wanted when we planned the last wedding."

Amanda smiled. "Well, it has to be opposite because that was a summer wedding and this is a Christmas wedding. How about you spend ten minutes on your phone and search winter wedding dresses," Amanda suggested. "Find a couple things you like and we'll see if they have anything here that's similar."

"I liked it when you made me a nice Pinterest board last time."

Amanda snorted a laugh. For someone who was all about being independent, there were still some things that Lily liked a little help with. "I'll keep pulling dresses I bet you'll like, while you search the web."

"What about this one? Simple. Long sleeves. I love the fur," Nadia said. "Maybe we should change the date and have a winter wedding, Blake. What do you think?" She held the dress up to her body.

"I thought you had your heart set on a summer wedding?" he replied. Not to mention that he wanted a summer wedding, as well. Snow was not his idea of wedding decor.

Nadia draped the dress over her arm. "I'm going to try this one on. We might need to reconsider the date if I like it." She got the attention of the woman who was manning the store to let her into a dressing room.

"You guys decided on a date?" Amanda asked.

"We sort of picked June nineteenth this morning. Taking this trip made her feel a little insecure. She needed to know that I was serious about getting married," Blake explained.

"Because asking her to get married didn't affirm you were serious?"

"I know. I don't understand what's gotten into her. Some of her friends got her all worked up about me being here without her."

"And with Amanda," Lily said knowingly.

It was as she had predicted. Nadia was jealous of Amanda.

"Don't worry," he said to Amanda. "She knows she was being silly. She felt bad about getting all worked up."

Lily stared down at her phone. "So it begins."

Amanda was busy stuffing her feeling about this down, down, down. He knew she was, because that was what she did when she got quiet like this.

"It's funny if you think about it. There are people who say you've been trying to seduce me this whole time. Hilarious, right?"

Amanda did not seem to think it was very

funny. "Does Nadia think I was trying to seduce you?"

"No! Not Nadia. Her friends who don't even know you, or me really, for that matter. Nadia knows we're like family."

Lily's eyes lifted from her phone and her gaze met his. She gave him that sympathetic look. She knew that Nadia had at least thought it.

"Um, excuse me?" The store clerk approached them. "The lady trying on the dress asked if Amanda could come back and give her opinion."

Surprise registered on Amanda's face. She looked to Blake, then to Lily.

"That's good. She wants your help. If she thought you were a man-stealing monster, she wouldn't ask your opinion," Lily offered.

Amanda took a deep breath before following the woman to the dressing room. This was what Blake wanted. He wanted them to be friends. Friends helped each other pick out wedding dresses. Then why did it feel so awkward?

"She dropped everything and came all the way out here? She's not going to be my sister's friend, Blake. It's impossible. I'm sorry, but it's true."

That wasn't true. Lily didn't know what she was talking about. She didn't know Nadia. She could not judge. "No, it's okay. She wants to be friends with Amanda. She came here because she was a little jealous, but once she got here, she realized it's fine."

Lily tilted her head. "Are you sure about that?"

"I have to be."

"Maybe it wouldn't be so terrible if Amanda stayed in Montana with me. Maybe it would make things easier for you and Nadia."

A flash of frustration hit him hard. "She has a life in San Diego. A job. A house. Your dad." *Me*, he wanted to say.

"I'm not saying she has to move here. I am simply suggesting that it could be an option. Amanda is all about family. If she needs to be around family, we have a lot of it here now."

"You know she doesn't consider the Blackwells her family."

"She's scared, Blake. Once Rudy comes back with Thomas, we're going to have a chance to mend the wounds that finding out the truth created. She'll come around on the Blackwells once that happens."

As if dress shopping hadn't been stressful enough, Lily managed to unintentionally make Blake's blood pressure skyrocket into the stratosphere. He had a plan and she wanted to put a wrench in it.

Amanda returned from the back. Her face was a little flushed.

"So?" Lily and Blake asked at the same time.

Amanda wore her best *I'm sorry* face. "You better not be too attached to that June nineteenth date because she's awfully attached to that dress. She sent pictures to her mom and her sister. Her mom loves it and her sister hates it. I guess that's okay, because hearing her sister hated it only made Nadia love it more."

Blake felt discombobulated. Nadia was here and wanted to get married this winter. Lily seemed certain that she could get Amanda to stay. What was happening? "She said she was not going to buy anything here. That's the first dress she's even looked at. She can't possibly think she's found the dress that fast, can she? That's not how it works, is it?"

Both Harrison girls shrugged. "I wish it

was how it worked for me. It figures that the bride not looking for a dress finds one and the one who needs it now can't find one that she even wants to try on."

"I will help you find one. There are a lot of dresses here. We'll pick one," Amanda promised. "What about the one on the mannequin back here. Come look." She took Lily's hand and led her toward the back of the store.

Nadia came out, smiling ear to ear. "I can't believe this. Who would have thought that in the middle of some tiny town in Montana, I would find the dress of my dreams? I have to buy it, Blake. I know I said I had no intention of looking while I was here, but this must be fate."

"I'm happy for you, but we agreed we wanted to get married in the summer," he said, trying to assert himself in the least offensive way.

"Well, I can't wear this dress in the summer. We're going to have to move it to winter. I'll let you decide. Do you want to get married this winter or the next?"

This was not a question he was answering in the middle of some dress shop. "I feel like we need to talk about this a little more."

"Blake, when a woman finds *the* dress, there's

no going back. I can't not wear this dress when we say 'I do.'" She waved over the clerk, who seemed to be helping Lily. "Ma'am, I'm ready."

Blake didn't want to make a scene, but he'd been pushed just a little too far. "I want a summer wedding!" He raised his voice loud enough to make the woman coming to help check Nadia out stop in her tracks.

CHAPTER FIFTEEN

AMANDA KNEW THAT SOUND. That was the sound of Blake's final straw. He wasn't the kind of man to lose his temper very often or very easily. For him to shout like that meant he was steaming mad about something.

"Why are you yelling at me?" Nadia asked, her hand pressed to her chest.

"I'm sorry. I didn't mean that." He paused. "I meant what I said. I didn't mean to raise my voice."

Amanda had to rescue him and give him a chance to calm down or he was going to be in the doghouse with Nadia. "I'll be right back, Lily." She ran to Blake's side and wrapped her hand around his wrist. "Hey, why don't you and I get some fresh air?" She smiled at Nadia. "Shopping isn't his favorite activity."

Without waiting for a response, she pulled him outside. The sun was blinding and Blake shielded his eyes with his hand.

"Are you okay?" she asked, knowing he wasn't. The question gave him permission to let it all out.

"What is going on in there? I thought we were coming here to find Lily a dress, and the next thing I know, I'm getting married in the winter instead of the summer because Nadia finds a dress with faux fur that she falls in love with? What kind of marriage is this going to be if we can't even compromise about when we should get married?"

Amanda let him vent all his feelings about that, and none of them were good. When he was finally finished, she took him by both hands. "Look at me," she said, standing in front of him. "Take a deep breath. It's not like you to lose your temper like that."

Blake was the chillest guy. He was an easygoing, go-with-the-flow kind of guy. This was not how he usually handled himself. Amanda admitted this had been building for a while.

"You're upset and tired. Maybe what you need to do is not pop her bubble right now. She thinks she's in love with that dress. Maybe you ask her to put it on hold while you two have a more reasonable conversation about what you want in the privacy of your room at the cabin versus in public in front of the nice woman running the bridal shop."

He hung his head. "You're right. Of course, you're right."

"You need to take a few more deep breaths and get yourself together. Then you need to go back in there and apologize profusely."

"I know."

His dad had been a yeller when Blake was growing up. It was not Mr. Collins's most redeeming quality. It was the one trait Blake tried very hard not to emulate. It sometimes made him more passive than assertive, but he usually felt that was a reasonable trade-off.

"Amanda?" The sound of her name made her turn around. Logan had a box in his arms and car keys in his hand.

"Hey, Logan. How are you?"

Logan put the box in the back of the blue pickup truck parked on the side of the street in front of him. "I'm good. Hey, Blake."

Blake took a very deep breath. "Logan," he said in his exhalation.

"What brings you guys to Overland?" he asked.

Amanda nodded in the direction of the bridal shop. "My sister and his fiancée are dress shopping. We are taking a break from all the discussions on tulle, lace and crystal beading."

Logan laughed. "I don't blame y'all for that. I'm happy to see you, though. I was disappointed I didn't get that call about breakfast."

The timing of this conversation could not be any worse. She felt her neck turning red from the awkwardness. "Funny story. See, my phone fell in a pond. Totally ruined it. I lost everything that hadn't been backed up to the cloud, including your number since it was the last one put in there."

He seemed pleasantly surprised. "Oh, well, that's a better excuse than I was expecting."

"We just got new phones this morning. I have the same number. If you text me, then I'll have your number again," she said.

"Great. I can do that. Maybe we can get together for breakfast?"

There was no way she could turn him down when he flashed her that smile with dimples in full effect. "That would be great."

"Great." Logan was still grinning.

"Great," she replied, not knowing what else to say.

"Great!" Blake chimed in. "Well, we'll see

you later, Logan. Lots of wedding planning yet to do before we head back to San Diego. Where we live. Where we've lived since we were born. Where we live permanently."

Amanda internally cringed. Logan's face fell and he took a step back. The poor guy did not deserve any of Blake's pent-up frustration.

"Well, hopefully we can see each other before you go back." He gave her a little wave goodbye and started for his truck.

"Hopefully," Amanda said, raising her hand in farewell.

Once Logan was safe inside his truck, she turned on Blake. "Not cool. I know you're having a minor crisis here, but it is not fair to treat Logan like that."

"Why are you leading this guy on? Are you really planning on dating this guy long-distance? What is the point of pretending you're going to call him?"

This was the same fight they had just ended without being resolved a couple of nights ago. She didn't understand why he was so bothered. Was he really so worried that she was going to move to Montana? If she did, it wouldn't be because of Logan.

"Being nice to someone and having breakfast with them—neither of those things are leading anyone on. Can you stay focused on your own problems and not make new ones with me?"

Blake threw his hands up. "I don't want you to move to Falcon Creek, okay? I want you to come back to California with me. Sorry if that's selfish or me being too involved in your love life or whatever you think I'm doing. I don't care. I don't want to get married in the winter and I don't want you to move. Nadia doesn't seem to care what I have to say about anything—do you?"

"Don't compare these two things because they are not the same. You and your fiancée need to talk about your wedding date. Plain and simple, that's an issue that you need to resolve because it involves both of you. Me going to breakfast with Logan doesn't have anything to do with you. It doesn't have anything to do with where I live or where you want me to live. You don't get to treat him like a jerk because he's being nice to me and because you and Nadia are having issues." She opened the door to the shop and went inside, leaving him out there to think about how he wanted to talk to the people in his

life. She wasn't going to tolerate it and neither was Nadia.

Speaking of Nadia, she was busy giving
her two cents about the dress Lily had tried
on. "I really like that little bit of crystal beading around the waist. It's not too much, but it
really elevates the whole look of the dress."

Lily spun around in front of the full-length
mirror in the back. The dress had a brocade
skirt, cut at the waist, and a crepe long-sleeved
V-neck on top. The crystal beading adorned
her waist in the front of the dress. Because they
only had one dress to try on in each style, it
wasn't exactly Lily's size. They had it clipped
in the back to make it fit better in the front. It
was supposed to be tighter fitting in the arms
than it was.

"What do you think?" Lily asked Amanda,
gazing at her through the mirror.

"You look beautiful. The more important
question is, what do you think?"

Lily slipped her hands in the pockets in
the skirt of the dress and checked herself out
from all angles. "It's what I was looking for.
Simple but not too simple. I love the texture
of the skirt. I like that I'll be able to acces-

sorize with a cool necklace. I feel pretty in this one."

Amanda realized how different this dress shopping experience was from the last. Lily hadn't even had an opinion the first time; she had wanted Amanda to just pick something. Maybe that was another red flag Amanda had failed to notice. Lily hadn't wanted to marry Danny, so it hadn't mattered what she looked like.

With Conner, it was different. It mattered, so she wanted it to be right. That was why she was so critical of everything they had looked at until now. She had been worried she wouldn't find the dress for this wedding, the wedding to the right man.

Amanda smiled at her sister. "I'm glad you found something you like."

"Where's Blake?" Nadia asked.

Amanda was about to say he was still outside when he appeared. "Right here. Can we talk for a second?" Nadia seemed hesitant. "I promise I will not raise my voice. I'm sorry I did that." He glanced over at Amanda when he said it, like he meant it for her, too.

They went outside, leaving Lily and Amanda with the saleswoman.

"I know I should try some more on, but I really like this one."

"When you know, you know. Why waste your time looking around for something else when what you want is right in front of you?"

"Good point," Lily said, taking one last look at herself. "Let's send a couple pictures to Fiona for one more opinion."

Amanda pulled out her phone to take the picture and noticed a text from an unknown number.

Great to see you again. Hope it wasn't the last time.

Logan. Was she leading him on by agreeing that they could get breakfast before she went back home? Why not go on an innocent date? Shouldn't she give guys a chance, because who knew—maybe she would find someone who didn't want kids. It wasn't like what she wanted was standing right in front of her. She glanced in the direction Blake and Nadia had gone. He may have been everything she wanted, but he wasn't the one she could have.

"Smile," Amanda said as she prepared to

take the picture. She took a few and sent them all to Fiona. It didn't take long for their baby sister to give her enthusiastic approval.

"So, you've decided?" the saleswoman asked.

"Yes. I would like to order this one."

"Wonderful! I'll need to take your measurements."

Amanda went to find somewhere to sit while Lily got sized and Nadia and Blake made up. So much for her telling him that she didn't want him to marry Nadia until he was truly sure about her. The woman wanted to buy a dress. How could Amanda interfere now?

She decided to text Logan back. One breakfast wasn't going to change anything. It was a chance to not be a third wheel for a few hours, though, and that had never been more desirable than it was today.

Doughnuts and coffee tomorrow at 8?

Logan was quick to reply. See you then!

Amanda dropped her phone into her purse. She had a date. In Montana. She had no idea what she was doing. She was trying to not fall apart like everything else in her life.

Lily had finished getting her measurements and walked up to the checkout counter with the saleswoman to put a down payment on her dress. This was really happening.

"Did your friend also want to pay the down payment on her dress?" the woman behind the counter asked.

Lily glanced at Amanda, who didn't want to interrupt those two to ask. She shrugged back at her sister.

"We're not really sure," Lily replied with a pasted-on smile.

Amanda could see them standing outside, deep in conversation. She could see Blake's face and he didn't look happy. It was killing her not to know what they were talking about. This conflict was stirring up those protective feelings again. He deserved to marry the perfect woman. The one who would make him smile all the time. Nadia had done nothing today but make him defensive and frustrated.

"I'm going to go out there and see what they've decided," she announced. Lily gave her a good-luck thumbs-up.

"Then I guess that's it," Nadia said when Amanda stepped outside. They both turned their attention to her.

"Lily is putting money down on the dress. The lady is wondering if you were going to do that, too, or not."

Nadia's eyes went back to Blake. "We're going to hold off for now."

The rush of relief that Amanda felt was indescribable. Maybe he had called the whole thing off like she had wanted. Blake held Nadia's hand and brought it up to his lips, dashing those hopes instantly. Amanda would have to be happy with the fact that they weren't going to get married the same time as Lily, at least. Blake had made it perfectly clear that he didn't want to get married in the winter, and it seemed that Nadia had listened and was willing to compromise.

They headed back to the ranch, and all Amanda wanted was to get Blake alone and find out what had happened. That was not a possibility. Nadia was attached at the hip to Blake the rest of the day. Hadley agreed to meet with them and take Nadia on a tour of the property and to the wedding barn.

Amanda realized this was what her future would be like. This was how it would be when they were married. Thinking about what it would be like and experiencing what it would be like were two very different things. There was no way she could share a cabin with those two. She had to give them their space and protect herself.

"Can I move into your cabin?" she asked Lily while they were eating lunch together in the dining hall.

"Sure. But why?"

"Do you really have to ask? I can't be in there with them. It's too weird."

"Of course you can stay with me. If you can handle my messiness."

If the choice was between some clutter and having to see Nadia and Blake be together, her sister's dirty laundry won every time. "After lunch, let's go back and move my stuff."

Lily took a bite of her salad. "What are you going to say to Blake?"

"I'll say it's because of Clancy. Nadia doesn't like him."

"She doesn't like Clancy? What kind of person doesn't love that guy? He's the sweetest dog ever."

"She's not a fan of his size or his interest in her." Amanda understood that Clancy's size would be overwhelming, but it was shocking that Blake would consider being with some-one who didn't love animals of all shapes and sizes. "It will be completely believable and she'll be relieved. Blake won't question it."

Lily shook her head. "And so it begins."

"Why do you keep saying that? What be-gins?"

"Don't worry about it. I'm sure Blake is going to make sure everything is hunky-dory." Lily went back to eating her salad.

Amanda wanted to believe that was true. "In other news, I have a breakfast date tomor-row morning."

Lily dropped her fork. "What?"

"I ran into Logan outside the bridal shop. He texted me and I asked him to meet me for breakfast." Her sister's eyes were wide and her mouth agape. "It doesn't mean anything. It's just a nice distraction."

"Conner is going to freak out."

Amanda's forehead creased. "Why would Conner freak out?"

"That's his best friend. He is Conner's Blake. He'll want to know that you're not going to break his heart."

Wow. This was not what Amanda needed to hear. "I'm eating breakfast, not trying to win the guy's heart. He knows I don't live here. I don't know why he even wants to spend any more time with me, but he does. I'm sure we're both on the same page that this isn't going to be something more than breakfast."

"Well, maybe he'll steal your heart and you'll move out here."

Amanda shook her head. "Why would you even want me out here? I thought you were trying to assert yourself as your own person, be independent. How would I fit into your new life exactly?"

Before she could answer, she heard a familiar voice over her shoulder. "If it isn't my two favorite Harrisons."

Conner pulled up a chair and sat down with the sisters. Lily leaned over and gave him a kiss. "If it isn't my second-favorite Hannah."

"Ouch," he said, pressing his hand against his chest.

"You know you'll never outshine your mother."

He smiled and gently tugged on the loose strands of hair that weren't pulled up in her ponytail. "Truer words were never spoken."

They were painfully cute together. They

were happy. They were going to have a wonderful life together.

"Guess who's having breakfast with your best friend tomorrow?" Lily said, getting right to it.

Conner's expression dampened a bit. "You're having breakfast with Logan?"

"Is that bad?" Amanda asked.

"Conner!" Ethan Blackwell came running into the dining hall, panic written all over his face. "We've got a horse tangled up in some barbed wire fencing on the southwest side of the grazing paddock. I need your help."

Conner didn't hesitate. He sprang into action. Lily followed. "I'm helping!" she shouted after the men.

"*We're* helping." Amanda couldn't stand the thought of an animal in distress. She was on her feet before Lily.

CHAPTER SIXTEEN

HADLEY PACED BACK and forth. "Ethan said he was going to find Conner and get out here as fast as he could."

Blake hated feeling helpless, especially when it came to an animal in danger. "I wish I had something to distract him with. He looks so afraid."

"I'm so glad you noticed him when we were driving by," she said.

"Is someone coming?" Nadia shouted from the car.

Blake walked over to her. "Yeah. We're waiting for them to get here."

"Could we go back to the cabin and Hadley can wait for them to come?" she asked.

"I want to help the horse, Nadia. If that poor thing injures its leg bad enough, they'll have to put it down. I don't want to see that happen, so anything I can do, I want to do." Helping animals was in his blood. It was a passion he'd had as long as he could remember. He'd thought he was weird for feeling that way until he met Amanda.

Conner's pickup truck towing a horse trailer came barreling down the dirt path and to a quick stop behind Hadley's car. Conner, Ethan, Lily and Amanda all jumped out.

Amanda seemed surprised to see him there. "What are you doing here?"

"We visited the barn and Hadley decided to show us where other bridal parties have gone to take pictures. I saw this guy and noticed he didn't seem to be able to move. Then I noticed the fence was all messed up. We called Ethan right away."

Conner grabbed tools out of the back of the truck, and Ethan had a small bundle of hay. "Lily, can you get the head collar and lead rope? We need to secure him so we can control where he goes and doesn't go. Amanda, I need someone to feed him some hay while we work to free him from the fence."

"I'm your woman," she said, taking the bundle of hay from him.

"What can I do?" Blake asked.

"You can help me and Conner cut him loose."

The five of them worked together to save the horse. Lily put the head collar on, and Amanda talked to him sweetly as she fed him hay.

"Blake, I need you to come over here and help me with the wire," Conner said. The horse neighed and shook its head. The wire had tightened around the horse's leg as he struggled to free himself.

Ethan tried to help calm him so he didn't do more damage to his leg. "We have to keep him as still as possible. Every time he moves, he cuts that leg. If we lose the leg, we lose the horse."

Amanda placed a gentle hand on the side of the horse's head. Blake knew her heart was breaking for this poor animal. The horse had no idea what was happening and had to be terrified. "It's okay, big boy. They're going to get you loose. Be patient, eat your hay, buddy."

"His name is Pirate," Ethan said. "He's not very old. I feel terrible he lost his way and got caught here."

"We've almost got it," Blake said. Conner had given him gloves and he was holding the wire so Conner could snip through it.

"They're almost done, Pirate. You're being such a good boy," Amanda said, holding out more hay.

"Lily, grab his lead and get ready to try to guide him forward," Conner directed. "Katie is going to be so upset about this. She's going to blame herself for the fence being damaged, which is why he thought he could get through here."

Ethan squirted disinfectant on the cut-up leg. "If Pirate heals, Katie won't beat herself up too much."

"Okay, Lily. Carefully, guide him forward," Conner said.

Lily clicked her tongue and pulled gently on the lead. Pirate was cautious. He knew the last time he had tried to go forward, his leg had hurt.

"It's okay, Pirate. You can trust us," Amanda said to reassure him. "This is one of those times I wish animals could understand me."

"You and me both, Harrison," Blake said, giving her a lopsided grin. That car ride seemed like ages ago. He felt like so much had happened since then.

Once Pirate was away from the barbed wire, Ethan was able to safely treat the wound. By a stroke of luck, it wasn't as serious as it could have been.

After wrapping it up in gauze, Ethan guided the injured pony into the trailer. Blake gravitated to the one person who understood what that rescue meant to him. Amanda fell into his arms, both of them laughing with relief.

"That was awesome," she said against his shoulder.

"Yeah, it was."

She pulled away. "I'm going to go back with Ethan and see if I can watch how he takes care of the horse now."

"I want to do that, too."

"You might have to take your fiancée back to the cabin first," Lily said, getting his attention.

Nadia was on her phone, typing something and talking at the same time. She seemed completely unaware of what was happening outside of her bubble. There was no way she would want to go back to Ethan's vet clinic and watch him work on the horse.

He jogged over to the car and tapped on the window. She put a finger up as she continued to talk to someone on the phone. He went to the other side of the car and climbed in the driver's seat next to her.

"I understand that, Ryan. I need you to get it done today. I'll finish my part, but I need you to do yours. Just because I'm not in the office doesn't mean nothing happens. I've taken vacations before and we all know that I work whether I'm in the office or not." She ended the call and rubbed her eyes. "Can we go back to the cabin? It's easier for me to work on my laptop than it is to work from my phone."

"Yeah, no problem. You can do some work back at the cabin and I'm going to check out the vet clinic. I'll have Hadley drive you back to the cabin."

That worked out perfectly. He opened the car door and her hand came down on his arm, stopping him from exiting. "What do you mean? I'm going to the cabin by myself?"

"You'll only be alone for a little bit. I want to see what they do with the horse and you have work to do."

"You're not going to be gone long, are you?"

"I'll be back before you know it," he assured her. Blake hopped out of the car and felt a little guilty for being so excited to be going in the opposite direction of Nadia. That feeling quickly faded when he was sitting in the back of Conner's truck with Amanda and Lily. There was no other place he wanted to be.

Ethan had an office downtown and a large animal clinic on the ranch. His equine examination and hospital area included two large hospital stalls and one isolation stall. He had a digital radiography, ultrasound and a surgical suite.

The black-and-white pony they had rescued was named Pirate because of the black spot on his head that surrounded one eye. He was brought into the radiography suite for an X-ray of his leg.

"I hope he's going to be okay. That was intense," Amanda said while they waited for the X-ray results.

"Living on a ranch is never boring," Lily said. "That's what really won me over. Every day is a new adventure."

"Are you saying I'm not the only reason you decided to stay?" Conner asked.

She popped up and wrapped her arms around his waist. He tucked her under his arm. "You were a very big reason but not the only one," she said, staring up at him with that dreamy look in her eye.

The way those two got lost in each other made Blake envious. He wondered if that was how he and Nadia looked to others when they were together.

"Do you want to help me take a group out in an hour?" Conner asked Lily.

"Yeah, sure. I need to help Amanda move her stuff into my cabin, but that shouldn't take long. She doesn't have that much stuff."

"Wait—what?" Blake's head swung in Amanda's direction. "What is she talking about? Why would you move into her cabin?"

"So you and Nadia can have some privacy. Plus, I don't think she likes Clancy very much."

"That's not true." As soon as those words left his mouth, in walked Hadley with Clancy on his leash.

"Hey, there's your mama." Hadley gave Clancy an ear scratch and handed him over to Amanda. "Nadia asked me to take him. She said she didn't feel comfortable in the cabin by herself with him. He's a sweetheart, though."

"Not everyone thinks so," Lily said.

Hadley was unnecessarily apologetic. "Sorry. I didn't know what else to do with him besides bring him here. I know you wanted to check on Pirate."

"No, it's fine. Thank you for bringing him to me. He's my dog. I'll take care of him. Lily, can I have the keys to your cabin?"

Blake stood up. "I'll take him back to the cabin. Nadia won't mind him being there if I'm there."

"Blake, it's okay. Stay and keep tabs on Pirate. I'll come back after I get him settled at Lily's."

Blake followed her and Clancy out. He didn't want her to move cabins. He didn't want Nadia to make her feel like she had to do that. Nadia was not going to change things between them. How many times had he promised Amanda that?

"You don't have to—"

"I do, Blake. I do." The way she said it made it impossible for him to argue. She wouldn't be changing her mind. Deflated, Blake went back into the clinic. After the X-ray, Ethan let Lily and Blake help him clean and re-dress Pirate's wounds. They placed him in the isolation stall so he could stay safe while he healed.

"I can't thank you guys enough for your help," Ethan said. "During the rescue and afterward. It's always scary when an animal gets itself in that kind of danger."

"We were happy to help," Lily said. "Can I bring my sister back later to check on him?"

"Absolutely! Pirate will be happy to have visitors."

"I'm going to help my sister get situated and then go on a ride with Conner and one of his groups. Maybe we can stop by before dinner."

"Perfect."

Blake thought Amanda was going to come back after putting Clancy in the cabin, but she didn't. He followed Lily back.

"You know, this isn't about Clancy," Lily said in a soft tone. "It's about my sister. It's always about my sister. I don't know why you thought this was going to be any different than any other relationship you've been in."

"Nadia will come around. She's smart and kind. She isn't going to want to come between me and Amanda. She knows we're just friends." He was probably trying to convince himself more than Lily.

She shook her head. "You keep saying that like just friends is what you two are. Like you can trivialize what you really have."

"I'm not trying to make it seem less than it is. I've always made it clear that she's my person. She's not just my friend."

Lily winced. "Exactly. Amanda is someone most men would want as a girlfriend or a wife. She's a catch."

Blake wouldn't disagree with that. He would have caught her if she had let him. No one seemed to understand. "Amanda doesn't want to marry me. She doesn't want to be my girlfriend. She lets me be her friend, so that's what we are. And now you're saying I can't be friends with her because I'm going to get married to someone else?"

Lily stopped and waited for him to do the same. "I don't know what my sister and you have talked about when it comes to your relationship. I have a hard time believing that she has never once thought about being more than friends. But regardless, I have a little advice for you."

There was little chance he'd be able to stop her. "I'm all ears."

"I made the mistake of thinking I could marry my childhood friend even though I knew I wasn't in love with him. What Danny and I had was always just friendship. The whole time we were engaged, I never felt like it was right. I pretended, but I wasn't the one making the decisions. I was only going along with what everyone else wanted."

Those seemed like good reasons not to try to win Amanda's heart. It obviously wasn't meant to be. It would end up like Danny and Lily. "I'm not marrying my best friend. I don't see where you're going with this."

"I'm getting there. When I met Conner, it was clearly different. I thought what Danny and I had was a friendship like you and Amanda, but it wasn't even close. When I met Conner, I realized that the way we connected was deeper. More. He is my person. My best friend. I wouldn't want to marry anyone else."

That was all well and good. Clearly, Conner felt the same way she did. They were fortunate enough for it to work out. Not everyone married their best friend. "I'm not sure where the advice is in there."

"I almost settled, Blake. And had I done that, I would have missed out on the love of my life. Be sure you aren't doing that. Make sure that your person knows exactly where you stand and that you know where she stands."

That was where her advice didn't follow. She assumed that he hadn't made sure he knew where Amanda stood. But that night at Cameron and Talia's wedding, after The Incident, Amanda had made herself very clear.

Blake could still picture her in that robin's-egg-blue dress. How her hair was up off her shoulders. The smell of her perfume and the softness of her skin when he touched her cheek. Those things had burned into his memory. He also remembered the way his heart had nearly beat out of his chest when she looked at him with those eyes. The ocean could not compete with their beauty. He had been lost in her eyes, but he had read the whole thing wrong. He thought he had seen something—desire, want, love.

No kiss would ever compare to that one. The way it had made him feel to let all his guards down and let her in was like nothing else. She had tasted like the champagne they had drunk too much of at the reception. He had loved her for so long and she had finally let him truly love her back. He had got carried away and had said too much.

I love you, Amanda. I've wanted this for so long. I've wanted you like this for so long. He had trailed kisses down her neck. When he'd touched her face, he'd felt the tears running down her cheeks.

She didn't feel the same way. She didn't love him or want him. She only wanted to be friends. There wasn't anything else between them. It had been a crushing blow. It was still hard to believe that he'd managed to let things go back to how they were after that. Somehow, he buried all that embarrassment and heartache and pretended that it was because he had had too much to drink and let the romance of their friends' wedding get him mixed up.

Blake was madly in love with his best friend, but she was not in love with him. Amanda didn't want him like that, and it wasn't fair for her to be sad that he had to go find it with someone else. If she didn't want him, she needed to be happy that someone else did.

CHAPTER SEVENTEEN

AMANDA LOVED HER sister but wished she was bothered a bit more by having all of her stuff strewn all over the place. Her cabin was a mess, and there was no way Amanda could leave Clancy there without cleaning up first.

"Wow. Did you do this?" Lily plopped down on the couch that was no longer covered in clothes, wedding magazines and a pizza box.

"Well, it wasn't housekeeping."

"It looks so clean. I should have had you stay with me from the start." Clancy jumped up on the couch next to Lily and snuggled up to her like he was a lapdog.

"You know that you're going to have to learn to pick up after yourself when you move in with Conner. The mess here was grounds for divorce."

Lily had been teased about her messy ways her entire life, so she didn't take offense. "He is perfectly aware of the fact that I may not always pick up after myself. I have a good excuse—I am super busy and this cabin isn't like a real house. I feel like I'm on vacation, and no one picks up after themselves when they're on vacation."

Amanda sat on the other side of her sister. "I do."

Lily, like Clancy had done to her, snuggled up against her sister. Amanda put her arm around her. Lily nudged her with her elbow. "You are not normal. But I love you anyway."

"Thanks?" Was that a good thing? It didn't exactly feel like it.

"I am going to go on a ride with Conner. You want to come with us?"

"I need to go grab my stuff next door. I didn't do that yet. I didn't want to bother Nadia."

"Blake's there now. It's probably safe."

Safe. Nothing was safe around Blake anymore. Her heart, most importantly. She wasn't sure why today was different from every other day Blake had been dating Nadia. They'd been together for two months. Maybe it was because when he spent time with Nadia, Amanda wasn't around. She didn't have to see them together. It was like it was happening in an alternate universe. Her world was still filled with lunches with Blake, business meetings with Blake, Monday night football at The Lion's Den Pub with Blake. They went surfing Saturday mornings. They texted each other funny memes all day long.

Nadia impeded on Blake and Amanda time very rarely. He had only begun to try to make them be friends the last month or so. Today had felt like a baptism by fire. Nadia all day. Amanda wasn't sure how many more days she could do this. She was ready to send them back to San Diego.

"Although, I feel like I should warn you," Lily said, resting her head on Amanda's shoulder.

A sense of dread fell over her. "Warn me about what?"

"I sort of encouraged Blake to think about how he feels about you and make sure he knows how you feel about him."

Amanda felt all her muscles tense. "I'm pretty sure he knows."

"I think he thought he knew why he wanted to marry her. I also think he thinks he knows how you feel, but I don't think he does."

That was a lot of thinking. Too much. "How I feel about what?"

"Him, obviously," she whispered.

Lily didn't realize what she was doing by starting this conversation. Amanda was never going to admit to how she really felt. "What did you say? Exactly."

"All I told him was that he better be sure before he goes through with this wedding. Have you seen the two of them together all day? What do they see in each other? They have very little in common."

"You don't understand."

"Help me understand. Why do you think you aren't in love with him?"

A knock on the door gave Amanda a chance to avoid answering that question. Blake was on the porch with all of Amanda's things.

"I figured you were going to need all this stuff if you're serious about staying here." She tried to read him. This was the first time in forever that she didn't feel they were on the same page about anything. When Nadia had walked in, everything he was feeling became a mystery to Amanda.

"Thanks," she said, taking the backpack on his shoulder from him. He carried in her bag.

Lily got off the couch and headed for the

door. "I'm going riding. See you guys for dinner."

Alone. Amanda had been waiting to get him alone all day so she could talk to him, but now that Lily had put things into his head, she wasn't sure she could have any conversation that wouldn't lead to both of them feeling terrible.

"Everything went okay with the horse?"

Blake stood in the middle of the room. He didn't seem to want to sit but wasn't trying to leave, either. "Pirate was good when we left. Ethan is an excellent vet. He's so good with the animals, knows exactly what they need to put them at ease."

"I'll have to go check on him before dinner. Did you and Nadia have any plans before dinner?"

"I guess she talked to Hadley about sitting down to look at dates."

"So it's official? You're going to get married here?"

He rocked back on his heels. "I guess so. She really loves the wedding barn. Hadley talked about how great it was in the summertime."

"Well, at least she's back to getting married in the summer."

"Yeah." Blake stared down at his feet. "Is there anything you and I need to talk about? Is there something you want to tell me that you haven't told me?"

There it was—the question that Lily had planted. "Not that I can think of. I know today was a little chaotic, but it sounds like you and Nadia worked things out. I want you to be happy. I want you and Nadia to be happy."

He nodded. "Good. Thanks. Maybe we'll see you at dinner."

"Why would I not see you at dinner?"

"I'm thinking Nadia would like something a little more intimate than a group dinner in the dining hall."

"Right." Amanda would bet money that Nadia was going to pick the intimate dinner, meaning sans Amanda. That was a no-brainer. "Thanks for bringing over my stuff. I appreciate it."

"Anything for you, Harrison."

How she wished that was true. Instead of telling him what she truly wanted, she let him leave and go back to his fiancée. She pictured Nadia greeting him, kissing him hello and thanking him for getting Amanda's stuff out of their cabin. She imagined Blake cradling Nadia's face and peppering it with kisses. *Anything for you, Nadia.*

The sharp pain in her chest wouldn't go away unless she got herself out of there. Amanda decided to go check on Pirate. When she got to the clinic, she found Tyler there instead of Ethan.

"Hey, I heard we owe you a big thank-you for helping out with this pony," Tyler said when he saw her.

"I didn't do much except feed him some hay to keep his mind on other things so the rest of them could cut him loose."

"It takes all hands on deck around here, so we appreciate it. I wanted to make sure he was in good shape before I break the news to Katie."

"Conner seemed pretty worried about that, as well."

"She takes it personal when the animals get injured on her watch. She's been thinking about hiring someone to take over as forewoman when she goes on maternity leave, and I think hearing there was broken fencing that we overlooked is going to push her to do that sooner rather than later."

Amanda stroked Pirate's head. He was a sweet horse. "She sounds like me. I tend to take it very personally if something doesn't go the way it should. I can't even read reviews online about our boxes because if someone is unhappy, I fret about it for days."

"Online reviews are the worst. Hadley and I probably spend a couple hours a day replying to online reviews. It's not so bad when they say something nice, but those bad ones? Man, they kill me."

Hadley and Tyler sounded so much like Amanda and Blake if Amanda and Blake could be together as husband and wife. If Amanda could have children like Hadley could. If there wasn't a Nadia tempting Blake away.

"You can't make everyone happy," she said, suddenly overwhelmed with emotion. The tears started running down her face.

"Are we still talking about reviews? Are you okay?" Tyler sounded afraid of the answer.

"Can I tell you something? Something I can't tell anyone in my real family? Not that you aren't my real family. I know that biologically you're my cousin, but you know what I mean, right?"

Tyler didn't hide his confusion, but nodded. "I get what you mean."

"I'm in love with my best friend," she admitted. Tyler stared back at her like a deer in headlights. "I know we said we were just friends and we are. We totally are. I don't want you to think that he's been unfaithful to Nadia. He doesn't even know I'm in love with him. He thinks I want to be friends. He once told me he loves me, and I told him it was never going to happen. And he believed me. He didn't even fight me about it. Part of me wonders if he said it and then regretted it, and then when I told him we had to be friends, he was relieved and was happy to go back to how things were. I didn't mean it, though. I told him that because I know he wants to be a dad. I know he wants to be like you and all of your brothers, with their pregnant wives and all the kids running around. That's his dream. It's all he wants out of life—a big family."

The tears were really coming now, but it felt good to say this out loud. She'd had these thoughts in her head for so long that once she opened the gates and let them out, they just kept coming like an avalanche.

"I can't get pregnant due to medical reasons. In fact, next month, I won't even have a uterus. No one knows that except my doctor. I haven't even told my sisters. None of them. I'm embarrassed. I don't want them to know because when they know, they'll look at me different. Forever. They won't talk to me the same. They'll constantly worry about hurting my feelings, so they won't want to tell me when they get pregnant. They won't be sure if they should invite me to be with them when they have a baby. They'll be sad for me, but they won't want me to know they're sad because they'll know that it will make me sad that they're sad."

"Should I get you some tissues?" Tyler pointed toward the exit. "I feel like you need tissues. And maybe Hadley. She's a lot better when it comes to feelings and how to say the right thing when someone is having big feelings. You're definitely having big feelings right now."

"Please don't tell your wife. Hadley is like the perfect person. You literally married the perfect woman. She does it all. My sister loves her. She's pregnant and will probably be an amazing mom. I'm fine." Amanda wiped her face with her shirtsleeves. "I'm fine. I just needed to tell someone all of that. I couldn't hold it in anymore and I didn't want it to come out in front of Blake or Lily."

Tyler touched her elbow. "I'm sorry. I wish I was better at this kind of stuff. I have always been the guy who pretended he didn't have any feelings. It was supposed to be easier that way. Then I met Hadley, and my feelings got too strong and there was no pretending they didn't exist anymore." Tyler took off his cowboy hat and scratched at the back of his neck. "All I can tell you is that as hard as it was to talk about my feelings, once I let the person I loved know they existed, it got better."

Amanda shook her head. She could never tell Blake everything. "I can't tell anyone else. Telling you really helped. That's all I needed. Thank you. Please don't say anything to anyone. Please."

"Of course. I would never tell anyone. I promise," Tyler said, showing his palms like he was being confronted by a dangerous animal.

"Thank you. Sorry for dumping all this on you. You're a really good listener."

She left the clinic and spotted Nadia standing outside the guest lodge. She couldn't pretend not to notice her. She had to go over and say something. What she wouldn't do for a mirror right about now. She had to look like she had been crying. Hopefully, Nadia wouldn't ask. If she did, Amanda would lie and say seeing the injured horse made her emotional.

"Nadia," she called out, crossing the street.

"Hi, Amanda." She smiled politely. "Blake went inside to find out how to get a ride into town. We were going to do a little shopping, and then we're meeting Chance Blackwell and his wife for dinner. He set it all up for me. Wasn't that sweet?"

Too bad there hadn't been anyone to take that bet earlier today. "That's Blake for you." He was always paying attention. Listening to what people said and doing what he could to make others happy. She really hoped Nadia appreciated how lucky she was to have someone like Blake love her. "You know, I'm sure you could borrow Lily's car."

"Blake didn't want to bother her. I figure we're two grown people—we should be able to call a cab."

"That is true. You two have fun. Tell Chance and Katie I said hi."

"Harrison." Blake jogged down the steps of the lodge. "We're going to town."

"So Nadia said. Have a good time." She started to move away, but Blake touched her arm.

"Hey, hold on a second. What's going on?" He led her away from Nadia. "Have you been crying?"

It was one thing to tell Nadia a lie, but it was another to lie to Blake. "I'm fine. I was visiting Pirate."

He glanced back at the clinic. "Is he okay? Did something happen?"

She placed a hand on his chest and regained his attention. When his gaze returned to her, she felt her heart skip a beat. "Pirate is good. I was in there talking to Tyler. I got a little emotional recounting the rescue. You know how I am about animals."

Blake pressed his lips together and nodded.

"You two have a good night. I'll see you tomorrow. Lily invited me to go cake tasting with her and Conner. I don't know if you and Nadia want to join us or if you two want to do your own thing."

"I'll talk to Nadia about it. See you tomorrow." He seemed sad, and as much as Amanda wanted to ask him what was wrong with him, she knew she had to let him go. Whatever was bothering him he'd have to share with his future wife. She would be his confidante now.

That sharp pain was back. Stronger than ever. Confessing everything to Tyler didn't change the fact that she still had to cope with the changes coming her way.

Her phone chimed with a text.

Looking forward to tomorrow. Hope you are too.

Logan wasn't Blake, but maybe she could convince herself that it was okay to pretend he could be.

Can't wait, she replied. She added a smiley face even though the tears had reappeared in her eyes.

CHAPTER EIGHTEEN

"You HAVE TO try these chocolate-frosted doughnuts. They are the best doughnut you will ever have." Blake slipped his hoodie over his head and fixed his hair.

"I don't eat doughnuts," Nadia said, coming out of the bathroom. She rubbed her lips together after putting on her lipstick. "Too many calories. Can't we go somewhere I can get some egg whites and turkey sausage?"

"We're on vacation. Try the doughnut."

"I don't like doughnuts. Isn't there somewhere we can go where you can get a doughnut and I can get egg whites?"

With that one admission, Blake realized they had never had breakfast together and that was why he had no idea that Nadia did not like doughnuts. Who didn't like doughnuts? Well, she hadn't had these doughnuts before, so she didn't know how amazing they could be.

He came up behind her and wrapped his arms around her waist. "Can you humor me and come with me to this bakery? Can we do this one thing this one time?"

"What is your fascination with a doughnut?"

"I can't explain it with words. You need to try it. You should have seen Amanda the first time she ate one. You would have thought she'd died and gone to heaven."

Nadia stepped out of his grasp. "So this is about Amanda? I should have known."

"This isn't about Amanda. It's about trying to include you in something that I find enjoyable. Is that so terrible?"

"Amanda loves the doughnuts, so you want me to love the doughnuts. I'm not Amanda. I don't save animals. I don't eat junk food. I don't have a big family with a lot of drama. I don't need you to rescue me or save me from all of my problems. If that's the kind of woman you want, then I suggest you go ask your best friend to marry you."

"Whoa. Where did that come from?" He'd been working very hard to be attentive to her. He also didn't like the way she was characterizing Amanda. She was not some damsel in distress. He did not have to save her. She did not usually have a lot of drama in her life, which was why he was here to support her.

Nadia stared down at her manicure. "Sometimes it feels like you ask me to do things because you do them with Amanda and you want to mold me into another version of her."

Blake had to hold back his laughter because that was not what he was doing. He didn't ask her to do things because they were things Amanda liked. He asked her to do them because they were things he liked. Just as he tried the things she liked and suggested. Shouldn't she want to do things that he enjoyed doing? And he could never say it, but the truth was Nadia would never be Amanda. No one could be.

"I don't want you to be like Amanda. Amanda is already in my life. I want you to be Nadia. And I'd like it if we shared our loves with each other."

He could see that she was biting the inside of her cheek. "Fine. We can try your doughnuts because you love them, not because Amanda does."

"This has nothing to do with Amanda. We won't even mention her the whole time we are eating doughnuts. I'm going to go ask Lily if we can borrow her car. I don't want to take a taxi again." Taxis were hard to come by in a small town like Falcon Creek, and Uber wasn't really much of a thing.

He knocked on Lily's door, hoping to see Amanda so he could explain why he was going to the bakery with Nadia alone. She would understand why she couldn't tag along. He would promise to bring her back her own dozen.

"Why are you up so early?" Lily asked, still in her pajamas. No Amanda on the couch. Maybe they were sharing the bed.

"Can I borrow your car? I promise I'll be back before you guys go cake tasting."

"Sure." Lily spun around and found her purse on the counter. "My sister makes it so much easier to find things." She handed him the keys.

"Tell Amanda I'll bring her back a treat."

"Sounds good," Lily said, shutting the door behind him.

Georgie was the only Harrison who was a morning person. Lily and Amanda would probably sleep all day if they didn't have somewhere to go. Nadia, on the other hand, had been up since six o'clock working on something.

"I promise you will be impressed with this place. It looks like a little hole-in-the-wall, but the food is so good."

Nadia was typing on her phone. "I am going to regret leaving San Diego. There is so much going on at work right now."

Blake had to refrain from reminding her that he hadn't asked her to come; she had done that all on her own because of her insecurity.

He reached over and squeezed her knee. "Well, I appreciate that you wanted to be with me."

When they got to the bakery, Blake jumped out of the car and ran around to open Nadia's door for her. This was their first breakfast date. He wanted her to be impressed. Holding the bakery door open for her, he reminded her, "You only need to eat one, but I don't think you'll be able to stop."

"What are you guys doing here?" Amanda asked.

Blake saw Amanda sitting at a table with Logan. They both had two Chocolate Junkie doughnuts in front of them and a coffee. "What are you guys doing here?"

"Breakfast date," Logan answered.

Blake had forgotten all about how Logan had mentioned breakfast the other day. He really had hoped Amanda would back out. "Us, too."

Nadia could not look more displeased. She had her back to Amanda and Logan, and ran her tongue over her teeth.

"I did not know she was coming here with him," Blake whispered in her ear.

"Sure." She didn't believe him. He knew exactly what she was thinking. She assumed he knew that Amanda was on a date and was showing up to crash it. Had he known she had a date, that was exactly what he would have done, but he wouldn't have brought Nadia to witness it.

Blake ordered his doughnuts and coffee, and left it up to Nadia if she wanted to eat there or take it back to the cabin. He didn't want to force her to stay here with Amanda.

"Aren't we going to join your best friend and her date?" she asked.

Blake glanced over his shoulder. Amanda and Logan were sitting at a table that seated four, but would they want Blake and Nadia to sit with them? He didn't have to ask because Logan was quick to invite them over.

"Come sit with us. We've got plenty of room as long as you bring your own Chocolate Junkie doughnuts."

"He knows I don't share," Amanda said before taking a sip of her coffee.

Blake pulled out Nadia's chair for her and pushed her in, and then took his seat across from her at Amanda and Logan's table.

"I was just telling Logan about how Lily once went surfing with us and challenged those two Australians to a surf competition."

"I will never forget," Blake said, smiling over his coffee.

"She dropped into that one wave that we both thought was going to wipe her out. That woman has no fear sometimes. I'm pretty sure those two guys will never underestimate a petite blonde woman ever again. I hope Conner remembers not to do that, either."

"Conner doesn't underestimate her. He also doesn't take unnecessary risks. He can't because he knows his mom needs him. Conner is the kind of guy people can rely on. Would you say your sister is the same?" Logan asked.

Blake found it interesting that all Logan wanted to talk about was Lily. Question after question was digging for more and more information about Amanda's sister. Blake sat back in his chair. He had been so darn jealous, but this was clearly not a date. This was a reconnaissance mission.

"Let me tell you something about the Harrison women, Logan. All of them have this undeniable spirit. Peyton is fierce. She's a boss. You don't mess with her. Georgie is smart. Not regular smart—doctor smart. Hence her being a doctor and all. Fiona is the youngest. She is light. She shines that light wherever she goes. You can't ignore it. Lily is joy. Lily loves life. She's good at living it to its fullest. She's smart, though. She knows not to push things too far. If Conner is the man you make him out to be, they are going to have one heck of a life together. She'll see to that."

Amanda grabbed his hand under the table and gave it a squeeze.

Logan nodded. "That makes me feel a lot better."

"Conner's your best friend," Blake said. "I'm sure you're like Amanda and a little skeptical that your friend could fall in love with the right person after only knowing her for a few days."

"Ten. They knew each other ten days and he wanted to marry her."

"I thought she was being completely reckless," Amanda said. "I didn't think there was any way she could have met such a great guy. I was sure he was hiding some demons."

"Conner is completely demon-free. She's not going to find a better man than him. He's got a heart of gold. Always has."

"I believe you. He's done nothing but impress me, and trust me, I have been searching for a flaw."

"He's not perfect, but he's a good man and I don't want him to get hurt by someone who is trying to escape a bad relationship or a troubled past."

Amanda put her elbows on the table. "Lily is not a troubled soul. She is a good person. She stayed here because of Conner. Because of what he unlocked inside of her. Not because she's hiding from something."

"Thank you for your honesty. It's nice to know that you care about your sister as much as I care about Conner. The fact that someone like you cares about her says a lot," Logan said.

Blake picked up on how that sounded a bit more flirtatious than the rest of the conversation. Just when he was starting to like the guy...

"You didn't do Amanda," Nadia said.

Everyone at the table swung their head in her direction. It was the first time she had said a word during the entire breakfast.

"What?" Amanda asked. She nervously glanced around the table, hoping everyone else was confused. She wasn't wrong. Blake didn't understand what Nadia meant, either.

"Blake didn't describe you. He talked about all of your sisters, but he didn't say what your special trait was. I'm curious. Logan thinks she's a good person. I'm curious what her best friend thinks."

It was a challenge. He could hear it in her tone. Blake wasn't going to censor what he thought about Amanda, though. He had left her out on purpose because he knew if he told everyone what he thought about her, they would know how he felt about her.

"Amanda. That's easy. Amanda is love. Amanda loves hard and she loves freely. She takes care of the people she loves. She protects the people she loves. She empowers the people she loves. Her heart is so big and it never stops giving. She makes it impossible not to love her back."

Amanda swallowed hard and her eyes were wet. Blake meant all of it. That was what she was. It didn't change the fact that she wasn't in love with him. Being loved by her was enough. It had to be.

"I'm ready to go back to the cabin." Nadia pushed her chair back and stood up. "I have work to do."

Blake got to his feet. "Have a good one," he said to Logan. "See you back at the ranch, Harrison."

Nadia didn't even bother to say goodbye as she stormed out the door and to the car.

"I didn't mean to make you mad."

"I'm not mad." She got in the car and slammed the door shut. Right, not mad.

"You asked me to talk about her. I didn't the first time so as not to upset you. It shouldn't upset you, though. Amanda loves me, but she's not in love with me. You have nothing to worry about."

Nadia laughed and shook her head. "I can see why you think that. When I came here, I was worried that your best friend was in love with you and would try to steal you away from me. I was so focused on Amanda's feelings and motives, I totally missed it."

"Missed what?"

"You're clearly in love with her, Blake."

"Nadia—"

"Don't try to tell me you love her, but you're in love with me. I definitely feel like if I asked you to choose right now—me or her—you would choose her."

"Let's not do this." Blake started the car. "I'm not going to do this."

"Exactly, because you would choose her." Her flippancy was frustrating.

"You're asking me to choose between two things that aren't going head-to-head with each other. It's like saying choose between your car and your favorite book. A car and a book don't serve the same purpose. Why would I need to give up my car to have a book or vice versa?" He needed her to see how absurd this was.

"That's not true, and you know it. I want to go back to the cabin to pack. I'm going back to San Diego. You need to choose. You can come with me and we'll get married and live happily ever after, or you can stay and be loved by the amazing Amanda, who isn't in love with you, and live miserably ever after."

"You're serious? You're really going to give me an ultimatum?" She wasn't the first to do that. The last girlfriend to do that was shown the door. Amanda didn't belong on the chopping block.

The difference between the last girlfriend who'd tried it and Nadia was that he had made a commitment to Nadia. He had made a promise to her by asking her to marry him, by giving her a ring. He had already told her once that he chose her above all others. He just hadn't thought she would ask him to give up Amanda in the process.

Nadia refused to even look at him. She stared down at her phone. "You love me or you don't. You're in love with me or you're not. We already know where you stand with Amanda. Either you want someone who's in love with you, too, or you don't."

CHAPTER NINETEEN

"I FEEL LIKE I need to apologize," Logan said when he dropped Amanda off at the ranch. "Believe me, if you didn't have plans to go back to San Diego, I may have worked harder to get to know about you instead of your sister."

Amanda stuck out her hand for a shake. "Never apologize for being a good friend. Conner is lucky to have you."

Logan's smile was slow and easy. He shook her hand. "He's like a brother. I knew you'd understand. I hope things work out for you."

"Work out for me?"

"I'm fairly certain we saw an engagement come to an end this morning. That guy is one hundred percent in love with you. I don't know if you wanted that to happen or not, so I'm just going to wish you luck and hope everything works out the way you want it to."

Amanda could have sat there and explained

that Blake was just being Blake. Surely, he had convinced Nadia that what he'd said didn't mean he didn't want to marry her. His sweet words didn't change what could or could not happen between him and Amanda.

Blake had basically said the same thing the day she almost drowned. He was kind enough to leave out the part about how he felt she made it impossible for other people to show her love this time.

Whatever had happened after they left the bakery would come out eventually. She glanced at Blake's cabin before going into Lily's. There were no signs of life. If they were fighting in there, they were doing it quietly enough not to disturb the rest of the ranch.

Lily was still in bed when Amanda got back, so Amanda climbed under the covers with her sister.

"Did you have a good date?" Lily mumbled, half-asleep.

"It was a good breakfast. Not so much a date, though."

Lily forced her eyes open. "What happened?"

"Logan asked me out so he could find out

more about you. He was still on the fence about giving his blessing."

Wide-awake, Lily sat up in bed. "He was on the fence about me? I thought all of Conner's friends liked me. Are there other people out there who think he shouldn't marry me?"

"You had to expect that his family and friends were going to question the speediness of this engagement. There hasn't been much time for them to get to know you. I think what's nice is that you know he has friends who really care about him and his happiness. They want to make sure no one is going to break his heart."

"Did he think I was going to do that? They think because I came here as a runaway bride, I was bad news. Didn't they?"

"Your runaway-bride status did not help your case, but you can also thank Blake for having your back this morning."

"Blake? How did he get involved in this?"

"He showed up at the bakery and crashed my breakfast with Logan. He said some really nice things about you, and I think what he said carried real weight with Logan."

Lily lay back down. "Wow. Blake Collins

had nice things to say about me. Wonders never cease."

Amanda gave Lily a playful shake. "Can you get up and get ready so we can go eat some cake?"

Her sister groaned and rolled away from her. "Conner will be here in an hour to meet us. Are Blake and Nadia coming?"

The decision to leave Lily out of what had happened with Blake and Nadia this morning was completely to protect Blake's privacy and feelings.

"I have no idea. We didn't talk about it at breakfast."

Lily got out of bed and stretched her arms above her head. "Can you find out?"

"Sure." Amanda also got out of bed and texted Blake about the tasting. He didn't reply, which wasn't like him. He and Nadia must be having a very intense conversation. Too intense to take a second to reply to Amanda's text. She hoped he was okay. As much as she had wanted to ask him to postpone his engagement yesterday, she didn't want his feelings for her to be the reason he did it.

She slipped outside onto the porch and sat on the bench to do a little spying. The cabin next door was still super quiet. From the outside there was no way to tell if there was anyone inside. Another text and no reply.

Tyler drove up on his ATV. "Good morning."

It wasn't unusual for Tyler to be out and about on the property. It was the first time he had driven out to the cabins. Amanda's stomach was already in knots, and seeing him made it worse. She knew she'd have to see him again after telling him all of her secrets, but she didn't realize how awkward that would feel.

"Morning. What brings you out this way?"

Tyler got off the ATV and glanced around like he wanted to make sure they were alone. "I felt like I needed to say something after everything that happened yesterday."

A sinking feeling told her there was more to it than that. "You told Hadley."

"Only Hadley," he said as he joined her on the porch. "She's my wife. I have a hard time keeping things from her, and she could tell something was weighing heavy on my mind."

Amanda rested her elbows on the railing and held her head in her hands. She really didn't want to hear Hadley's take on what she had told Tyler, but she knew that was why he was there. "Please don't worry about me. Pretend we never had that conversation yesterday. Wipe it from your memory."

"Trust me, I know you told me because you hoped that because we don't really know each other very well that I would pretend it didn't happen."

That was exactly what she had been hoping.

"I'm sorry, but I can't do that. I'm not here to make things worse, though. I just wanted to say that I think you should talk to Blake. It's not really fair to not let him know all the facts."

"He doesn't need all the facts. I already know what my news will do to him. You know how you feel? How bad you feel for me? Multiply that by a thousand. That's how he'll feel. He'll feel so bad for me that it will change our relationship. Everything about it. I don't want to do that. I like how we are."

"He is going to feel bad, but he also kind of deserves to know how you feel about him. He might be in love with you, too," he whispered.

Amanda's anxiety had her shaking. She turned around and leaned against the railing so she could watch the front door. She didn't want Lily to make a surprise appearance and overhear any of this. "He might, but I can't be what he needs me to be. Telling him would trap him into something that would rob him of what he wants most of all."

"Hadley pointed out that there are lots of ways to get that. Not to mention we're concerned that you're going to have surgery and not have anyone be there for you when it's over. You need to let someone in your life know what's happening."

"I really appreciate your concern. I promise that I will let someone know what's happening when I have to go in for surgery." And by someone, she meant someone who was not Blake and who would think they were driving her home after getting a mole removed.

Tyler took off his hat and stared down at it as he spoke. "Hadley and I know better than anyone what happens when you don't tell the truth because you're afraid of what being honest will lead to. It almost always backfires. The truth comes out eventually, and then the people you weren't honest with aren't just dealing with the truth but the lie, as well."

"I appreciate the advice. I know what I'm

doing. Sometimes it's better to keep things to ourselves. Sometimes saying everything that's on our minds is hurtful. I don't want to hurt Blake. I also don't want him or Lily to worry about me, so it's better they don't know."

"It's better that I don't know what?"

Amanda felt all the blood drain from her face. She spun around and saw Blake standing between the two cabins.

"It's better I don't know what?" he repeated, coming closer.

Tyler put his hat back on and grimaced. "I'm sorry, Amanda. I didn't mean to—"

Force her hand? Because that was what he had unintentionally done. She stalled, knowing there was no way she was going to fast-talk her way out of this.

"Good morning, Tyler." Lily came out onto the porch. She had a cup of coffee in her hand and a smile on her face.

"Hey, Lily."

"What don't you want me or Lily to know, Harrison?" Blake joined them on the porch. He moved slow like he did when they encountered sick or injured animals. Like he didn't want to spook her.

"What's going on out here?" Lily asked.

"I'm going to head back to the lodge. I'll see y'all later." Tyler backed away toward the steps, but Blake stopped him.

"Could you stay, instead? So that we know whatever Amanda says next is really what she needs to tell me and Lily."

Lily's brows scrunched together. "You need to tell us something?"

Amanda gripped the railing as it began to feel like the ground was moving under her feet and she was about to lose her balance.

Blake moved closer, and with each step Amanda was sure he could hear how fast and hard her heart was beating. "After breakfast, my fiancée decided that I am in love with you, but I told her it really doesn't matter how I feel about you because you have always been very clear that you are not in love with me. I've been mulling that over a lot since we got here. I've been trying to figure out what it is that keeps you from loving me the way that I love you. What is wrong with me that makes me not worthy? I've been obsessing over it. And the more I think about it, the more it doesn't make sense. The more I know I'm missing something."

He stood in front of her, his jaw ticking as he paused. His eyes were full of nothing but hurt and pain, and it tore a hole in Amanda's heart. This was what all the lies were supposed to protect him from, and instead it had made things worse.

"I think you are in love with me. I think you have been in love with me as long as I have been in love with you. I think there's a reason you won't let me love you, though. I think whatever it is is so bad that you think it would crush me."

Amanda's cheeks were wet. The tears flowed without permission like they had yesterday.

"Are you dying?" he asked, his voice cracking with emotion. Tears welled in his eyes. "You have cancer, don't you? The thing on your back is cancer, and you didn't want us to know because it's bad. Is that it? You have to tell us because we deserve to know the truth, Amanda. You aren't softening the blow by not telling us."

"You have cancer?" Lily gasped.

This had spiraled out of control. The horror on Lily's face was devastating. She couldn't let her sister think the worst. She went to Lily and grabbed her by both hands. "I do not have cancer. I am not dying. I would not keep something like that from you. I am not dying."

"You swear? You swear on Mom's grave?"

"I swear on Mom's grave that I am not dying and I do not have cancer. I swear."

Lily and Blake both looked to Tyler. Their distrust was another blow to her nerves. "Did she tell you she had cancer?" Blake asked him.

Tyler shook his head. "There was no mention of dying or cancer. I don't know anything about that at all. I really feel like y'all need to talk about this as a family and I should go. I don't think she's going to keep any more secrets. I think she's learned that secrets and lies only make things worse." He backed down the steps, got on his ATV and drove off.

Blake pressed his back to the railing and slid down to the ground. He pulled on the front of his hair. "What is it, then? Can you tell us what it is because I can't do this anymore. I can't."

Lily was breathing normally again now that the fear her sister was dying had passed. Amanda let go of her and went over to Blake.

Sitting next to him, she placed a hand on his knee.

"This is going to sound so ridiculous now that you got yourself worked up that I was dying."

"Harrison, what is going on?"

"I have endometriosis. According to my doctor, I have the worst case she's ever seen. It's so bad that when we get back to San Diego, I have to have a hysterectomy."

"Oh, Amanda!" Lily sat down on the other side of her and hugged her tight. "How did I not know about this?"

"I didn't tell anyone except Mom. She's the one who told me to go to the doctor when things started to get really bad. She came with me to appointments. Would take care of me when the pain was so bad I couldn't do anything."

"I don't know what all that means. What is endometriosis?" Blake asked.

"It's a disease that affects the uterus. Stuff grows in there that shouldn't and it hurts. It can lead to infertility." Saying the word aloud was even harder than she'd imagined. She hated that word more than cancer.

"But it's treatable?" Blake turned his body in her direction. "You're seeing a doctor?"

"I've seen a lot of doctors. And they all say the same thing. My case is the worst, and I should end my misery and have a hysterectomy."

His denial was so strong. "You don't have to do that. You're twenty-nine years old. We can go to better doctors. We'll find the best doctor."

Amanda had to remind herself that he was only hearing about this for the first time. She'd had years to process what was happening and her sad reality. He still had that pointless hope. "I've seen the best doctors. I've been to the specialists. I've gotten second opinions, and third and fourth opinions. They all say the same thing. I'm never going to have a baby."

"Oh, Amanda," Lily said again. She hugged Amanda's arm, wetting it with her tears.

"I didn't want to tell you or any of our sisters because I don't want you guys to treat me different. I don't want you to think that I can't handle being happy for you when you get pregnant someday."

"I'm glad Mom was there for you. I'm sorry

you felt like you had to handle this all by yourself once she was gone. I could have gone to doctor appointments with you. Georgie's going to be ticked that you didn't let her consult."

"Georgie will get over it," Blake said. His voice still sounded off, gruff and pained. "I would sure hope none of you would give her a hard time about keeping this private."

"No one's going to give her a hard time," Lily assured him. "How about you? Can you not give her a hard time?"

"Can I talk to her by myself? I need to talk to her alone."

Amanda nodded and wiped away her tears. "Lily, can Blake and I have a minute?"

"Sure," she said, pulling herself up. "Come here, first." She held her arms open for a hug. Amanda stood and let her sister hug her tight. "I love you. I will be there for you when you need me. Let me, okay?"

"Okay." Amanda didn't want to let Lily go. Talking to Blake, although necessary, was terrifying. This was the moment she had been dreading and attempting to avoid.

Lily let go and wiped Amanda's face for her. "Your mascara is a mess."

"I didn't think I was going to cry over cake samples."

Lily kissed her cheek. "Don't be afraid," she whispered in her ear.

If only it was that easy.

CHAPTER TWENTY

BLAKE'S BRAIN WAS having a hard time organizing all his thoughts and feelings. He had come over here so sure that he needed to confront her about an illness that was possibly going to take her life. Every crushing thought he had been having had seemed justified when he'd heard what Tyler said to her.

She wasn't dying, though. She was going to live a long life. Yet she still didn't want him to be her partner in it.

"I'm so mad at you," he said. If he was going to insist that honesty was the best policy, he had to practice what he was about to preach. Anger was only one of the many feelings that he had messing with his head right now, but it was the strongest.

"I'm sorry. I don't want you to be mad at me."

"I fooled myself into believing that you don't hide things from me. I know you do it with your sisters all the time, but I truly believed that you were honest with me, that you let me in on how you were feeling about things."

She fidgeted with her hands. "Most of the time that's true. You have always made me feel safe to tell you what was going on with me."

"So why did you keep this to yourself? Especially after your mom died."

"Mom died so suddenly. I had a person to talk to about it and then I didn't. I wasn't sure how to bring someone up to speed with what was going on after keeping you out of the loop for so long."

"Let's sit." He put his hands on hers to stop her and walked her over to the bench by the front door. "I wish you would have told me from the start."

She pulled her knees up and wrapped her arms around them so he couldn't get too close. "It first started when I was in high school, and I was not going to talk to you about my uterus."

"This has been going on since high school?" How had he missed that she was dealing with some disease that caused her chronic pain?

"Like I said, it's been a long time. Telling you now seemed so overwhelming. I knew you'd have all these questions and beliefs that you could make it better. It would be hard for you to understand that we were way past the simple solutions."

"I'm not an idiot. I would have understood eventually."

"Of course you would have. But when my mom died, we were adults and I had a firm grasp on what you wanted out of life and that I couldn't give it to you."

It was like the light bulb went on. Her resistance to even give them a chance made sense now. "This is why you want to only be friends?"

Tears were rolling down her face so fast and she was clearly unable to speak. He didn't care how she was sitting—he was going to hold her regardless. She collapsed against him and sobbed in the crook of his neck. Rubbing her back, he just kept repeating, "I've got you."

Lily came out with a box of tissues and quickly retreated back inside. Blake let her cry until she couldn't cry anymore. When she finally came up for air, he waited patiently for her to get her thoughts together.

"I can't have children. I will never be able to have children, Blake."

"I don't care about that," he said, fighting the emotion that placed a huge lump in his throat.

"Don't say that," she choked out. "Don't say that when I know you don't mean it."

Blake's jaw quivered. "I do mean it. I don't care about that. I care about you. I have loved you for so long and all I have ever wanted is for you to love me back. If you're in love with me, nothing else matters."

Amanda shook her head. "Since forever, you have told me how you can't wait to have a family of your own. To hold your son or daughter in your arms. You have told me time and time again how you want a big family like mine, a house full of children. You seriously told me you asked Nadia to marry you because you're worried about running out of time to have all those babies."

Blake covered his mouth with his hand. He had said those things. He had *felt* those things. He thought about how that must have made her feel when she knew she had a problem. How many times had he unknowingly caused her so much pain?

"When you held that baby at Jon and Lydia's, even people who didn't know you could see that you were meant to be a father. I've known for a long time that I couldn't have you. I could never ask you to settle for me when there are women like Nadia out there who can love you and give you the children you deserve to have."

"Maybe we can talk to Georgie and she can find us a doctor who can make it happen. Let's try."

Amanda held his face in her hands. Her blue eyes were rimmed red. Her mascara had made a mess of her face. "I have tried. No one has tried harder to find a way. All I've ever wanted to do was find one doctor who would say it was possible. Had any of them given me even a glimmer of hope, I would have come to you and poured my heart out. I dreamed about being able to do that. You have no idea."

"There are a lot of ways to have a baby. We could adopt. We could adopt as many babies as we wanted."

"I knew you'd say that. I knew you'd immediately jump to adopting without thinking about what that would mean. None of our babies would look like you or me. The world would be deprived of the handsomeness that's sure to be a son of Blake Collins. Your sweet disposition. Your kind heart. Your surfing ability. That strong jaw. Those long eyelashes."

He put his hands on top of hers. "You are more important than all of those things."

She gave him that dismissive head shake again and let go of him. "That's how you feel right now when the emotions are raw. But when you have time to think about it, really think about it and what you want and what you would have to give up, I'm not sure that's how you'll still feel."

"I love you. I don't need time to think about that. I have thought about that for *years*."

"I love you, too. That's why I never wanted to put you in the position of having to choose. Asking you to pick between me and your unborn children is horrifying. That's an awful ultimatum and I know how you feel about those."

"You understand that now that I know you're in love with me, we can't ever go back. I can't just be friends ever again. Either we're together or we have to go our separate ways, because I can't be with you but not be with you anymore."

Amanda dropped her gaze to her hands in her lap. "I know. I don't think I could do it, either." Her head lifted. "I need you to think about it. You have to really think about it and decide what you can live with."

"Or live without." That was the real question. Who could he live without? Amanda or the children he'd imagined for years that he would have someday?

"I need you to know that it's okay if you choose Nadia. I will understand. I don't blame you for wanting to go ahead with marrying her and having the family you wanted with her."

Blake hadn't been thinking about Nadia. She hadn't crossed his mind even once during this conversation. When he thought about losing her, he felt nothing. He had made promises to Nadia because he wanted a family, not because she was his one and only. He needed to be careful not to do the same thing to Amanda. He didn't want to let his emotions push him to say or do something he would later regret.

"I can't think straight right now. All I want to do is stop you from hurting, and the last thing I want to do is make you promises that I can't keep once I'm not caught up in all this emotion." He stood up. "I need to take care of something and then I want to talk again. Can we talk again?"

Amanda balled up a tissue and held it in her fist in front of her mouth. He could see her trying so hard not to start crying again. She nodded.

"I'll find you later. Will you let Lily be there for you? I don't think you should be alone right now."

She nodded again and went inside the cabin. He retreated from the porch and crossed the path to his cabin. He felt dizzy, like he hadn't eaten all day. The weight on his shoulders was so heavy. The person he loved more than anything in this world had been harboring a secret for years. A secret that had kept her from opening up her heart to him all this time.

Nadia was at the café table, on her phone and her laptop at the same time. Blake sat down across from her and waited for her to finish so he had her full attention. He did what he could to calm his breathing and relax.

Every time he thought about Amanda, he thought about how he had inadvertently hurt her. He couldn't do that anymore. Would she ever not feel guilty around him? Maybe the best thing to do was to walk away and give her a chance to have a relationship with a man she could be honest with from the beginning.

What was best for her? He wasn't sure.

He watched Nadia conduct her business. He cared about her. He could see them making a life together if he wasn't carrying a torch for his best friend anymore. They could have children and raise a family together. It would be easy. Did he want easy?

The answer came to him so surely and so clearly. He wanted Amanda.

"Can I help you?" Nadia asked when she ended her call.

"I can't go back to San Diego with you."

"I knew you were going to say that." She closed her laptop.

"You deserve someone who doesn't need to think about it. Your husband should never make you feel like you aren't the one. I care about you and I think you are an amazing woman. The fact that you ever felt like anything less makes me a complete jerk. My head and my heart aren't on the same page. You were right to call me out."

"I hope I haven't set you up to get your heart broken. You're a good man, Blake. I hope she's worth it. Just like I deserve someone who thinks I'm the one, you do, too."

"I appreciate that."

Nadia slipped her engagement ring off her finger and set it on the table in front of him. "I guess it's a good thing I didn't buy a dress the other day. I have a car picking me up in an hour to take me to Bozeman. I fly out tomorrow morning."

"I'm sorry I rushed what we had and that I made promises before I was really ready to back them up. That's on me."

She slipped her laptop into her briefcase. "I should have been more cautious. We were moving very fast. You were too good to be true. I really wanted you to be true."

"I'm sorry for that, too."

"Can you not be here when I leave? I don't think I can handle an emotional goodbye."

"Fair enough."

Nadia went into the bedroom to pack up her things. Blake pinched the engagement ring between his fingers. He had asked Amanda to help him pick this ring out because he thought she didn't feel anything romantic for him. He had been asking her to help him plan a wedding. She had shoved down all of her feelings for him and done everything he asked. She was a gosh darn martyr.

He stuck the ring in his pocket and went outside. He walked to the clinic and decided to check on Pirate. Ethan was there with another horse.

Ethan lifted his head. "Hey, there."

"Just coming to check on Pirate. How's he doing?"

"He's about the same. He needs time. These things don't heal overnight."

Blake knew that. That was the way life worked. It didn't make it fair. In this world, things could get wrecked in an instant but take much longer to heal. Or maybe never heal at all.

"Ethan, I've got ten—" Tyler stopped dead in his tracks. "Hey."

"Hey," Blake said. The fact that Amanda went to Tyler about everything that was going on in her life was still mind-boggling. She'd been so vocal about not viewing the Blackwells as her family but as strangers who didn't know anything about her, but she had chosen to open up on the most crucial aspect in her life.

"You've got ten what?" Ethan asked.

"Can I talk to you a minute?" Blake asked Tyler.

The man stood still, his lips pressed together. He was as open as a clam.

"Everything okay?" Ethan asked. He glanced back and forth between Tyler and Blake.

"I just have a couple questions," Blake explained. "I don't mean to put you on the spot, but you're already on the spot and you're the only one who can help me out here."

Tyler nodded. "Sure. Come on."

Blake followed him outside.

"What happened that made her tell you all of that really personal stuff?"

"I don't know, man." Tyler tapped his foot against the paddock fence. "She probably chose me because I had nothing to do with anything. Maybe she also figured I was the kind of guy who wasn't going to say anything."

"But you did say something. I want you to

know that I appreciate that you encouraged her to come clean."

"You should thank my wife for that. She was the one who pointed out that secrets and lies ruin the best things in life. We didn't want that for Amanda."

"She's really fortunate that this family is full of good people. You all have been really great to her and to Lily." Family was so important. It was everything. Without it, what did anyone really have?

"Lily and Amanda are family. And because they are, I want you to know that the thing she said that stood out above all the crying about not being able to have children was that she loves you. She loves you so much that all she thinks about is how to protect you from what she sees as her shortcomings. I know about thinking you're not good enough for the person you love, so when she implied that about herself, it hit home. I hope you keep that in mind. I don't know how things went after I left, but I hope Amanda comes out of this okay."

Blake let that sink in. She loved him. He let himself feel it. Family was everything, but family wasn't defined one way. Family was more than the people who shared your DNA. It was more than who grew up in your home or who took on the responsibility of raising you. Family could be a lot of things, but it was always love.

Amanda wasn't okay right now, but she would be. If Blake had anything to say about it, she would be more than okay.

CHAPTER TWENTY-ONE

WHEN AMANDA WALKED back into the cabin, the last thing she expected to hear was Peyton's voice. Or Georgie's. Or Fiona's. But there on Lily's computer screen were three video chats. The whole gang was here and they were all up-to-date on Amanda's health condition.

"I can make a couple calls. I know an ob-gyn in Philly who specializes in infertility. Maybe she can help."

"Don't call anyone," Amanda said, coming up behind Lily.

"Amanda," they all said at the same time. Then they all started talking at the same time, and she couldn't make out anything any of them were saying.

"Guys, guys, guys! Stop. I can't hear you when you all talk at once."

"Amanda, I love you," Fiona said. "I am so sorry that this is happening. You need to let me know when you are having surgery because I am coming down to San Diego to be with you."

"I can't believe you didn't tell me. I can't believe that Mom didn't tell me. I went to medical school. I could have helped if you would have let me."

"I got diagnosed when we were in high school, Georgie. You were not qualified to treat my endometriosis when you were fifteen and had one year of high-school biology under your belt."

"Fifteen? Holy moly. How did I not notice that Mom was taking you to doctor appointments?" Peyton asked.

"You probably had your hands full watching the other three while she was taking care of me because that's what you always did. You were Mom's backup."

"We're all here for you now, Amanda. You don't have to go through this alone," Lily said, wrapping her arm around her waist. "We are going to find a way to get you all the kids you and Blake want."

"I could be a surrogate!" Fiona offered. "It would be a way better job than I have now. You and Blake can make a whole bunch of babies in a petri dish and I will be your incubator. I would do that for you."

"That's very sweet of you, but I'm not sure that's going to happen." Amanda wasn't even sure Blake would choose to be in her life at all. She wouldn't fault him for staying with Nadia. Why wouldn't he want things to be easy? Being with Amanda was never going to be easy.

"Are we not going to talk about this Blake thing? Since when are you in love with Blake?" Peyton asked.

"Since forever," Fiona said.

"I seriously doubt that," Georgie challenged. "She has not been in love with him forever. I don't think Amanda even realized that boys could be more than friends until junior year of high school."

"Not to mention that man has always been dating someone else," Peyton said. "I want to know—when did he fall in love with you?"

"They started out friends and somewhere around college they both fell in love with each other," Lily chimed in.

"Wrong," Fiona said. "Always and forever. You two wouldn't admit it, but he's always been your person and you've always been his. Always."

Amanda was holding on by a thread. Listening to them dissect a relationship that might not exist by the end of the day was too much. "I can't talk about Blake right now, you guys. I love you and thank you for being here. I appreciate it."

"Love you!" they all said at the same time before all signing off.

Lily turned and hugged Amanda. The twins stood there for several minutes in silence. It was exactly what Amanda needed.

"Leave it to Fiona to offer up her uterus as a backup," Lily said eventually. They both laughed.

Amanda pulled away. "I have done a lot of research about freezing my eggs. The bad news is that eggs from a woman with endometriosis are way less viable. The chances that a baby with my egg would survive are low. I don't know if I could go through that or put Fiona through that. She would blame herself if it didn't work."

"Then you'll use my eggs."

"What? No." Amanda scrunched up her face. "No, I'm not taking any of your eggs."

"Why not? We have identical DNA. I would do that for you because I know if the tables were turned, you would do the same for me. Don't give up on Blake because you can't have his babies. We can figure out a way to make you guys babies."

Lily's phone rang, but she ignored it.

"I'm not taking your eggs or using Fiona's uterus. I don't even know if Blake is going to still want to be with me."

"He's going to because he loves you."

Lily's phone rang again.

"Someone really wants to talk to you. You should answer it," Amanda said.

"It's Conner. Hey, can I call you back? My sister needs me right now. Oh! We totally forgot. Stuff has happened over here. I'm not sure we can eat cake right now."

The cake tasting. Amanda had completely forgotten that they were on their way to do that when Tyler showed up. Cake sounded delicious. Maybe if she ate enough cake, she could go into a sugar coma and forget all about her problems.

"Let's go eat cake. I want to eat cake," she said to Lily.

"Are you sure?"

She nodded.

"Never mind—we're coming. We'll be there in a few minutes. Amanda needs to wash her face."

Dried mascara was not a good public look. She went back into the bathroom and freshened up. She felt like a new woman, or at least a woman whose entire life had flipped upside down but she now had a clean face.

Cake would be a sad replacement for what she really wanted, which was Blake. She wanted Blake to want her even though she wasn't what he deserved. She was proud of herself for not falling for it when he said none of it mattered. She could have taken advantage of his empathy and fear. She hadn't done that, though. She'd told him to think about it. She allowed him time to get clarity. Clarity that could lead to him not being a part of her life anymore.

That could have been the biggest mistake of her life.

"I WANT YOU to remember that these are our traditional flavors, but if there is something you want, all you have to do is let us know and we can get it made for you."

Hadley had everything perfectly arranged

as usual. The ranch had a baker in house who, based on the photos they had seen, could make wedding cakes that rivaled anything they'd seen at the fanciest bakeries back in San Diego.

"Let's start with the classic white cake with vanilla buttercream."

Amanda didn't even care about being a third wheel today. She was going to eat her feelings away one piece of cake at a time. So far, she was in love with the butter pecan cake with caramel filling. She was going to have Hadley order her an entire cake to take back to the cabin.

"Amanda." Blake sounded out of breath. "I've been looking all over for you guys."

"Cake?" Lily offered.

"No, thanks. Can I steal Amanda away or do you need her to help you pick?"

"We got this," Conner said.

Blake took her by the hand and led her outside. They walked in silence for a bit. There were several guests playing with the animals in the petting zoo. Another group had just returned from the morning adventure ride. Two little boys were playing catch with a baseball.

Finding somewhere private to talk proved

more difficult than Amanda had thought. Blake took them past the main house, which Tyler and Hadley called home. They went up a hill to a lookout spot. There was a wooden bench under a huge weeping willow tree.

The sun shone bright today, casting its glow on the grazing fields. Amanda thought it was beautiful, but it made her homesick at the same time. She missed the way the sun danced on the waves of the ocean. She missed the smell of salt water in the air. She missed how things seemed easier when they were back home. Although coming here to Montana had given her peace of mind about her sister's well-being, she was ready to go home.

"Nadia left for Bozeman. She flies home tomorrow morning."

Amanda was surprised but unsure if she should feel relieved just yet. "Are you going with her?"

He shook his head and sat down on the bench. "I told her I couldn't be with her. I felt like a real jerk, but I had to be honest with her. I am not in love with her the way a man should be in love with his wife."

Guilt mixed with relief, making Amanda feel more confused. "I'm sorry. I know how excited you were at first about the prospect of getting married and starting a family."

"Can you sit down?"

People told others to sit when they were going to give them bad news. That was a universal sign that whatever came next was going to be so bad that the person might pass out or become so distraught they wouldn't be able to stand.

Cautiously, she took the seat next to him. He could have sent Nadia home and planned to walk away from Amanda, as well.

"When Big E and your dad come back with Thomas Blackwell, are you going to stop loving your dad?"

Amanda straightened and cocked her head. "Why would you ask me that? Of course not."

"Do you think that once you get to know Thomas, it will make you love your dad any less?"

"No. Nothing will make me love my dad any less than I do. In fact, once I meet this guy who left his wife and kids to fend for themselves, I will probably love my dad even more. Rudy Harrison was there for us, cared for us, taught me how to tie my shoes and how to ride a bike. He helped me when I couldn't figure out algebra. He dried my eyes when Tommy Garfield broke my heart senior year. He's the best dad I could have ever asked for."

"I hate Tommy Garfield," Blake said. "But that's beside the point. The reason I'm asking you about your dad is because for someone so set on me being a dad, you seem to have forgotten how you define family."

"I don't understand."

"I love you, Amanda. I've loved you longer than I realized. I know you think I can't grasp what it means that you have to have this hysterectomy, but what I do get is that we're going to have to do things differently. My son might not have my eyes, but he's going to love watching all the superhero movies with me because I am going to teach him that those are the best movies ever."

Amanda's heart knocked against her rib cage. She had sat through more superhero movies because of Blake. It was only fitting that he would watch them with his children, as well.

"All I want is for you to be happy," she said, reaching up to trace the line of his jaw.

He took her hand and kissed it. "I am happiest when I am with you. No one else laughs at my bad jokes the way you do. You're the only one who makes me smile by simply breathing."

This was the biggest risk she was ever going to take. She had to trust that Blake knew what he was doing. "I'm so afraid that you're going to regret choosing me."

"Do you believe that your dad regrets marrying your mom? Raising you and your sisters as his own? Any fears I've got that I can't have the family I want disappear when I think about the Harrisons. Your family is the family I have wished I could be a part of for sixteen years."

Amanda ran her fingers through the hair above his ear. She couldn't remember the exact moment she fell in love with Blake. Maybe it was when they were thirteen and he helped her rescue a runaway family of kittens or when they were eighteen and he danced one dance with her at prom even though he was prom king and they were both there with other dates.

"I love you, Blake. And I want nothing more than for you to be part of my family." She leaned forward and he didn't hesitate to capture her lips with his. It wasn't their first kiss, but it was the sweetest. It was the kind of kiss that made her believe that anything was possible. Families began when two people dared to love one another. Blake and Amanda could do that. Would do that.

EPILOGUE

"YOU WERE SUPPOSED to turn right."

"We're supposed to turn right at the next right," Rudy said. He was exhausted, not because he was physically tired but because Elias Blackwell was the single most annoying human on the planet.

"I'm not even sure this is a good idea. What is this guy going to tell us that we don't already know?"

Rudy couldn't care less about what Elias thought was a good idea or not. Thomas Blackwell's commanding officer had retired last month. He'd had a very large party, and many of those who had been under his command came from near and far.

It was possible that Thomas was at the party. It was also possible that he wasn't. Someone who had been there may know more about where Thomas might be. Navy men and women stuck together even after they were done living side by side on a ship.

"Is it hard to earn one of these medals?" Elias folded and unfolded the certificate that had come with Thomas's Medal of Honor. Rudy had known that Peyton had it, kept it hidden somewhere. That child had always wanted to stay connected to him. Probably because she was the only child who remembered that he existed.

"It's hard. You never would have been able to do it."

"Pfft! You don't know me, Harrison. When I put my mind to something, there's no stopping me. If I had wanted a medal, I would have gotten a medal."

"That's not how it works. You don't get one because you want one. You earn it because you put your life on the line for someone else. I don't know you that well, but you don't come across as the kind of guy who would stick his neck out for anyone other than himself."

Elias wore a scowl. "You said it—you don't know me very well."

"When we get there, can you please let me do the talking? We will get more information out of him if he hears from a fellow officer, not some cowboy."

"Why do you always act like being a cowboy is such a bad thing? Lily fell in love with a cowboy. I bet Amanda would, too, if she stayed longer."

"Amanda loves the sand and the surf as well as her best friend, who rides those waves. Blake and Amanda are happy and we're going to leave it that way."

Rudy checked the mailboxes that lined the street for the number 501, home of Admiral Cole Larson. He was their best lead yet, but there was no guarantee he'd have any information. Finding Thomas was proving to be harder than they'd thought.

Rudy put the RV in Park and put the keys in his pocket. "Don't embarrass me, Elias."

The old man got a chuckle out of that one. "Who—me?"

* * * * *

Don't miss Montana Dreams,
the next installment of
The Blackwell Sisters,
coming next month from USA TODAY
bestselling author Anna J. Stewart and
Harlequin Heartwarming!

For more great romances in the Harlequin
Heartwarming series,
visit www.Harlequin.com today!

Get 4 FREE REWARDS!

We'll send you 2 FREE Books plus 2 FREE Mystery Gifts.

Love Inspired books feature uplifting stories where faith helps guide you through life's challenges and discover the promise of a new beginning.

FREE
Value Over
$20

Get 4 FREE REWARDS!

We'll send you 2 FREE Books plus 2 FREE Mystery Gifts.

Love Inspired Suspense books showcase how courage and optimism unite in stories of faith and love in the face of danger.

FREE Value Over **$20**

THE WESTERN HEARTS COLLECTION!

19 FREE BOOKS in all!

COWBOYS. RANCHERS. RODEO REBELS.
**Here are their charming love stories in one prized Collection:
51 emotional and heart-filled romances that capture the majesty
and rugged beauty of the American West!**

YES! Please send me **The Western Hearts Collection** in Larger Print. This collection begins with 3 FREE books and 2 FREE gifts in the first shipment. Along with my 3 free books, I'll also get the next 4 books from The Western Hearts Collection, in LARGER PRINT, which I may either return and owe nothing, or keep for the low price of $5.45 U.S./$6.23 CDN each plus $2.99 U.S./$7.49 CDN for shipping and handling per shipment*. If I decide to continue, about once a month for 8 months I'll get 6 or 7 more books but will only need to pay for 4. That means 2 or 3 books in every shipment will be FREE! If I decide to keep the entire collection, I'll have paid for only 32 books because 19 books are FREE! I understand that accepting the 3 free books and gifts places me under no obligation to buy anything. I can always return a shipment and cancel at any time. My free books and gifts are mine to keep no matter what I decide.

☐ 270 HCN 5354   ☐ 470 HCN 5354

Name (please print)

Address   Apt. #

City   State/Province   Zip/Postal Code

Mail to the **Reader Service:**
IN U.S.A.: P.O. Box 1341, Buffalo, N.Y. 14240-8531
IN CANADA: P.O. Box 603, Fort Erie, Ontario L2A 5X3

Get 4 FREE REWARDS!

We'll send you 2 FREE Books plus 2 FREE Mystery Gifts.

Harlequin Special Edition books relate to finding comfort and strength in the support of loved ones and enjoying the journey no matter what life throws your way.

FREE Value Over **$20**